W9-AFN-760

While My Pretty One Knits

Meet the Black Sheep Knitters

Maggie Messina, owner of the Black Sheep Knitting Shop, is a retired high school art teacher who runs her little slice of knitters' paradise with the kind of vibrant energy that leaves her friends dazzled! From novice to pro, knitters come to Maggie as much for her up-to-the-minute offerings like organic wool as for her encouragement and friendship. Her only detractor? The owner of a rival shop who resents Maggie's success. . . .

Lucy Binger left Boston when her marriage ended, and found herself shifting gears to run her graphic design business from the coastal cottage she and her sister inherited. After big-city living, she now finds contentment on a front porch in tiny Plum Harbor, knitting with her closest friends.

Dana Haeger is a psychologist with a busy local practice. A stylishly polished professional with a quick wit, she slips out to Maggie's shop whenever her schedule allows—after all, knitting *is* the best form of therapy!

Suzanne Cavanaugh is a typical working supermom—a Realtor with a million demands on her time, from coaching soccer to showing houses to attending the PTA. But she carves out a little "me" time with the Black Sheep Knitters.

Phoebe Meyer, a college student complete with magenta highlights and nose stud, lives in the apartment above Maggie's shop. She's Maggie's indispensable helper (when she's not in class)—and part of the new wave of young knitters.

While My Pretty One Knits

Anne Canadeo

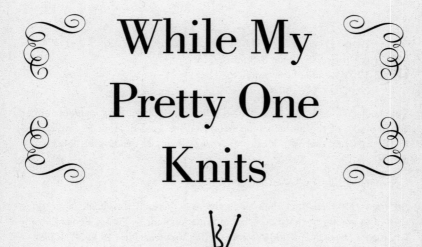

Pocket Books
NEW YORK LONDON TORONTO SYDNEY

Pocket Books
A Division of Simon & Schuster, Inc.
1230 Avenue of the Americas
New York, NY 10020

First Pocket Books trade paperback edition May 2009

Designed by Joy O'Meara

Manufactured in the United States of America

10 9 8 7 6 5 4

Library of Congress Cataloging-in-Publication Data is available.

ISBN-13: 978-1-4165-9809-1
ISBN-10: 1-4165-9809-X

This book is dedicated with love and gratitude to my grandmother, Anna Cavaliere, who lived to knit beautiful things and loved to tell—or listen to—a good story even more. Grandma had a sharp, irreverent sense of humor. She liked to stay up late, knitting and watching old movies, and I watched them with her. Mysteries were among the tales she loved best and I hold many memories of sitting beside her as knitting needles clicked intently while we watched her favorites like *The Big Sleep* or *The Curse of the Maltese Falcon*, episodes of *Columbo* and *Perry Mason*, of course. I can still hear the pounding theme music and see my grandmother's mesmerized expression. She sometimes tried to teach me how to knit, but the lessons never seemed to stick. What did stick is best evidenced in this book. A thoroughly creative soul, I'm certain she's been standing by, directing my progress, stitch by stitch. I hope she is pleased with the finished product.

While My Pretty One Knits

Chapter One

"Maggie, you've got to be kidding . . . do you want to kill me?" Lucy Binger tried to stare down her best friend, but it was no use.

Maggie Messina had already settled in to her furniture moving stance—knees bent, jaw set, a determined grip on the far end of an antique love seat.

"Come on, Lucy. You can do this." When that coaxing tone failed, she said, "It's the absolute last time, I *promise*."

Lucy shot her a dark look, then finally took hold of her end and hoisted the couch up. Taking the high road, she thought, by not harping on the fact that they'd moved this particular piece of furniture around the shop three times, each trip reportedly the last.

"I owe you one," Maggie said.

"You owe me a few," Lucy replied with a grunt.

"Absolutely . . . watch the molding, please?"

Maggie swung her end through the doorway while Lucy hung on to the other side for dear life.

Lucy was trying hard not to destroy the decor, but angling the couch around the coral-colored walls, tall armoires, and baskets brimming with yarn was no mean feat.

Maggie's knitting shop, the Black Sheep, covered the first floor of a meticulously restored Victorian, the kind real-estate brokers might call "a jewel box." Lucy knew that was just a clever way of saying the rooms were small and tight, designed for diminutive, nineteenth-century folk, but these days more suited to retail space.

Finally, they reached the corner Maggie had staked out as the sofa's latest landing strip. Or close enough, Lucy decided. She dropped her end, then collapsed on the cushions, her long legs dangling over one side.

"Okay, furniture is set. How about the fireworks?" Lucy turned her head and caught Maggie's eye. "Don't you need a permit for that?"

"All right. I did get a little carried away. But Cara's practically famous. It's a big deal for me, having her here. I'm expecting a full house. Did I tell you?"

Lucy smiled and nodded. Maggie had told her. A few times.

"So Cara was a student of yours, right?" Lucy folded one arm under her head. "When was that again?"

"Almost ten years ago." Maggie sat on an armchair near the love seat and rubbed the back of her neck. "She went to college in New York after high school, the Fashion Institute of Technology."

"Did she stay in touch?"

"Oh, a little. When her first book came out, I sent her a note and she wrote back. She'd returned to Boston by then and was writing for *Knitting Now!* Cara comes back to town fairly often to see her family. She stopped in to say hello one day and mentioned she was working on a new book about felting. So I asked if she'd give a talk here and she agreed. Pretty good for me," Maggie added. "Her publisher is sending her out to five or six cities. Bookshops and the big arts and crafts chain stores."

"That is a coup. You must have been one of her favorite teachers."

"Maybe." Maggie's tone was modest, but Lucy knew she'd been very popular with students. Maggie not only looked half her age, but had the kind of energy and outlook that would always make her seem young.

Maggie had left teaching four years ago, after her husband, Bill, had died. She'd always talked about opening a knitting shop some far-off day, perhaps when she retired. But at that low point in her life, she needed a new plan to pull her through and didn't see any reason to put off her heart's desire.

"Cara was one of those kids who hung out in the art room. You know the type. I encouraged her, I guess. I had a feeling she'd do something with herself in the real world."

Lucy wasn't sure if the wondrous world of knitting had that much overlap with the real world. But she knew what Maggie meant and Cara Newhouse was clearly a bona fide success in both realms.

Felting Fever, the book Cara would sign tomorrow, was her second in less than two years. Her first, *Ready, Set, Knit!*, had turned out to be one of the bestselling titles for novice knitters ever. All before Cara had even hit thirty.

Slouching toward thirty-three, with no national book tours penciled into her datebook, Lucy knew she was a little jealous.

"I'm not sure if I'm allowed to say, but Cara might have her own TV show soon." Maggie picked up a fringed couch pillow that had slipped overboard and slapped it back into shape. "Some producer type is coming tomorrow to tape her demonstration. It's just a screen test. It won't actually be on TV," Maggie clarified. "But the *Plum Harbor Times* is sending a reporter. We could make the front page."

"I bet you will," Lucy agreed. Cara's appearance would be

good publicity for the shop. It didn't take much to appear above the fold in the *Plum Harbor Times.* The pages of the local paper were filled with blurry photos and fluffy articles about student groups, Scout troops, and Rotary Club members honored for canned food drives and other good deeds. Town trustees debated passionately about traffic lights, trapping raccoons, or keeping skateboarders off Main Street.

The truth was, truly bad things rarely happened in Plum Harbor. It was just that kind of place. When Lucy and her sister Ellen visited their aunt Laura in the summers all through childhood, Lucy had accepted that fact without question. Now that she was an adult and living here full-time—at least, trying it out for a while—the happily out-of-synch atmosphere still amazed her. While other people in other places were striving to be on the cutting edge of trends and fashion, Dare to Be Dull could easily be Plum Harbor's village motto.

Lucy had never found living in Boston particularly difficult, except the year her marriage to Eric underwent a meltdown—and that could have happened anywhere. Boston was only about an hour and a half away, sometimes two with traffic, but it might as well have been another galaxy. Some hardy souls made the daily commute, but too few to consider the area a bona fide suburb. And it wasn't a summer destination any longer, either. It was something in between, what people called an ex-burb, which was why Lucy liked it.

"Anything left on your list?" Lucy really didn't want to move a muscle, but felt obliged to ask.

"I think we're finished, thanks."

Maggie rose and headed for a table that held stacks of Cara's new book. She began to unpack more copies from the brown cartons on the floor, now hidden by a long tablecloth.

Maggie was almost ten years older, but Lucy sometimes

found her friend's energy level downright annoying. Lucy teased her about slugging down Red Bull on the sly, but they both knew Maggie was too much of a health food freak for that lapse. Maggie was obviously part border collie, restless and cranky unless she had a productive job to do.

Maggie hummed while arranging the books on the table. Lucy glanced at her watch, then closed her eyes. It was almost seven. She couldn't believe it. She'd dropped by the shop around three, just to see how things were going, and had found Maggie totally overwhelmed. Lucy had rarely seen her in a true panic about anything, but that afternoon, her dear pal had been about to unravel. Lucy didn't have the heart to desert her.

That was the trouble with working at home and being your own boss, Lucy had noticed. She was too easily distracted. There was always some excuse to avoid her freelance assignments. Even housework distracted her, and that was saying something.

Some days, she practically tied herself to her desk chair, then ended up roaming the Internet instead of working. Answering e-mails, checking her horoscope or pseudo-news items. "Stars Without Makeup" was always amusing, and, on a certain level, a deep comfort.

Of course, she had to check out her favorite knitting bloggers, like the Yarn Harlot. Then there was always knitting itself, the perfect distraction from work because you were doing something productive.

Lucy was still a neophyte knitter, but she was definitely hooked. Polishing off a few rows when she got stuck in some graphic design dilemma cleared her head and settled her mood. As for hanging out at the Black Sheep, the shop was her home away from home. Once inside the door of the cozy knitters' haven, it was easy to lose track of time.

Phoebe Meyer, a college student who worked part-time for

Maggie and lived in the apartment above the shop, had conveniently escaped the set-up marathon at about four. Phoebe had classes on Thursday afternoon, but would be back soon. The others would be here any minute, too.

It was almost time for their group's weekly knitting night.

They'd all told Maggie they should skip tonight's meeting as she had enough to do. But Maggie insisted. Since the group had formed over a year ago, they'd rarely missed, traveling from house to house, holding it here at the shop.

Tonight was Maggie's turn and Lucy had a feeling Maggie would be better off with the distracting, relaxing presence of her knitting friends than hanging out there alone, fussing over the book display and cookie trays.

The knitting group had first met right here, in the Black Sheep, at one of Maggie's beginner classes last summer. There had simply been good chemistry and a true connection between them—five women at different stages in life, with different occupations but similar interests. And they were united by a common desire to master enticing strands of yarn and unwieldily sets of needles.

By the time Maggie's course was over, they knew a knit stitch from a purl, how to read a pattern, and repair a yarn over. They had also come to know one another, stitch by stitch, creating an intricate, unique pattern of friendship. Ending their knitting nights together seemed unthinkable. It seemed like just the beginning.

Lucy thought of the knitting club as a night out with gal pals . . . without the pomegranate martinis. They were known to share a good bottle of chardonnay or pinot noir from time to time, though, along with something tasty to eat.

Mini-quiche and green salad were on the menu tonight, a preview of the finger food Maggie would serve tomorrow. Maggie had popped a cookie sheet into the oven a short time ago and the warm buttery smell made Lucy's stomach growl, though she was too tired to get up and sneak a taste test.

The shop door opened and Dana Haeger strolled in. She took two steps and stared around. A row of chairs blocked her path.

"Maggie, what have you done to this place?"

"You mean you like it, right?" Maggie glanced at Dana briefly, then turned back to the book display.

"Absolutely. It looks great." Dana wove a path through the chairs in the other direction, and smiled down at Lucy. "Have you been here all afternoon schlepping folding chairs?"

"Just about," Lucy admitted. She sat up and rubbed the small of her back.

"What a pal you are."

"I'm not sure 'pal' is the word I'd use at the moment," Lucy replied.

Dana smiled, and slipped off her coat. She dropped it on the love seat, along with a duffel-shaped tote with long leather handles she used as her knitting bag. "Something smells yummy. Did you guys cook, too?"

"Mini-quiche, from Value Barn," Lucy replied. "Maggie bought half a ton for tomorrow. She had a few dozen to spare."

"Sounds good to me. I'll make some coffee."

Dana headed for the storeroom, which had once been a kitchen and still had all the basic equipment. Lucy followed and watched as she set up the coffeemaker.

As usual, Dana looked smart and professional in a brown tweed suit and cashmere sweater. A psychologist with a busy practice, she had an office a few blocks down Main Street. She also had hours on staff at a local hospital clinic. She often stopped in at the knitting shop during the day, counting the breaks as her own special therapy.

Dana hit the start button on the coffeemaker. "I'd like to write a book one of these days. One of those self-help, how-to's with a snappy title? *Three Secrets to Happiness, Wealth, Love, and Great Sex . . . All the Time . . . Or Your Money Back.*"

"I think that's four secrets," Lucy noted. "But I would definitely read it. Wait a second . . . maybe I *have* read it?"

"Yeah, so did I." Dana smiled at her.

The coffee had dripped into the pot, the scent energizing. Dana poured out two mugs and handed one to Lucy.

They both turned at the sound of Suzanne Cavanaugh's voice, greeting Maggie with a shriek. "What happened to this place? Where's our table?"

Lucy emerged from the storeroom just in time to see their fellow knitter, Suzanne, spin in a confused circle, searching for their usual meeting place.

"We moved the table up front for the refreshments," Maggie explained. Along with the quiche, Maggie would be serving muffins and cookies, coffee, and tea. She went the distance, Lucy had to hand it to her.

"Why don't we just sit up here? There's room for everyone." Dana led the way back to the front parlor and the love seat. "Just grab a few more chairs and make a circle."

Maggie checked the time. "I guess we'd better start without Phoebe." Maggie toted a chair over and unfolded it. "She's probably stuck at school. That European history class."

Maggie had barely finished the thought when the shop door swung open.

But it was not Phoebe. Not even close.

Lucy heard Maggie's quiet, sharp breath as a short, dark-eyed woman stepped into view. She pushed back the hood of a voluminous Aryan knit wrap, its workmanship and detail impressive, even at a distance.

It was Amanda Goran. For a moment, Lucy didn't recognize her. She looked so different. Then she spoke and her voice—thin, nasal, totally irritating—dispelled any doubt.

"Hello, Maggie. I saw the lights on and the door was open. . . . Are you giving a class tonight?"

"Not exactly . . ."

"I didn't think so. Not with the big event tomorrow. Wow, look at this place. You must expect a real crowd."

Maggie forced a small smile. "It's a hot ticket."

Lucy could sense Maggie's discomfort. Or maybe it was just curiosity about this unexpected honor.

Amanda rarely set foot in the Black Sheep and *never* wearing such a cheerful expression. Well, it was as close as Amanda ever got to cheerful. She probably had more enemies than friends in Plum Harbor, but she considered Maggie her number one archrival. For a long time Amanda's shop, the Knitting Nest, had been the only choice for local knitters, until the Black Sheep hopped onto Main Street.

Amanda had resented the quick success of Maggie's store, which had easily eclipsed her own. She'd always taken it personally. Maggie usually laughed off the feud as all in Amanda's head, though her contentious rival had managed to get under Maggie's skin more than once in the past few years. Still, Maggie tried hard to rise above Amanda's pettiness and ignore her.

"Can I help you with something?" Maggie started to rise from her chair.

"Don't get up." Amanda waved at her. "I just wanted to say hello." Amanda took a few more steps inside and fingered a skein of yarn that sat in a basket on a side table. Then she read the label and nodded. "Organic. Nice. . . . Wow, look at that price. Are you trying to put me out of business, Maggie?"

The accusation was delivered with a small surprised laugh.

Maggie managed another tight smile. "A new supplier. She's giving good discounts to build her business. Would you like her card?"

"That's okay. I'm not getting involved with any new labels right now. I'm trying to take a step back from the Nest."

"Really?" Maggie didn't bother to hide her surprise. Lucy was surprised, too. Amanda was devoted to her shop. Obsessed with it, Lucy would say.

"I'm looking for a manager," she added. "If you think of anyone, let me know."

"Yes, I will," Maggie promised.

Amanda plucked a ball of yarn from another basket and slipped on her reading glasses for a closer inspection. Maggie glanced at her friends. Everyone had pulled out their projects and had busily set to work, but of course, they still soaked up every word of the exchange.

Taking a step back from the knitting wars? Lucy wondered. What had enticed Amanda to suddenly retreat from battle? Whatever it was, it seemed to agree with her.

Amanda rewound the wool and carefully set the ball back in the basket. "You really have some nice stock in here Maggie. And so well displayed."

Had Amanda actually given Maggie a compliment? Lucy saw Maggie's eyes widen. She was speechless.

Amanda slipped her wrap around her arms and turned to go. "Looks like I'd better get here early tomorrow for a good seat."

"Yes, you really should," Maggie replied, finding her voice again. "Cara will start at eleven, but we'll be open at nine."

"I'll come when you open, then." She flashed a grin, displaying dazzling white teeth. "See you, ladies."

The others looked up from their work and nodded good-bye as Amanda swished through the doorway.

Maggie raised her hand and waved. "Good night, Amanda. See you—"

The door snapped closed and they sat in absolute silence.

Lucy imagined Amanda lingering on the porch, about to pop back in for a sneak attack. She slowly looked around at her friends. "Did that really happen?" Her gaze came to rest on Maggie. "Is she really coming here tomorrow?"

"I'd worry about that, if I were you." Suzanne's clicking needles echoed her concern. "You know Amanda. What if she makes a scene? What if she's coming just to screw things up?"

Suzanne was their official Fretting Queen. But this time, Lucy thought Suzanne had a point.

"I thought about that, too, when she called to sign up," Maggie admitted. "But I had plenty of room left and I didn't feel right being rude to her. Maybe she won't even come." Maggie touched her forehead with her hand. "I can't remember the last time she stopped in here like that. Or maybe I just blocked it out of my memory?"

Dana finished a row and turned her work to the other side. She was making a long, belted cardigan with a shawl collar using taupe-colored wool with a touch of angora. Lucy thought it was going to look fabulous on her.

"I'm sure any visit from Amanda is always fraught with drama," Dana said. "Funny how she'd seemed so conciliatory tonight. And she looked terrific."

"Didn't she? I almost didn't recognize her," Lucy admitted. "Even her teeth were sort of . . . glowing."

"Looked like veneers to me," Suzanne agreed. "You can't get there with the home strips."

"Her hair looked really good, too," Lucy noted. "I wonder where she had it done."

Amanda had changed her dowdy Dutch boy style for a ragged

razor cut and a brighter color. Her plain features were enhanced by serious makeup, Lucy had noticed. Eyes, lips, foundation—the works. It didn't look like drugstore stuff, either. Definitely department store quality.

"A new and improved Amanda," Maggie summed up. "Her personality included. I think she actually gave me a compliment."

"Could you believe it? What was that about?" Suzanne shook her head.

Dana set her knitting down and checked the pattern. "I've always thought she was a perfect candidate for antidepressants. Argumentative. Paranoid. Maybe she started taking some medication. There are some terrific new drugs out there now."

Dana was rarely at a loss for a diagnosis, but in this case, Lucy thought it was a smart call. Amanda did seem transformed from the inside out.

"She lost some weight, too. But everybody loses weight when their marriage breaks up." Suzanne sounded very knowledgeable for someone who had married her high school boyfriend and seemed to be living happily ever after, juggling her part-time job in real estate with the 24/7 job of running a home and raising three children.

Lucy had some personal experience with the divorce diet. She'd dropped twenty pounds during her breakup with Eric, and, just like Amanda, had splurged for the requisite overpriced haircut. By now, she had gained about half the weight back and her long wavy hair had returned to its former dirty blonde color and unruly style.

"Amanda and Peter are not divorced yet. They're not even legally separated," Dana clarified. "They're living apart, but I don't think they've signed anything. Jack knows the attorney who's representing Peter, and I hear Amanda is tough as nails negotiating."

"Why am I not surprised?" Maggie murmured.

Dana's husband, Jack, had had a full career as a county detective before returning to school for a law degree and now practiced in town. Between the two of them, Dana and Jack were privy to the inside story on many residents of Plum Harbor. Not that she lacked in discretion or professional ethics in any way, Lucy thought, Dana didn't mind adding a few insider footnotes to stories that were common knowledge.

"She'll never find a guy like Peter, willing to put up with all *her* quirks, that's for sure." Suzanne rolled her eyes. "Why did they split up in the first place?"

Dana took a snip of black yarn and tied a marker at the end of her row. She shrugged. "Who knows? I did hear that one day she just cleared all the furniture and the handcrafted things he makes and dumped it all in a pile on the sidewalk. Before Peter could get over there, half of it was gone."

Lucy had not been in the Knitting Nest for ages, but she did recall Peter's wares took up a good portion of the space.

"He's a good craftsman. His pieces have simple lines but are very artistic," Maggie said sympathetically. "Knowing Amanda, anything could have set her off."

Dana pursed her lips, concentrating on her stitches. Lucy sensed she knew more about the Gorans' marriage than she would say. Dana glanced up at her friends, then down at her needles.

"What did she do with all the empty space in the shop?" Lucy asked.

"Moved in a huge spinning wheel . . . and a big display of her dog sweaters." Maggie's gaze remained on her knitting but Lucy saw her laugh. Maggie acted as if she didn't give a thought to the Knitting Nest, but somehow she managed to keep up with any changes there, Lucy noticed.

"Kicking Peter out of the shop does make more room for the dogs. How convenient," Suzanne said. She'd been fishing through her big tapestry knitting bag for something and finally came up with a crumpled copy of her pattern.

Suzanne was a fast but impatient knitter and she hated to follow a pattern. Everybody teased her about it. Or maybe she was just multitasking so much, she didn't have time to check instructions. On any given night, poor Suzanne ended up frogging half her work, ripping out half as many rows as she'd finished. She was making a chulo hat for her thirteen-year-old daughter, Alexis, but had never worked with three colors before.

"Andrea and Peter never had children. The dogs obviously take up the emotional slack. Transference," Dana offered.

There seemed to be plenty of that. Amanda was as devoted as any mother to her furry darlings. Lucy wasn't quite sure how many she had now. A pack of mixed-breed hounds she'd adopted from shelters and rescue groups. That was another reason customers avoided the Knitting Nest. Amanda always kept two or three of her canine crew in the shop with her and some people were uncomfortable around dogs, or simply didn't like dealing with all the cold, wet noses and the pet hair getting into their projects.

"Maggie . . . can you fix this . . . please? This snowflake is turning into a spider." Maggie stuck her hand out and Suzanne handed over her project. White, blue, and pink bobbins of yarn dangled from the piece.

Maggie examined Suzanne's knitting, then picked up a few stitches to get her back on track.

"I, for one, am all in favor of a kinder and gentler Amanda Goran. I think it's very hard for a person to change. I give her a lot of credit. Whatever the reason behind the transformation, I wish her well," Maggie said as she handed Suzanne back her knitting.

The front door of the shop swung open. They held their breath and looked up to see who was coming in this time.

Phoebe, finally.

She clomped in, big black boots scraping the wooden floor. Her cheeks were ruddy from the cold, her dark eyes bright. A fuzzy, multicolored scarf of her own creation looped around her neck, dangling down the front of her black peacoat. A streak of magenta in the scarf matched the one dyed in her dark hair.

She swung her book bag off her shoulder and smiled.

"Hi, guys. Sorry I'm late . . . did I miss anything?"

Lucy got home around ten. She felt tired but needed to make up lost time on her current work project—designing a set of pamphlets explaining employee health insurance benefits. She knew she'd be out again most of the day tomorrow and didn't have that much breathing room on the deadline.

The assignment seemed boring and endless, though she'd only been working on it a week. But it was paying the rent, Lucy kept reminding herself.

She kept at it until half past one, then decided to quit for the night. Before shutting down the computer, she quickly checked her e-mail. A message from her sister Ellen reminding Lucy she was expected at a dinner party at Ellen's house in Concord this coming Saturday night. Lucy had forgotten all about it . . . conveniently. The mere thought of sitting through one of Ellen and Scott's get-togethers made her want to run to her bed and put a pillow over her head.

Ellen had been sympathetic enough during Lucy's divorce, but now acted as if it had been an unfortunate but fairly common ailment, like whiplash or a compressed disc. Lucy could not expect to recover and return to a normal life if she didn't bare down and commit to "the therapy." If Lucy was still not "moving on" with her life at this point, to Ellen's way of thinking, well . . . maybe she was just plain lazy.

Secretly, Lucy had to agree at least a little with this diagnosis, though she wasn't sure what she could do about it. Especially when "the therapy" took the form of one of Ellen's get-togethers, where Lucy knew she would be surrounded by happy—or presumably happy—suburban couples. With the exception of one unattached, presumably straight man that Ellen always invited as the latest candidate.

Ellen's well-intentioned matchups were, without exception, disastrous. Lucy sometimes went through the motions just to avoid hurting Ellen's feelings . . . or avoid her nagging. This time, however, she typed a quick note, claiming she had a bad deadline and could not possibly come to Concord . . . as much as she wanted to.

There was also a message from her mother, who was down in Nicaragua, building houses and latrines in a poverty-stricken village. Her mother's idea of a great tropical vacation, bless her heart. Isabel Binger taught political science at the University of Massachusetts in Amherst, but was on a sabbatical this year.

Lucy and Ellen had been raised near Amherst, in the town of Northampton. Their parents had divorced when Lucy was in college. Her father, Harry Binger, had retired from his law practice and immediately moved down to Myrtle Beach. He'd always hated the cold winters in the northeast and its brief golfing season. Lucy had visited him once at his condo community. She found the place a lot like the Jersey shore but with palm trees and miles of real golf courses, instead of miniature ones—though there were a lot of those, too.

Her father had married a woman named Sheila who shared his values and priorities—well-maintained greens, dry martinis, and watching a lively panel of celebrity guests on *Larry King Live*.

While it was easy to say Ellen had taken after their father and Lucy was clearly her mother's child, Lucy knew that it was never so simple as that.

There were a few other messages from work associates and friends in the city. Many couldn't believe that she was still living out here. At first, neither could Lucy.

During her summers growing up, Lucy's parents more or less dumped her and Ellen with their aunt Laura, who was a schoolteacher with summers off, for weeks at a stretch, as if Laura's home were some convenient free summer camp. But Aunt Laura looked forward to it, being unmarried and without kids of her own. Once the girls were in high school and college, summer jobs and their social lives reduced their visits to Plum Harbor down to a weekend or two. Then when she got busy with her career and marriage, Lucy had not come up very often at all.

Aunt Laura seemed to understand. She was not the whining or judgmental type. When Laura died last spring, the cottage that had always been her home was left to Lucy and Ellen.

Lucy had just left her office job and set up her own business so she decided to take a long summer in Plum Harbor. It seemed a good place to clear her head and regroup after so many life-altering changes in such a short time.

Ellen was happy to have Lucy stay in the house, instead of renting it out to strangers. Lucy's older sister, who was married with two girls, came out for a weekend only once with her family.

Plum Harbor wasn't really Ellen's speed anymore. She was more of a Nantucket or Martha's Vineyard type now. Lucy basically had the place to herself. Ellen hadn't even wanted any of the furniture, with the exception of a small, tiger oak secretary and a mohogany ballroom chair. They were the only pieces of any value, of course. But Lucy knew she was still getting the better of the bargain.

Lucy's own belongings, her half of the furniture she'd shared with her ex-husband, made a curious mix with Aunt Laura's home decor—early American meets early IKEA. Lucy was still trying to sort it all out.

The village did get somewhat desolate in the winter, as Maggie had warned. It was especially so after the holidays, when it was like watching an ant hill, Lucy decided. At first there doesn't seem to be any activity, but if you keep staring, you'll eventually see a steady stream of coming and going, a flow of quiet, methodical industry. The empty beach and open spaces had a strange, subtle beauty this time of year, making their summer glory seem obvious and ordinary.

Looking back now, she wasn't sure if she would have stayed if it hadn't been for Maggie. She had wandered into the Black Sheep one day, purely by chance and didn't even know how to hold knitting needles. But one thing led to another and it was impossible now to trace back to the moment when she and the sisterhood of traveling knitting totes had become true friends, or the moment Lucy realized she was totally hooked on knitting—something she at times considered a mixed blessing.

Early the next morning Lucy dressed quickly, leaving the house with her hair wet and altogether skipping makeup. She'd definitely duck any photographers from the *Plum Harbor Times.* She had promised Maggie she'd come to the shop by nine to help with any last-minute details.

By the time she parked in front of the Black Sheep, the dashboard clock read 8:55. Lucy was surprised to find the shop dark, still closed up tight, and Maggie's car nowhere in sight. She walked up on the porch and peered into the bay window. Maggie was definitely not in there. Neither was Phoebe.

She waited a moment, thinking she might walk up the street

and pick up some coffee. But before she could decide, Maggie's dark green Subaru pulled up and Maggie jumped out, white plastic shopping bags dangling from each hand and a bouquet of flowers tucked under her arm.

"Oh, good, you're here. Could you grab this stuff while I open the door?"

Maggie handed over a bag, then unlocked the front door.

"After I picked up my order at the bakery, I realized I wasn't serving anything healthy. So I ran over to the supermarket for some fruit. Berries. Nice ones. You'd never expect it this time of year."

"Good idea." Lucy nodded. Knowing Maggie, there would be more than enough food, with or without berries. But Maggie did want the event to be perfect.

While Maggie carried the shopping bags inside, Lucy went back to Maggie's car, where she found several white cardboard boxes from the bakery in the trunk. She carried them inside and walked back to the storeroom.

Maggie was working near the sink, arranging flowers in a tall vase. She glanced at Lucy over her shoulder. "Could you take these outside, please? I think the counter near the register would be a good spot."

The vase was slippery and Lucy carried it carefully. She had just set it down in its assigned spot when the shop door swung open. A tall, thin blonde stood in the doorway. She paused and looked around, then stepped inside. Her long, swishy shearling coat was the real thing, Lucy noticed, not a faux version from L.L. Bean. Under that, Lucy caught a glimpse of an attractive three-quarter-length sweater made of multicolored yarn.

The young woman had barely shut the door behind her when Maggie seemed to fly through the air, appearing out of nowhere.

"Cara! So good to see you." The women shared a quick hug

and Maggie stepped back. Cara Newhouse smiled down at her former teacher.

"Good to see you, too, Maggie. . . . Wow. Look at this place. The flowers. Everything. You shouldn't have gone to so much trouble."

Maggie shook her head, but looked pleased. "I wanted to do something special now that you're so well known."

Cara seemed embarrassed by the praise. "Don't be silly. I'm no celebrity."

"You are in the knitting world. Which counts for a lot around here." Maggie turned to Lucy and waved her over. "I want you to meet my good friend, Lucy Binger."

Lucy stretched out her hand as Maggie introduced them. "Nice to meet you, Cara."

"Thanks. Nice to meet you, too." Cara nodded and smiled.

"We put a table for the demonstration back there." Maggie pointed to the far side of the shop's main room. "We thought that would be the easiest place for everyone to see. But we did leave an aisle, so you can walk around as you talk," Maggie explained.

"I can walk around. I can work at the table, I'll do whatever you'd like," Cara said agreeably.

"How about the TV people? Where do you think they'll put the camera?"

"Oh, they're not coming. They called this morning and canceled." Cara shrugged as she took off her long coat. "I don't mind. I'm really not ready. This will be good practice. I'm going to audition at the studio next week."

Maggie looked disappointed for a moment, then quickly recovered. "Just as well. A camera crew in here today would have made it even crazier."

Phoebe had come down from her apartment, Lucy noticed. She poked her head out of the storeroom and waved at Maggie.

"I need another basket for the muffins. Are there any more back here?"

"Looks like I'm needed," Maggie said. "I'll be right back . . ."

Cara started toward the table and Lucy offered to help with the large tote bags she was carrying. Cara handed one over. It was filled with all kinds of things: knitting tools, yarn, measuring sticks.

"I feel like Mary Poppins when I start pulling all this stuff out of my bags."

Cute, Lucy thought, though she'd be hard-pressed to figure out anything else Cara had in common with the original Nanny 911. Cara looked every inch the knitting world diva and soon-to-be TV host. She was a perfect TTB—Lucy's ex-husband's acronym for tall thin blonde. She had the type of figure that looked good in long, draping sweaters and shawls, and . . . okay, a body that would look great draped in almost anything. Or nothing.

Lucy studied Cara's three-quarter-length sweater coat, knitted in a tweedy, medium-weight wool. The coat was embellished with fringe on the cuffs and hem, and wonderful felted flowers that covered snap fasteners. Her black top, black pants, and boots set off the piece perfectly.

"Nice jacket," Lucy complimented her.

"Thanks, the design is in my book. I'm going to talk about it and show everyone how to make the flowers," she promised with another toothpaste-ad smile. "I can make the stuff just fine, but I can get a little confused if I have to stop and explain how I do it," she admitted with a laugh. "So please ask a lot of questions."

"Okay, I'll remember that," Lucy promised.

Cara was different than Lucy had expected. More down to earth. Modest even. Not nearly the prima donna she could be. Maybe it was just Maggie's description of Cara's success that had given that impression.

As for Cara's concerns about her show-and-tell skills, Lucy didn't think Cara needed to sweat it. Just look at her. What producer would care if she didn't know a knitting needle from a chopstick?

Just as Cara finished setting up, the audience began to arrive. Phoebe handed out programs. Lucy noticed Dana come in. She waved, but was too far away to make her way over. Suzanne was late, as usual. Lucy hoped she could save a good seat.

Where was Amanda Goran? Amanda had definitely not been one of the early birds, as she'd promised last night. Lucy would have noticed that entrance. Had Amanda slipped in under the radar somehow? Lucy looked around but didn't see Maggie's notorious rival in the rows of guests already seated.

Amanda's absence suddenly made Lucy worry. She wondered if Maggie had noticed, too. Was Amanda planning to make some scene that would undermine the event? Or had she just chickened out? No matter what she'd said last night, from Amanda's point of view, coming here this morning was a sign of submission. Even defeat. For everyone's sake, Lucy hoped Amanda had decided to just stay in her own territory.

The audience was mostly women, with a few men sprinkled in here and there. About fifty guests, Lucy estimated, probably the largest turnout for a Black Sheep event to date. While Plum Harbor was a small village, little more than two square miles around, the Black Sheep did draw customers from all the neighboring towns and Cara was well known in the community.

The reporter from the *Plum Harbor Times* had arrived. Lucy saw Maggie and Cara pose for a photo in front of the flower arrangement. Cara held up a copy of her book and they both smiled for the camera.

Everything was going perfectly. At precisely eleven, Maggie stepped in front of the group and gently raised her hands for quiet, revealing her past life as a schoolteacher, Lucy thought. The chattering voices stopped.

"Thank you all for coming to the Black Sheep this morning," she began. "We try to present speakers and classes that will enrich and inspire your love of knitting. Today, we have a very special guest, Cara Newhouse. Cara will be talking about her new book, *Felting Fever*, and giving some great tips on the process."

The audience answered with a smattering of applause.

Maggie continued. "A lot of you have told me you'd love to try this technique, but feel intimidated. Time to let go of your fear of felting, ladies." She smiled widely as she urged Cara forward. "Here she is, consulting editor and writer for *Knitting Now!* and two other bestselling books. Plum Harbor's own Cara Newhouse . . ."

Lucy watched Cara stroll front and center. She turned to the audience, her smile growing even wider as the welcoming applause rose.

Cara was just about to speak when the front door flew open.

Suzanne stumbled into the shop. She stared at Phoebe, looking pale and wild eyed, her lipstick smeared. Lucy's heart kicked into overdrive.*What in the world happened? Was something wrong with one of Suzanne's kids?*

The entire audience grew quiet as all eyes turned toward the doorway.

Suzanne's chin trembled. She glanced around the room. "Didn't you hear what happened to Amanda Goran? She's dead!"

Chapter Two

Lucy quickly stepped over to Suzanne and grasped her arm. "Come and sit down, Sue," Lucy said. She led Suzanne to a chair and Phoebe appeared on Suzanne's other side.

Maggie still stood next to Cara at the front of the assembly. Her face was pale as paper and she covered her mouth with her hand. The noise level in the room quickly rose, everyone talking at once. Lucy could tell from the chatter that most, if not all, had known Amanda.

It was big news, all right. Sad and shocking. It was simply . . . unbelievable.

"Better put your head between your knees." Phoebe rested one hand on Suzanne's shoulder. "You look like you're going to lose it."

Suzanne shook her head, resisting the first-aid lesson. "Please, Phoebe . . . I just had my hair done."

Lucy handed Suzanne a bottle of water she'd scooped off the buffet table. "Take a few deep breaths. You'll be okay."

Suzanne sighed and twisted the cap off the bottle. "Just goes to show, you never know. She was right here, last night. Standing right in that doorway. And she'd never looked better."

Lucy shared the thought, then added, "And for once, Amanda hadn't been her usual witchy self, had she?"

Suzanne sighed and shook her head, then took a sip of water.

"How did you hear about it?" Phoebe asked.

"I had an early appointment at the Cut Above. I dropped the kids off at school and went straight over. A woman came in just as I was going out. She'd just heard at the village hall. She said it was a real mess," she added, her voice trembling again. "Very . . . bloody."

Bad news traveled fast, especially in a small town.

The Black Sheep would definitely be bumped off the front page of the local newspaper now. Lucy wondered if Cara's talk would even go on.

She looked back at Maggie, who stepped forward and tried to quiet down the group. "This is terrible news. What a shock. I'm sure we all sympathize with Amanda's loved ones right now. It's a loss for our whole community. Especially our knitting community." Maggie's voice trembled as she delivered her impromptu speech. "Out of respect for Amanda, I think we should bow our heads and have a moment of silence."

The request seemed appropriate and well spoken. Maggie had gracefully sidestepped any mention of her own feelings for the deceased, Lucy noticed.

After a few moments, Maggie lifted her head. Cara stood close beside her, looking suitably solemn. "We can continue with the presentation, if enough of you want to stay," Maggie suggested. "Can I see a show of hands?"

Practically everyone in the audience raised their hand. Lucy did notice a few women gather up their bags and coats, then wiggle through the rows to exit. One of them dabbed a wadded tissue to her eyes. She'd been crying. A true Knitting Nest loyalist—a small but sincere faction.

Maggie waited a moment. "Okay, let's try this again. Here's Cara."

Cara took her place once more in front of the group, her smile tentative. She began her presentation, glancing at some note cards on the table, recalling how she'd learned to knit as a little girl, right here in Plum Harbor, taught by her grandma Nattie. And how she rediscovered the hobby in college with a roommate while studying fashion design in New York City.

"One day it all just came together for me. My lifelong love of knitting and newfound interest in design. I knew what I wanted to be," she said brightly. "Working for *Knitting Now!* and writing my books help me share my passion and know-how with others, like you. Which is what I love best."

Cara's speaking style had all the wit and depth of a beauty pageant contestant delivering her essay on world peace, and Lucy found it hard to focus as snarky comments broke into her thoughts, like pop-up ads.

Thoughts of Amanda Goran were equally if not even more distracting, and Cara's chipper tone seemed oddly out of synch with the solemn mood that had fallen over the room after Suzanne's grave announcement.

Lucy forced her attention back to the show just as Cara picked up a copy of *Felting Fever* from the table. "As you may already know, felting is a process that dates back to ancient times. Some of the earliest knitted objects discovered by archeologists were felted, like socks found in Egyptian ruins, for instance. There are a few ways to felt. Blending loose fibers or felting knitted or woven objects."

She closed the book and walked over to her display items set out on the table. "Socks, hats, place mats, toys, these adorable handbags . . ." She picked up a small bag and wiggled it over the audience, like live bait. "Just about anything you knit can be felted."

Cara stepped back and opened her book. "As I say right here in chapter one, 'Heat and agitation. That's really all there is to it.'"

Cara's description sounded to Lucy just like her social life lately. Or lack of one. Of course there were other stages—attraction, flirtation, connection . . . rejection.

"Only animal fibers can be felted," Cara noted, breaking into Lucy's rambling thoughts. "Super-hot water and the motion from a washer, or motion by hand, make the hair cuticles open and tangle. Like getting the frizzies." Cara touched her own blonde locks, though her own bad hair days were probably few and far between. "The fibers merge and melt into one another, and you get this lovely fabriclike finish. The hot water makes everything tighten and shrink."

So, Lucy realized, when she'd accidently washed sweaters on the wrong cycle and they'd shrunk to Munchkin size, she'd actually been felting? Who knew?

"There are many ways to create special effects. Marbles, braiding . . . umm . . ." Cara paused, checking her notes. "And all of those advanced techniques are explained in depth in my book." Cara smiled again, looking as if she'd lost her train of thought.

Lucy heard two women in the row behind her whispering intensely about Amanda, and she noticed at least two other women up front, doing the same, their heads close together as they commiserated.

Cara was trying her best, but the bad news continued to ripple through the group like an earthquake's aftershocks. Everyone felt shaken and scared, still trying to catch their balance.

Lucy glanced over at Suzanne. "How are you doing, Suzanne?" she whispered.

"Okay, I guess," Suzanne whispered back. "I can't stop thinking about it. I keep expecting her to be here. Then I look around and remember . . ."

Lucy nodded. She felt the same. It was as if Amanda was in the room, her silent presence upstaging the star performer. If Amanda had been here right now, Lucy was sure she'd be sitting up front, sneering—dismissing Cara as all flash and no fiber. Lucy herself was reserving judgment. Cara seemed a bit unsure of her subject matter, but the dreadful news must have shaken her, too. It wasn't easy to give a perky presentation under these circumstances.

Lucy leaned toward Suzanne again. She hated to be rude, but she couldn't help it. "How did it happen?"

"I'm not exactly sure. There was some sort of accident in her shop this morning. She had a head wound. Maybe she fell? I did hear that she died before the ambulance got there . . ." Suzanne's hushed voice trailed off.

Lucy leaned back in her chair and sighed. No matter what you thought about the woman, it was very sad.

Lucy forced her focus back to Cara, who stood at the display table. She was scrambling now to recapture her audience. She was using a knitted rectangle about the size of a place mat as an example, and now showed how the piece looked before and after felting. "We just fold it like so, shape a bit, sew up the sides, add handles, and voilà . . . you've made this adorable handbag."

She chose one of the handbags on display and handed it down to the audience to pass around. Lucy examined it when it was her turn.

The leap from mundane mat to designer original took a little more than a mere "voilà," but Lucy got the idea. You could make cool stuff this way quickly. It was a good technique for knitters like herself who craved instant gratification. Right now most of her projects screamed, "I have number twenty-five needles and I'm not afraid to use them!"

Phoebe examined the felted handbags Cara had on display with interest. "Check this out. This is sick."

"Absolutely," Lucy agreed. Lucy already knew that coming from Phoebe, "sick" was a good thing.

Suzanne leaned closer, her voice hushed. "God, I love that coat."

"She said she was going to talk about it. Why don't you remind her?" Lucy suggested.

Suzanne shook her head. For someone who rarely filtered a word of what she was thinking, Suzanne could be surprising shy in a group.

"Would you, Lucy?" Suzanne asked.

Lucy shrugged. She raised her hand and Cara smiled at her. "A question?"

"My friend and I were wondering about your jacket?"

Cara looked grateful for the nudge. "Oh, right. This is my own design and the pattern is included in *Felting Fever*. The body of the coat is mostly a seed stitch, with some popcorn on the hem and cuffs," Cara explained. "The flower fasteners are felted and have snaps underneath. The technique for the flowers is a little advanced . . . but not too hard." She paused, staring down at the yarn flower, then back at Lucy. "Well, you can read about that on your own. I won't take up everyone's time now explaining."

Cara briefly met Lucy's glance, then her gaze swept the room. "Any more questions?"

A few more hands popped up. Cara finally wrapped up, thanking everyone for coming and offering to sign copies of her book.

"I wish I could make that jacket," Suzanne sighed. "I'd have to felt my butt to look halfway decent in it."

Lucy cast her a sympathetic smile, but as usual, Suzanne spoke the truth. The busy design would have been a disaster on Suzanne's "real-women-have-hips" figure.

"It looks good on her. But it's a little fussy for my taste. I like the fasteners, though." Lucy thought the felted flowers, which also embellished the handbags, were an interesting clever touch.

The audience rose from their seats and dispersed around the shop. Some headed straight for the free food, the other group swarmed around Cara, barely giving her room to breathe as she found a seat and began to sign copies of her book and answer one-on-one questions.

Lucy thought Cara looked relieved. It couldn't have been easy, getting up there after such horrific news had been announced. You had to give her credit.

As Lucy had expected, the talk around the cake table was mainly about Amanda and mostly questions. When had it happened? How had she died? Who had found her . . . and where?

Suzanne knew very little, just what she'd heard at the hair salon and had related to Lucy. Still, she had as many people crowded around her as Cara, which must have been just a bit annoying for the almost-famous guest speaker.

It was over an hour later when the last mini-quiche, muffin and berry had been consumed and the final autograph signed. Maggie's friends hung around, helping to put the shop back together, all but Suzanne, who had to hit the real-estate office before her children got home from school. Cara also remained, packing her belongings.

Maggie dropped into a folding chair, looking exhausted but relieved. "I thought that went well. Considering that dreadful news about Amanda. What a shock. I've hardly had a chance to take it all in."

"It's just terrible," Dana said. "Suzanne said she fell and hit her head?"

"I'm not sure if it was a fall," Lucy replied. "She did have a bad head wound. Some sort of accident, I guess?"

"It's a shock. Very sad," Maggie agreed.

"Did you guys know her well?" Cara glanced around the group of friends.

"A little," Lucy replied. She wasn't sure how to describe Amanda's relationship with their circle. She exchanged a look with Dana. Wasn't the feud between Maggie and Amanda common knowledge around town? Obviously Cara was not in the loop.

Maggie glanced up at Cara, then back at the carton of books she was packing up. "We knew each other. But we didn't get along very well," Maggie admitted. "Amanda always looked at me as some sort of evil genius, scheming to put her out of business. Still, I wouldn't wish such an end on anyone, even my worst enemy."

"Of course not," Cara said quietly. She took the carton and placed it with her other belongings.

"Did you know Amanda at all?" Lucy asked Cara.

Cara shrugged as she slipped on her coat. "I must have seen her around town. I'm not really sure. She had a shop on Hobson Street, right? I think I've only been in there once or twice. I didn't really get into knitting until I was away at college. And since Maggie opened the Black Sheep if I need anything when I'm in town, I come here."

Lucy nodded, remembering the biographical tidbit from her talk.

Maggie sighed. "Amanda was very talented. She should have stuck to designing, I think. She wasn't much of a businesswoman."

"Was she married? Did she have a family?" Cara was winding a scarf around her neck, another felted creation in a shade of French blue that matched her eyes perfectly.

"She was married but they didn't have any children," Dana replied.

"Oh . . . well, it's still sad," Cara answered. She pulled a pair of matching blue mittens out of her pocket, then turned to Maggie again. "Guess I'll take off. Thanks so much for having me here. It was really fun."

Maggie jumped up from her seat. "Thank you for coming, Cara. I appreciate it, really. And good luck with the TV show. Let me know what happens, okay?"

"Oh, I will, Maggie. See you soon." Cara gave Maggie a hug and finally headed out.

Lucy helped Maggie with the last of the furniture arranging to get the shop back to normal, then decided it was time to go, too. Once she got home, she would kick off her boots, yank off her bra, find the thick, comfy socks—which she'd knitted herself, though one had turned out slightly larger than the other—and plant herself at the computer to make up for lost time.

As she was leaving, a few customers wandered in and Maggie ran over to help them. Lucy waved from the doorway as she stepped outside.

Driving home, she couldn't help thinking about Amanda and her untimely end. *Just goes to show, Gather yea felted rosebuds while ye may . . . or something like that,* she thought.

Maggie had said all the right things about Amanda, but Lucy wondered what Maggie really felt, hearing that her arch rival had suddenly been wiped off the playing field. Along with the shock they all felt, the news must have brought Maggie some private moment of relief, if only to realize she was no longer subjected to Amanda's ill will and bouts of harassment.

The next morning, after a halfhearted attempt to clean up the cottage—a routine that basically consisted of collecting armfuls of dirty mugs and newspapers, and throwing in a load of laundry—Lucy decided a walk into town would be a good way to clear her head after the previous night's work marathon.

The bright winter sunlight made her blink and the dry cold air burned her lungs as she attempted a speed walk down the winding side streets to the village.

She made it all the way to the town docks and village green, which fronted the harbor, then started back up Main Street, heading for the Schooner. The Schooner was a coffee shop that had been opened in the 1950s and had not changed much since then in menu, attitude, or decor. The turquoise leather booths and chrome trim were so far out of fashion they were back in.

Edie Steiber, who had inherited the grill from her father, ran the place. She sat behind the cash register like a Buddha in a cardigan—a Christmas cardigan, Lucy noticed, though it was well past Valentine's Day. Edie had her own style, you might say. Reading glasses dangled around her neck on a beaded cord as she wiped down a stack of plastic menus. Her perch was right near the entrance, at the end of the long counter, and she prided herself on greeting just about everyone who came in or out by name.

"Hey, Lucy. You're out early. Coffee?" Edie asked as Lucy walked in. Lucy nodded and took a seat at the counter.

"Large, please. To go."

As Edie poured the coffee, Lucy checked the rack near the register that usually held the local paper, but it stood empty. She riffled through the other slots that held copies of the *Boston Globe* and *U-Sell It*, but didn't see any stray copies. Had Edie missed her delivery this morning?

"Looking for the *Plum Harbor Times*?" Edie set the paper cup of coffee on the counter, the plastic lid balanced on top. "I might have a copy down here somewhere." She leaned over and peered under the counter. "Sold out the stack in an hour. That poor Amanda Goran, what a terrible thing. . . . Oh, here it is."

She pulled out the paper and laid it on the counter. Lucy had already taken a sip of coffee, but the gulp of hot liquid stuck in her throat.

"Local Merchant Murdered," the headline read.

A photo of Amanda holding up a knitting project and a picture of the Knitting Nest surrounded by yellow crime-scene tape ran alongside the story.

"She was murdered?" Lucy stared at Edie. "I heard it was an accident."

"Someone broke into the shop and bashed the poor woman's head in. That was no accident, hon." Edie tugged her sweater a little tighter around her chest and ample stomach, as if the conversation gave her a chill.

"Oh my God, that's horrible. . . ." Lucy quickly scanned the article. Amanda had died from a head injury, as Suzanne had reported, but it had not been caused by a fall or some random accident. She'd died in her shop yesterday morning after being struck repeatedly on the head, the *Plum Harbor Times* reported. Peter Goran, Amanda's estranged husband, had found her around ten o'clock. He'd put in the call to 911, but it had been too late.

"I've been living here all my life. It's hard to remember the last time something this violent ever happened." Edie shook her head. "People are horrified. They can't stop talking about it. It's a frightening world we're living in today. I just hope they catch whoever did this. Catch them and make them pay."

Lucy stared blankly across the counter. Amanda's death had been shocking enough. Was it really a cold-blooded murder? Who would do such a thing? Sure, Amanda had a knack for rubbing people the wrong way, hoarding every slight—real or imagined—and rarely sparing anyone her opinion. Plenty of people in town had tangled with the proprietor of the Knitting Nest, that was for sure. But did anyone dislike her enough to kill her? Lucy couldn't imagine it. Not in this town.

"Must have been a break-in," Edie speculated. "I've had problems myself. I had to put a thick metal door with a bar at the kitchen entrance in back. Looks like Fort Knox."

Lucy nodded at the story. She was still shocked practically speechless by the newspaper headline. It could have been some random act, committed by a total stranger, Lucy thought. Though any criminal mind who found the Knitting Nest a temptation had to be completely desperate . . . or a real dimwit.

"It's all the drugs at the high school," Edie added. "The kids are desperate. And daring. They see all this violence in the movies and those video games and say, What the heck. It doesn't mean a thing to them."

"Drugs at the high school? I never heard that."

Edie nodded knowingly. "Oh yeah. It's bad. People don't like to talk about it. Brings down the real-estate value and all that baloney, but believe me, it's going on here, same as everywhere. We're just close enough to the city, that's the problem."

Edie did have a point. Plum Harbor seemed to be a long way from civilization but it was actually quite close to Boston and no place on earth was really immune to the insidious problem.

Lucy reached in her pocket and pulled out some bills, then paid for the coffee and paper. As she was leaving, she passed a group of women seated in a booth by the door. She couldn't help but overhear their conversation, more speculation about Amanda's murder, of course.

As Lucy headed up Main Street toward the Black Sheep, she had no doubt the same conversation was going on behind each storefront—the variety and hardware stores, busy with Saturday-morning shoppers. The antique stores and bookshop. The deli and post office. As Lucy passed each doorway, she imagined the shock and speculation voiced within. Edie had her own theories, but she'd been right about one thing. Amanda's murder was frightening, especially to the shopkeepers, who must now wonder if it could happen again, to one of them.

The Black Sheep didn't open on Saturdays until eleven, but Lucy had a feeling she'd find Maggie there. She wasn't surprised to find the shop door open and she walked in. Maggie sat in an armchair in the front room. She had some knitting out, though the needles lay idle in her lap. The newspaper sat open on the tea table in front of the couch.

"I guess you've seen the news about Amanda," Lucy said.

Maggie stared up at her. "Can you believe it?"

"It's hard to get my brain around it," Lucy admitted. "Do you really think she was murdered?"

"That's what the police say. The paper doesn't give much information, but there must be a good reason. It must have been awful for Peter to have found her like that."

Lucy didn't answer. The mere thought made her shudder.

The shop door opened and Dana swept in, her large travel mug in hand. From the look on her face, Lucy could tell she was up to speed on the news.

"My ten thirty canceled, so I have a little time," she said, sitting down.

A little time to talk about Amanda's murder, she meant. The newspaper article had been sparse with details and reasons why the police were investigating. Lucy hoped Dana might be able to fill in a few of the blanks.

"Did Jack hear anything about Amanda?" Lucy asked her.

"Yes, what are his police friends saying?" Maggie leaned forward eagerly.

Dana sat down and twisted open her mug. "It's a huge case.

Jack can't remember the last time this town had a murder to investigate." Same as Edie said, Lucy thought. "That's why the county detectives were brought in. It's beyond the scope of the village police force."

"I read that in the paper," Lucy said.

"Peter Goran found her," she added. "Jack's buddy said the poor man came out of the shop covered with blood. He was really in shock. Quite a sight when the ER and police got there." Dana shuddered.

Lucy cringed at the image. "He must have been trying to revive her."

Maggie slipped on her reading glasses, then picked up her knitting. Her fingers jumped nervously across the row of stitches as she tried to find her place. "I guess he tried to help her. But it was too late. . . . How awful."

"He told the police he went over to the Knitting Nest yesterday morning to talk to Amanda about some point they were haggling about in their separation agreement," Dana continued. "He heard the dogs barking, really going crazy. When she didn't answer, he used his own key to get in."

"And found her," Lucy added.

"She was on the floor in her office. He thought at first maybe she'd fallen and struck her head. But the wounds were not the type you'd get from a fall. More like someone had struck her on the head with a blunt object."

"The police can tell all that so quickly?" Lucy asked.

Dana nodded, sipping her coffee. "It's pretty basic medical examiner's stuff. They're doing a full autopsy, of course. Jack says the report won't be in for a few days. I think they had to send the body to Boston."

Maggie took a breath. "Poor Amanda. She didn't deserve this."

"And the shop was a mess. Her office was turned upside down. Whoever broke in must have been looking for cash, or anything valuable they could get their hands on."

"Sounds like Amanda walked in on a robbery," Lucy said.

"Maybe. Just a case of bad timing." Dana shrugged.

"What about the dogs?" Lucy asked. "Wouldn't they have tried to protect her?"

"I've heard crooks have ways of dealing with dogs. They toss them some meat or sticks of butter," Maggie said.

"Amanda wouldn't have been subdued so easily," Lucy replied. "She wouldn't have given in meekly if she came face-to-face with an intruder."

"No, she was never meek . . . but she didn't have much luck, did she?" Maggie sounded genuinely grieved for her former foe.

The shop door opened and they all looked up to find a couple standing in the doorway. Lucy didn't recognize them. The man was about Maggie's age, tall and thin, dressed in a long, navy blue, all-weather-type coat. A brimmed hat shadowed his thin face. The woman looked younger, wearing a tailored wool coat over dark pants. They didn't look like a married couple, Lucy thought. In fact, they didn't seem to match at all, except for their serious expressions.

"Good morning. I'm Detective Walsh. From the Essex County Police. This is Detective Reyes," he added, introducing his partner. "We're looking for Ms. Messina?" He stared around at the group of women and removed his hat.

Maggie's eyes widened. "I'm Maggie Messina." She stood up and put down her knitting. "Can I help you with something?"

The county detectives had not stopped by for advice on their cable stitch, Lucy was sure of that.

As Maggie walked toward them, the two detectives took out

official ID from their coat pockets and flashed the cards for her to see.

"We're gathering information about Amanda Goran," Detective Reyes said. "You may have known her?"

"Of course. We were just talking about Amanda," Maggie replied. "Very sad news."

"Yes, it is." Detective Walsh agreed and nodded. The expression in his eyes suggested he'd seen a lot of sad situations, Lucy thought, and would see a lot more before he was through.

"We'd like to ask you a few questions, Ms. Messina," Detective Reyes said. "Is there somewhere private where we can talk?" She glanced over at Dana and Lucy, sparing a small smile.

Maggie shrugged. "I don't mind talking to you here. These are my good friends. You might want to speak with them, too. They knew Amanda. At least a little."

Detective Walsh tilted his head. "I've heard that you knew her through your business. That the two of you were rivals. Is that a fair description?"

Obviously, the Black Sheep was not their first stop, though they probably didn't have to question too many people in order to hear about Amanda and Maggie's contentious relationship.

"I guess you could call us rivals," Maggie replied, "though you make it sound like we were dueling with knitting needles or something."

"Point taken." The detective responded with a small smile. Lucy thought it looked as if it pained him just a bit, but he was making the effort, possibly to get Maggie talking.

"How would you describe your relationship with her, Ms. Messina?" Detective Reyes followed up in a quiet tone.

"There was some friction," Maggie admitted. "Mainly on her side."

For a small person, Maggie had a surprisingly strong, deep

voice. She could summon an authoritative edge, too, honed during years of managing surly high school students.

Detective Walsh took a slim pad and pen from the breast pocket of his coat and flipped it open. "What do you think Ms. Goran's grievances were. Did she ever tell you?"

Maggie shrugged. "I'm not sure where to start. Amanda acted as if I had no right to open a knitting shop because of her place, which was over on the other side of town and didn't even get enough traffic to stay open regular hours. I think she would have resented anyone opening a knitting store within twenty miles of here." Maggie shrugged and glanced at Detective Walsh. He showed no reaction. She looked over at Detective Reyes, whose expression seemed a bit more sympathetic. "I didn't take it personally. I mean, I tried not to. Though she made it personal," Maggie explained.

Detective Reyes nodded. She was pretty, Lucy noticed, though obviously downplaying her looks, with her dark hair pulled back in a clip and little or no makeup. Lucy guessed it was still difficult for a woman in law enforcement and hard to rise to the rank of detective. "How long have you had this business, Ms. Messina?" she asked.

"Oh . . . about three years. I used to teach at the high school, in the art department. I'd always wanted to open a knitting store when I retired. But Bill—my husband—died about four years ago," she explained simply.

Lucy heard the catch in her voice. Maggie still grew emotional talking about Bill. She'd carried on with her life, but there remained a great yawning gap that could not be repaired.

"There wasn't any reason to put it off after that," she added. "And I needed something to keep me going."

Detective Reyes answered with another sympathetic nod. Detective Walsh made a note in his book. Neither of them said very much, Lucy noticed. They just let Maggie do the talking. She was probably giving too much information now, more than the police wanted to know.

"Did you know Ms. Goran before you started your business?" Detective Walsh asked.

"Oh . . . I don't know. I guess so," Maggie said vaguely. "I knew who she was. I used to buy most of my yarn back then from catalogues or ordered online. I did go into the Knitting Nest once in a while, in an emergency. But it always seemed very drab and dingy to me."

"But after you opened your own shop, you got to know her better?" he persisted.

"I wouldn't go that far. I really didn't know her at all," Maggie clarified. "Only at a distance. Which was enough for me," she added tartly.

The detective stared at Maggie a moment, then looked down at his pad again. "Let's get back to her grievances. You said there were quite a few. What else besides opening this store?"

"It all boiled down to one thing, Detective. My shop was more successful than hers. She was jealous. Extremely jealous. She considered herself above me, in her knowledge of knitting and even in teaching the craft. Maybe she was, who can say? All I know is I was better at running a business. My shop is in a better location, and it's more comfortable and attractive to customers. It's just more fun to come in here," she said bluntly, as if he'd been arguing with her. "But I never set out to steal her customers or put her out of business. Is that what you've heard?" she asked. "Because if you have, it just isn't true. If anything, it was completely the opposite. She always tried to make problems for me. Big ones."

"Really? How so?" His eyebrows quirked up with interest. Detective Reyes crossed her arms over her chest, listening to Maggie with a serious expression.

Lucy exchanged worried glances with Dana. Was it time to stuff a few skeins of yarn into Maggie's mouth? Clearly Maggie felt she had nothing to hide, Lucy reminded herself. It was probably better if she answered all these questions now, so the police could cross her off their list.

Maggie took a deep breath. She stared straight ahead, looking uncomfortable and self-conscious. "Well, I remember when I was open about a month or so, Amanda spread rumors that I was cheating customers, changing the labels on ordinary yarn to pass it off as organic, so I could charge more. Or that when I set up classes, I tricked students into buying a lot of expensive yarn and needles from the shop. That sort of thing. But none of it was true."

"I see." He nodded, though it was impossible from his expression to tell if he believed her or not.

"Did you ever confront Ms. Goran about this?" Detective Reyes asked.

Dana shot Lucy a look. Lucy could tell what her friend was thinking. This part of the story didn't show Maggie in her best light. Was there some way they could interrupt? Spill coffee? Call Maggie over for a knitting emergency? Too late. Maggie was already answering.

"I did try to speak to her about all the misinformation she was spreading around. Though I'm not sure I'd call it a confrontation." Maggie's voice shook a bit, sounding a little nervous now.

"How did you resolve it?" Detective Reyes asked politely.

Maggie nervously played with some bangle bracelets on her wrist. "First, I tried to call her, but she wouldn't speak to me. She kept hanging up." Maggie spoke slowly, her tone markedly more careful. "So I tried to talk to her face-to-face. I went to her shop. Well, she denied the entire thing. She acted as if I was imagining it, which of course, I was not. Not one bit," Maggie assured him.

Lucy felt a twinge. Amanda had been the obsessive one, that was for sure, but in telling the story, Maggie sounded like the nutjob. It was ironic and unfortunate now for Maggie.

Detective Walsh scribbled a note. "Were there any customers there at the time?"

Maggie shrugged. "A few. She never had that many customers there at one time."

"So you spoke with her. Told her to stop spreading rumors. She denied she was and then you left," Detective Reyes repeated the story as Maggie had told it. Then she paused, her tone becoming more personal, even a bit coaxing. "Is that how it went? There was no argument or confrontation, Ms. Messina?"

Maggie sighed as she crossed her arms over her chest. Lucy thought she looked cornered, caught in a lie, though she had no reason to feel guilty about anything.

"The situation deteriorated a bit, I guess. Maybe I raised my voice. I don't really remember. It was a long time ago. I was angry. She had no right to sabotage my business, just because her shop wasn't doing well. I needed to make it clear that she wasn't going to intimidate me. I told her to stop, or I'd take legal action."

"I see," Detective Reyes replied. She glanced at her partner, then looked back at Maggie. "How long ago would you say this happened?"

Maggie shrugged. Her cheeks were flushed and she definitely looked flustered now. "Oh, I don't know. I'd say I was in business about a year or so by then. So maybe it was about two years ago? Maybe more."

Detective Walsh made another note. "Did you ever follow through on that threat?"

"No, I did not." Maggie shook her head, her curly brown hair bouncing around her face. "Amanda pulled plenty of other nasty tricks, believe me. But I ignored her. I could see there was no reasoning with her. Frankly, it didn't matter. My shop did well, no matter what she said."

Detective Reyes nodded. She seemed to believe Maggie's side of the story. Walsh was harder to read. He showed little reaction to the information.

"So you ignored her after that point . . . two years ago, you said," he added, checking his notes.

"Yes, I did. Mostly," Maggie hedged. She took a deep breath. "Listen, Detective. I don't know how far you've gotten with your investigation, but there are lots of people around here with far more serious grudges against Amanda Goran than I had, believe me," Maggie promised. "It didn't take much to start an argument with her and she didn't waste any energy keeping her opinions to herself. You must have heard that by now."

Lucy could tell from her tone that Maggie was starting to lose her patience. Lucy cringed, wondering what was going to come out next.

Detective Reyes tipped her head in interest. Detective Walsh maintained his poker face, not reacting one way or the other.

"Who else do you think had a grudge against Ms. Goran?" Detective Reyes asked.

Maggie considered the question a moment. "Well, let's see. She had a problem with a coworker at Sally's Arts and Crafts—that big chain store in the mall," Maggie clarified.

"I know it well," Detective Reyes replied. "My girls love that place. They try to drag me there at least once a week." She shook her head and smiled. "Go on."

"Amanda took a part-time job there for a while, since the shop wasn't earning much. I heard she found out a woman she worked with was stealing crafts supplies and selling the goods at flea markets. Amanda turned the woman in, and the woman went to jail for several months. She ended up losing custody of her kids because of it, too. So when this coworker got out, I heard she began to harass the Gorans. Made phone calls and sent threatening notes, that sort of thing. I heard Amanda went to the police. She may have even filed for an order of protection. That wasn't too long ago," Maggie pointed out. "Maybe you should look into it."

Detective Walsh made a note or two, Lucy noticed. But he didn't look impressed. Or surprised. He probably already knew about that episode since the Gorans had complained to the police.

"Anyone else?" he asked evenly.

"Yes, there was, " Maggie piped up. "I heard she had some friction with a neighbor. Very recently, too. Amanda thought the man was mistreating his dog, leaving the animal out all day in all kinds of weather. Amanda loved dogs. She couldn't stand to see anything like that."

"So we've heard," he replied.

"Well, Amanda just walked into the yard next door while the man was at work one day and took the dog. After he'd figured out what had happened, she wouldn't give the dog back. I think he got physical, tried to force his way into her house. Peter, her husband, may have fought with him. I'm not sure. But I do know the police were called, and they all went to court. It was in the newspaper. I think the neighbor was renting the place and lost his lease over it. He couldn't have been happy about that."

"I'm sure he wasn't," Detective Walsh agreed mildly.

Detective Reyes didn't say anything. She looked down a moment and adjusted the strap on her shoulder bag. A subtle gesture but probably a bad sign, Lucy thought.

Walsh hadn't made any notes about that story, either. He appraised Maggie with a long look. "You seem to know a lot about Ms. Goran. You seem to have taken a real interest in her activities."

Lucy saw Maggie's cheeks color. It did sound like that, didn't it? As if Maggie was practically obsessed with Amanda . . . not the other way around.

Maggie shrugged. She rearranged some items on the counter, a display of crochet hooks with enamel handles. "It's a small town. You hear things."

"I'm sure. Especially if you run a shop like this one," Detective Walsh replied.

A shop full of women who sat knitting and dishing dirt all day was what he really meant, Lucy thought.

"When was the last time you saw Ms. Goran?" Detective Reyes asked her.

"Thursday night. I was here with my knitting group—Lucy and Dana," Maggie noted, glancing at them. "And another friend, Suzanne Cavanaugh. Amanda saw the lights on, so she stopped in and said hello. She had signed up for an event I held here on Friday. I think she just wanted a sneak preview."

"And what sort of event was that?" Detective Reyes continued.

"An author came in for a presentation and a book signing. Cara Newhouse. She grew up in town and was a student of mine. She's pretty well known now." A copy of Cara's book happened to be on the counter and Maggie picked it up to show them.

"Can you describe the conversation with Ms. Goran that night?" Detective Walsh asked. "Was there friction between any of you?"

"No, none at all. She seemed in a remarkably good mood. She was very polite, almost friendly."

"That surprised you?" he asked.

"It surprised everyone." Maggie glanced over at Dana and Lucy. They looked at the two police officers and nodded.

"Can you remember anything specific?" Detective Reyes asked. "Anything she said?"

"Oh, I don't know. We talked for a minute or two. She was

sort of nosing around. She asked about some organic wool that's on display." Maggie pointed out the yarn in question. "She noticed that it's a good price and asked if I was trying to put her out of business . . . in a joking way," Maggie hurried to add. "I offered to put her in touch with the supplier, but she wasn't interested. She said she had decided to pull back from her business and was looking for a manager. We were all surprised at that, too," Maggie told them. "I mean, the Knitting Nest is—was—her life. She was devoted to that shop."

Detective Walsh made a quick note, then looked up. "Anything else?"

Maggie thought a moment. "She told me that my shop had good stock and nice displays. I think that was the first and only time she ever gave me a compliment. Then she said she was going to get here early for a good seat on Friday. But of course . . . she never made it."

Maggie sighed, either swept by a wave of sympathy for her former foe, or tired out by all the questions.

"Okay, let's talk about Friday morning," Detective Walsh said. "Can you tell me where you were between, say, seven and nine that morning, Ms. Messina?" He wasn't looking at his pad anymore, he was staring straight at Maggie.

Lucy sat up straight, suddenly alarmed. This was the kind of question police ask if they suspect a person of having committed the crime . . . wasn't it? Maggie didn't seem to notice that. Maybe because she was so completely innocent?

She paused and took a breath. "Well, let's see . . . I got up early to get ready for the event. I had a lot of errands to do. I guess I left my house around seven and went to the bakery to pick up some muffins and cookies I'd ordered. Then I stopped at the florist right on Main Street. And then, I drove over to the supermarket. I needed some fruit," she explained. "I guess I got back here around . . . a quarter to nine? Lucy was waiting for me," Maggie added, glancing over at Lucy again.

As Lucy recalled, it was actually just nine when Maggie finally arrived, but she was not about to correct her.

"I'm pretty sure I saved the store receipts," Maggie added. "It was all a business expense."

"You were at the grocery store the entire time, buying fruit?" Detective Walsh asked.

"Not the entire time," Maggie clarified. "I drove down to the harbor and sat in my car a few minutes. I did some knitting, to settle my nerves. I hate to start the day in a rush, it really sets me off on the wrong foot."

Lucy knew for a fact that was true: Maggie often knit by the harbor to destress. But Maggie had been so keyed up on Friday morning, it was hard to imagine she'd come to a full stop like that for a knitting break.

The police also seemed to be having trouble imagining it.

Walsh glanced at his partner. Detective Reyes looked back at Maggie. "Did anyone see you down there? Did you speak to anyone?" Detective Reyes asked her.

Maggie's brow crinkled a moment. Then she shook her head. "I can't think of anyone specifically. I saw a few people pass by, jogging or walking their dogs. I didn't meet anyone I know."

Walsh looked back at his notes and flipped the page. "So maybe you sat in your car about half an hour . . . forty-five minutes?"

Maggie paused again. "Maybe. I finished about half a sleeve for the sweater I've been working on."

Maggie sounded proud of her progress, then her expression fell. She'd suddenly realized what he was asking. The gap in time would have made it possible for her to drive over to the Knitting Nest, kill Amanda, and return to meet Lucy at the Black Sheep by nine. Or even sooner.

"You don't think I had anything to do with Amanda Goran's death . . . do you?" Maggie stared at Detective Walsh, looking stunned. When he didn't respond, she turned to Detective Reyes.

"Our job is to question people who knew her," Detective Reyes replied.

"Like you just told us, Ms. Messina, she rubbed a lot of people the wrong way," Detective Walsh added.

Lucy didn't find his answer exactly reassuring. She could see Maggie had not, either.

"Believe me, it was far more likely that she would have tried to finish me off than I ever would have harmed her." Maggie punctuated the insight with a strained laugh.

Detective Walsh flipped his pad closed and slipped it back in his breast coat pocket. "One more question, please. I noticed a green Subaru parked out front. Is that your car?"

Maggie nodded. "Yes, it is . . . why do you ask?"

He paused, as if judging whether or not to tell her. "A car fitting that description was seen parked at the Knitting Nest early yesterday morning."

Maggie took a breath. Her cheeks colored again. Surprised by the question, or trying to control her temper, Lucy couldn't tell which.

"There are a lot of green Subarus on the road these days. That doesn't mean anything."

He flashed a brief, tight smile. "Nothing means anything until it means something, Ms. Messina . . . know what I mean?"

Good one, Detective, Lucy thought. If that wasn't a Zen koan, it really should be.

Detective Walsh drew a white business card from his wallet. "Thanks for your time. If anything comes to mind, even if it seems insignificant, please give me a call."

Maggie took the card without looking at it.

"You're welcome, Detective."

A shrill ring sounded and Detective Walsh reached into his coat pocket and flipped open his phone. "Walsh," he answered curtly. He focused on the conversation a moment, then looked at Detective Reyes. "I have to take this. I'll meet you at the car, Marisol."

She met his glance and nodded. He walked quickly to the door and let himself out. Detective Reyes turned back to Maggie. "I'm sure this situation is upsetting, Ms. Messina. We appreciate you taking the time to speak with us."

"It *has* been upsetting," Maggie admitted. "But I want to help the police find whoever did this. I didn't like her, that's true, but she didn't deserve to die that way. No one does."

Detective Reyes held out her own card. "Please feel free to call me, as well, if anything else comes to mind." She glanced around as she headed for the door. "This is a very nice shop. I can see why you do a good business here."

And I can see why Amanda Goran may have been jealous, Lucy thought the detective was also saying.

"Thank you," Maggie said politely.

The three women watched as Detective Reyes stepped outside. Maggie shut the door behind her. A long silent moment passed before anyone dared to speak. Maggie returned and dropped onto the love seat.

"Did that really happen?" She stared at each of them in turn, looking shocked and frightened. "Can the police possibly think that I killed Amanda Goran?"

Dana touched Maggie's arm. "Let's slow down a minute. The police have to interview a long list of people she knew. Detective Reyes just told you that. They must have heard about the bad vibes between the two of you and come to check out your side of the story."

"Probably . . . but that doesn't make me feel better. I think they got the impression *I* was the crazy one. Especially Detective Walsh. Didn't you notice the way he kept looking at me? Could anyone possibly think I'd kill Amanda over competition between our shops? That's utterly . . . absurd."

Lucy agreed. It was absurd, laughable even. Under different circumstances. But it hadn't helped to dredge up all those old stories about Amanda. Lucy didn't think this was a good time to point that out to her, though.

"Dana's right," Lucy said calmly. "The police must be questioning everyone who had problems with Amanda, and that's a long list. Longer than we even know."

"And what about Peter?" Dana leaned back and crossed her legs, covered by knee-high, black leather boots. "Peter had a truckload of problems with his wife and definitely has the most to gain by her death."

"Certainly more than I do," Maggie cut in.

"Absolutely," Dana agreed. "Jack said their separation agreement was never signed. So Peter still stands to inherit any property or savings they held in common. He'll collect any insurance benefit, too."

"He did find her body," Maggie reminded them.

"And came out of the house covered with her blood," Dana added.

Maggie picked up a skein of yarn from the table. She fitted it on her wooden umbrella swift, which was clamped to the table rim, and started rolling the yarn into a ball.

"That's how it always ends up in the movies," Maggie reminded them. "The husband or wife did it. It's a known fact that most murder victims are killed by someone familiar to them. I must have read it somewhere."

"I've heard that, too, but . . . sorry, I just can't see it," Lucy admitted. "Unless Peter Goran has a dark side. A very hidden dark side," she added.

Maggie suddenly stopped rolling and looked up. "The police think I have a dark side. Why can't Peter Goran have one?"

"Oh, Maggie. No they don't," Dana insisted.

Maggie met her glance but didn't seem much calmer. "Thanks, Dana. But I think I'd better call your husband. I think I need to find a good lawyer."

Chapter Three

Soon after the detectives left the Black Sheep, customers began to drift in. Dana returned to her office and Maggie gathered materials for a class that would start at 11:00 called It's a Wrap!: Ponchos, Stoles and Wraps for Beginners.

Lucy lingered, paging through a new pattern magazine that featured spring styles. She couldn't help but overhear the conversations swirling around her, mostly about Amanda Goran's murder. The event had shaken the town but truly shocked the knitting community. Just as she was about to leave, she saw a man walk in the store. He stood at the counter and gazed around curiously. Lucy walked up to him. "Can I help you with something?" she asked him.

"I'm looking for Ms. Messina?"

Lucy looked him over. Middle-aged, wearing a dress shirt and tie under his down jacket. Another detective? Oh . . . she hoped not.

"And you are?" Lucy asked.

He offered her a business card and an eager smile. "Gladiator Security. I wondered if she wants to update her alarm system. There have been some serious break-ins around town," he added in a solemn tone.

"So we've heard," Lucy replied.

It had started; Plum Harbor shopkeepers were circling the wagons. This guy was enterprising, she had to hand it to him.

"Ms. Messina is back there, at the big table. The woman with the curly brown hair," Lucy told him.

Maggie might be annoyed at her later for not just turning the salesman away. But Lucy was so relieved to find out he wasn't another police officer, she didn't think of brushing him off until it was too late.

Lucy spent the rest of the day and night at home at her computer, slogging away on her freelance project. Once she was immersed in her work, it was easy to forget that it was Saturday night and she had no social life. Probably not the healthiest way to cope with the situation, she knew. But what the heck, so far it was workin' for her.

On Sunday morning, she woke to the sound of Suzanne's chipper voice on the answering machine.

"Hey, Lucy. This is your wakeup call. We're going to that free yoga class this morning, remember? I'll be by to pick you up in ten minutes."

Yoga class? Since when did Suzanne do yoga? Then Lucy remembered. The yoga studio Dana belonged to was holding an open house today—bring a friend and get a free class—so she and Suzanne had agreed to try it.

They must have ganged up on her at a weak moment, Lucy realized as she staggered out of bed. She did need a regular exercise routine, no arguing with that. The sands of time were shifting all over her body. Sitting on her butt all day in front of the computer wasn't helping matters. But yoga? Dana seemed to thrive on it and had promised to take them out for breakfast afterward. What else did she have to do this morning anyway.

A short time later, Lucy was seated next to Suzanne in the Cavanaughs' huge SUV, aptly named a Sequoia. The interior smelled distinctly of stale french fries, crayons, and abandoned cleats. Fearing they were late, Suzanne flew down side streets and practically took the last turn on two wheels. She maneuvered the buslike vehicle into a space with remarkable ease, then shut the engine, whisking a sheen from her forehead with her sweatshirt sleeve.

"Whew . . . feels like I had a workout just getting here. I could definitely use some stress-busting stretches." She smiled at Lucy and grabbed her purse from the backseat. "There it is, Nirvana Yoga Center."

"Look . . ." Lucy pointed to the building directly across the street. "The Knitting Nest."

Suzanne turned, her expression suddenly serious. "Oh, right. I didn't realize."

They sat for a moment and stared at the storefront, the first floor of a large old cedar shake building that was badly in need of tending. Yellow crime-scene tape that surrounded the front entrance now hung a bit slack, a few strangling pieces blowing in the wind.

It was a damp chilly day and the gunmetal gray sky made the scene even more ominous. The shop windows were dark and the place looked forlorn and deserted. Lucy couldn't help thinking about Amanda and her gruesome end.

She felt a hand on her shoulder and jumped. "Come on, we'd better go," Suzanne said quietly.

Lucy nodded, grabbed her bag, and hopped out of the SUV. By now, Lucy had seen the newspaper photo of the Knitting Nest covered in crime-scene tape countless times, but standing in front of the place gave her a jolt and brought the reality of Amanda's murder home all over again.

Lucy and Suzanne were the last ones to arrive at the class. They found places in the back of the room near Dana and set up mats. Then they settled down for some serious stretching.

Lucy soon decided that the yoga class was a bit like eating a sandwich made with really tasty bread, but a filling she didn't particularly care for. She enjoyed the warm-up stretches and the cooldown—"picture your happy place"—segments. But she was sure that forcing her pathetically out-of-shape body into contorted poses, like Downward Dog and Blossoming Lotus, was not leading anywhere near a happy place. More likely to a chiropractor's office.

Their teacher, Wanda Gruber, was kind and encouraging. She spoke in a slow soothing voice and her own lithe form seemed to be made of some inhuman, rubberlike substance.

Dana, who had been practicing for years, could also bend her slim figure into amazing configurations. She could even stand on her head. Lucy realized that feat had ceased to be impressive at say . . . age ten? But it did seem like an achievement of some kind at this point in life. Dana had studied ballet and modern dance, from elementary school all the way through college.

Lucy, on the other hand, had played soccer during her formative years. Defensive fullback. What else did you need to know?

When the class was over and the students busily rolled up their mats, Wanda walked around to chat with the visitors.

"Did you like the class?" she asked Lucy.

"Interesting," Lucy replied. "I'm sure once you get into it, you don't hear all those cracking and popping sounds, right?"

Wanda laughed. "Students come in here with years of stress and bad body postures to release. I think you did really well."

Lucy would hardly go that far. She'd barely muddled through without totally embarrassing herself and splitting the seams on her yoga pants. Lucy glanced out the window at the dark gloomy day, the specter of the Knitting Nest filling her view.

"I never noticed your studio before. But I don't come down this street much."

"We opened about a year ago. It's a little out of the way and it's taken people a while to find us. It might sound awful to say," she added, "but there's been a parade coming through here the last few days. They all want to see the Knitting Nest. A little ghoulish, if you ask me."

"Yeah, it is pretty tacky," Lucy agreed, though she could relate to the crass interest. "Did you know Amanda Goran at all?"

Wanda swallowed and nodded quickly. "She was a bit standoffish when I first opened." A kind way of describing Amanda's prickly personality, Lucy thought. "But we'd become pretty friendly lately. She took a few classes here and whenever she had to go into the city for the day, I'd check on her dogs."

Lucy's eyes widened and she took a moment to reply. No way could she picture Amanda doing yoga. But Wanda's claim that Amanda took frequent trips into Boston was even more intriguing.

"I'm sure Amanda must have appreciated that," Lucy said finally. "She really loved those dogs."

"Oh yes, she did. It was a very spiritual connection," Wanda agreed in a wistful tone.

"Did she go into Boston a lot?" Lucy knew the question was a bit nosey, but now she was curious.

"Oh, a few times a month, I'd say." Wanda shrugged. "To see friends, she told me. But I thought maybe she was in a relationship. Technically, she was still married to Peter, of course. But she did have a certain glow lately,"

"Yes, she did." Lucy had seen it with her own eyes. It was a bona fide glow, not just owning to Amanda's cosmetically whitened teeth. A romantic relationship would explain the makeover and weight loss, too.

"Well . . . I hope she was happy," Lucy added. Happier than she seemed most of the time I knew her, she nearly said aloud.

Wanda nodded solemnly. "I think she was happy. And is at peace now. I was heartbroken when I heard the sad news. But I always try to lift my vision, Lucy. Amanda's death served to remind me that it is so important to be here now. To be focused and aware. To be grateful for the simple things. To allow ourselves to be happy . . . to simply . . . *be*."

Wanda's philosophical insights left Lucy with a slight wave of vertigo. The speech sounded vaguely familiar. Hadn't she read it on a package of Celestial Seasonings tea?

Wanda leaned forward and bowed slightly. "Namaste, Lucy—the divine in me honors the divine in you."

Lucy stood wide-eyed for a moment, then in a reflexive reaction, found herself bowing toward Wanda. "Right . . . Namaste. And thanks for the class."

Wanda smiled and drifted into the group.

Dana and Suzanne had been standing nearby, talking with some of the other students. Both had already pulled on their sweatshirts, jackets, and shoes. Lucy rummaged through her tote bag to catch up. They walked outside and stood on the sidewalk, near Suzanne's car.

"I'm parked right down the street," Dana said. "I'm still taking you guys out to breakfast, right?"

"That's right," Suzanne answered. "You got two free classes and I'll never do the macerena again. I can at least get a bacon-and-egg sandwich out of the deal."

"Sorry, Sue. They don't serve egg sandwiches at the Sprout. You can get an egg-white omelet and some tofu bacon," Dana told her with a smile. "And they serve really awesome oatmeal. Hand-cut oats, with dried cranberries."

"Be still, my beating heart." Suzanne rolled her eyes. "I should have slept late and made my gang waffles for breakfast . . . with piles of real bacon on the side."

Lucy stood nearby, only half listening to the exchange: her real focus was on the Knitting Nest. The conversation she'd had with Wanda Gruber about Amanda echoed in her thoughts.

As Lucy stared at the shop, she realized that she hadn't really known Amanda very well at all, had she? Sure, she knew of Amanda's critical sour side—the traits that had defined the woman publicly—but there was more there, Lucy realized, a lot more. Maybe that brash, bitter façade was a curtain and a completely different person was hiding behind it. Like that scene in *The Wizard of Oz,* when the thundering Wizard is revealed to be a timid little man. "Pay no attention to the man behind the curtain," he says. But of course, it's too late.

"Lucy . . . are you okay?" Suzanne stood a few steps away. Lucy turned to see Suzanne staring curiously at her.

"Wait . . ." Lucy took a deep breath. She wondered if her eyes were playing a trick on her. She'd been thinking about Amanda so much this morning. Maybe she'd just . . . lost it.

"What's the matter?" Dana had started up the street toward her car, but now turned and came back.

Lucy paused. She knew her friends were going to think she'd gone crazy. "I think I just saw someone in Amanda's shop."

Suzanne squinted at her. "Saw someone? What do you mean?" Dana stared at Lucy, too, but didn't say anything.

"I was standing here, staring at the shop, and I saw a shadow or a person or something in there. I'm sure of it." Lucy knew she was rambling now, but she couldn't help it.

"There couldn't be anyone in there, Lucy. That place is taped up like a UPS box going to Tierra del Feugo," Suzanne said.

"Maybe you just saw a reflection off the window. From a passing car?" Dana offered.

"Could be . . . except a car hasn't passed for a while now," Lucy replied. When they didn't answer, she added, "I'm going over to check it out."

Lucy knew that sounded a bit crazy, but she was curious now to find out if she'd imagined it. She felt certain she'd seen something. But the doubts of her friends were making her question her own perception.

Suzanne reached for her arm as she started to cross the street. "You can't go in there. It's a crime scene . . . duh? What if the police drive by and see you over there? You'll be arrested."

"Lucy, if there really is someone there, it could be dangerous," Dana pointed out. "Maybe we should just call the police right now."

Lucy considered the suggestion. "By the time they come, whoever is inside will be gone and we'll be standing here for hours in the cold answering questions." From what she'd seen so far, the police had no shortage of them. "Besides, we'll draw attention to Maggie and that might upset her."

Her friends didn't answer but she could tell from their expressions that they more or less agreed.

"Just stay here and watch for patrol cars. I'll be right back. I'm not going to do anything stupid," she promised.

I hope, she added silently. Without waiting for their approval, Lucy ran across the street to the Knitting Nest. Peering in the front window seemed too obvious. And Suzanne was right about the police catching her. It would be just her luck if a patrol car passed as she slipped under the yellow tape and pressed her face to the front window. There had to a side window, she thought, or one in back.

A paved alleyway, about the width of a car, separated the building from the one next door. Lucy crept down the passageway and finally came to a small window on the side of the building, close to the back.

She stood up on tiptoes and peered in. Despite the fact that it was daytime, the interior was very dark, especially at the back of the shop. Lucy could barely see anything at first. Gradually, her eyes adjusted and could make out the shape of a counter and register up front, cube-shaped shelves on the walls.

In the back of the store, a large oddly-shaped object took up most of the space. She realized it must be a spinning wheel.

The shop looked empty and silent. She watched for another minute, then decided her imagination had indeed been working overtime and her eyes had been playing tricks on her. She was also getting a cramp in her calf muscle from being up on tiptoes so long.

She was just about to give up when a hooded figure came into view. The form moved across her field of vision in an instant, then quickly merged into the shadows.

Lucy jumped back and smothered a scream. There *was* somebody in there. Now she really did need to call the police. If only she could get one more look, maybe see their face? Or what they were doing? She couldn't even say if it was a man or a woman.

Maybe there was another window in the back and she could get a better look. Then I'll call the police, she promised herself.

Lucy took a breath. She looked back toward the street and saw her friends, still waiting on the sidewalk. They motioned for her to come back, but she shook her head. She just wanted one good look at whoever was in there. That shouldn't be too hard.

She tiptoed farther down the alley, her footsteps crunching on patches of old frosty snow. Could someone inside hear her, she wondered? She tried to walk even more softly as she came to the end of the building, but it was almost impossible. Her sneakers kept slipping and sliding on the frosty surface.

At the end of the building, she took a deep breath, readied

herself, then peered around the corner, taking hold of a drainpipe for balance. She didn't realize until it was too late that she'd leaned too far. The drainpipe bent under her weight and her feet flew out from under her.

She shrieked, landing facedown in a snowy patch in the backyard.

Seconds later, she heard the back door fly open. She lifted her snow-covered face just in time to see a figure run out of the building. Head lowered and hands stuffed in the front pocket of a black sweatshirt, the culprit dashed through the small snowy yard and disappeared into a clump of bushes, crossing into the property of a house behind the shop.

"Lucy . . . are you all right?" Suzanne called.

Before she could answer, her friends were beside her. Lucy looked up and spit out some dirty snow. "I'm . . . okay. What an idiot I am."

"Here, let me help." Dana took her arm and hoisted her up.

"What happened? Did you see anything?" Suzanne asked.

Lucy nodded. "Someone was in there. I saw them for just a second, so I came back here to get a better look. They must have heard me and they ran out of the house." She pointed to the opening in the bushes where the intruder had escaped. "They ran right through the bushes. I didn't even get to see their face."

"Wow . . . that's creepy," Suzanne said.

Dana leaned closer. "What did they look like? Was it a man or woman?"

"I'm not sure," Lucy said honestly. "It all happened so fast."

"We need to tell the police." Dana's tone was firm. "It probably has nothing to do with Amanda's murder, but they need to know. Everyone in town knows the shop is deserted, so this guy broke in and was looking for something left to steal."

"Probably," Lucy agreed, though something in her gut told her otherwise.

"You didn't do anything that awful," Dana pointed out. "You just looked through the window. But the police need to know the building isn't secure. It's still a crime scene."

"Detective Reyes seemed nice. You ought to call her," Suzanne suggested.

Detective Reyes had seemed approachable, Lucy thought. But maybe that was just because she was a woman, and compared to Detective Walsh, it wouldn't take much to make a good impression.

"I hate to get involved," Lucy admitted. "And if I call up Walsh and tell him we've been snooping in windows at the crime scene, it draws his attention back to Maggie. And she's freaked out enough about having been interrogated yesterday."

Maybe that was not a good reason to avoid telling the police, but Lucy didn't want to be the cause of more angst for her best friend.

Dana seemed to understand. "All right. I hear you. Let's leave the detectives out of this for now. We can go down to the village police station and tell them, like responsible citizens doing our civic duty. It's their job to pass it on to the county detectives if they think it's important enough. The village cops will need to come out here anyway and check the shop again."

"Good idea," Suzanne said. She looked at Lucy. "What do you think? We can all go in together."

Lucy nodded. "Okay. I'm in. Let's just get out of here. I'm getting the creeps."

"Me, too," Suzanne agreed. "And all this tension makes me hungry. And the police station is practically next door to the Schooner. How convenient." She glanced at Dana, who just sighed.

"I'll follow you in my own car," Dana said simply.

Sounded to Lucy like Suzanne was going to get her preferred breakfast after all.

The Plum Harbor village police station was in the same building as the Village Hall. Lucy had never been inside before. It was a modest operation, she thought. The three women practically filled the anteroom in front of a counter and heavy glass window. The fluorescent lighting reminded Lucy of a gas station bathroom, for some odd reason, and the walls were covered with inky photos of wanted criminals and descriptions of their crimes, which made for some unsettling reading as she waited to speak to the officer at the desk.

Flanked by Suzanne and Dana, she stepped up and explained to a burly officer behind the window why she had come. First, how she'd come out of a yoga class at an exercise studio on Hobson Street, right across from the Knitting Nest, and thought she saw someone inside the shop. So she went around back and by the time she got there, the person was running out the back door of the building.

Lucy knew she had simplified the story a bit. But she wanted to keep this report short and sweet.

The police officer took down her information, then asked Dana and Suzanne if they had anything to add.

"You should have called right away," he told them. "We might have had a car in the area."

"We did think of that, Officer," Lucy replied. "But it would have been too late. I mean, this guy was really moving."

He glanced at her but didn't reply. Finally, he handed Lucy a form and asked her to sign at the bottom, then gave her a copy.

"That's it?" she asked him. Wasn't he going to give her a summons or something for crossing the yellow tape?

"That's it," he said gruffly. "Just stay out of crime scenes, Ms.

Binger. If you see something that doesn't look right, you call the police and let us handle it."

"I will," Lucy promised, backing away from the window. "I mean, not that I plan on doing anything stupid like that again. . . . It was really none of my business."

Suzanne took Lucy's arm and yanked her along. "Thank you, Officer. You've been very helpful."

A short time later, seated in a rear booth of the Schooner, Lucy found the comforting smells of unhealthy breakfast foods a balm to her soul. Edie was not around, she noticed, but their attentive waitress quickly served mugs of incredibly good coffee, then took their orders.

"Well, that wasn't too bad. At least I didn't get a ticket for crossing the yellow tape," Lucy said.

"He let you off easy. But you'll probably get a follow-up call from Walsh or Reyes," Dana warned her.

"I figured that," Lucy said.

"Who do you think was in there?" Suzanne asked. "Just some kid, messing around?"

"I didn't realize we had so many delinquent teenagers around here. There suddenly seems to be swarms of them, the main suspects in every situation. Is that possible?" Lucy asked her friends.

"Well . . . unfortunately, it is," Dana replied. She had a stepson, named Tyler, who was in his first year of college and a son with Jack, named Dylan, who was a freshman at Plum Harbor High, so she had some firsthand knowledge to offer.

"There is a bad element in the high school," she added. "The school board formed a task force last spring to get control of the situation. But I get your point. It does seem an easy answer, the last few days, doesn't it?"

Lucy didn't reply. She'd only seen the darting figure for a few seconds, but that quick glimpse had chilled her to the bone. She just had this feeling the Knitting Nest intruder was not some random teenager, looking for pawnable leftovers.

"If it wasn't a kid just scrounging around, who could it be?" Suzanne said.

"I don't know," Lucy said honestly. "But there's a lot we don't even know about Amanda. I was talking to Wanda, the yoga teacher, and she told me that Amanda was going into Boston a few times a month. Wanda thinks Amanda must have had a secret relationship going on."

"A secret relationship . . . with a man, you mean?" Suzanne's mouth hung open. She hardly noticed the waitress slip her order under her nose.

Dana looked surprised, as well. "Before she and Peter broke up?" she asked Lucy.

"Wanda told me she'd been looking in on Amanda's dogs whenever Amanda went into the city and it sounds like that arrangement was going on for a while. When did the Gorans spilt up?"

"In January, I think," Dana replied. "About two months ago."

"Sounds like Amanda had a little somethin' on the side." Suzanne thoughtfully savored a bite of her breakfast sandwich. "No wonder she was looking so good."

"It would explain the makeover and the attitude change," Lucy agreed. She'd thought the same thing when Wanda told her.

Dana shook her head, looking confused. "From what Jack heard, there was no mention of an affair in their separation papers. Of course, that doesn't mean she wasn't having one. Or Peter wasn't having one, for that matter."

Dana had ordered a virtuous-looking bowl of oatmeal, though she had to settle for raisins instead of dried cranberries. The

Schooner wasn't into trendy toppings. She blew on a spoonful and took a bite.

"Well, if it's true, it would explain a lot of things," Suzanne said.

Lucy nodded, her fork poised with a bite of superthin pancakes—the Schooner's specialty, which was hard to resist especially after the morning's stressful adventure.

If Amanda was having an affair during her marriage, it would explain the changes they'd all seen in her that fateful night, Lucy reflected. But it raised more questions than it answered.

After breakfast the three friends went their separate ways. Suzanne ran back home to shower, change, and show a house and Dana was meeting her husband at their health club to play tennis. Lucy decided a brisk walk home from town would burn off at least one pancake and work out a few kinks from the yoga poses.

Maggie's house was not usually on her way, but on impulse she turned down Straight Path Lane. Maggie lived on one of the prettiest streets in town, in a neat pearl gray cape with dark blue shutters and a fuchsia pink door.

As Lucy walked up the path to the front door, her friend's face appeared briefly at the living room window. The front door swung open before she had the chance to knock.

"Hey, there . . . how was the yoga class? Did I miss anything?" Maggie shut the door and followed Lucy into the living room.

"You did miss something. But it didn't have anything to do with yoga."

They walked into the living room and Lucy quickly related her snooping adventure. Maggie sat in the middle of the living room couch, her expression growing more and more surprised.

"Lucy, you shouldn't have gone back there. That was dangerous. And dumb."

Lucy winced. "Yes, we're all in agreement on that one. But it seemed like a good idea at the time."

"Did you call the police or the detectives?" Maggie asked.

"Well, by the time we talked it over, we figured the culprit was long gone. So we drove into town and I reported it in person at the village station."

"Oh . . ." Maggie seemed surprised. "Whose idea was that?"

"Dana thought it was the right thing to do. I guess word will reach the county detectives sooner or later. I just felt weird calling them directly."

She glanced at Maggie and sensed that Maggie understood the reasons for her hesitation. "You mean because of the way they questioned me?"

Lucy sighed. "A little," she admitted. "I didn't want to get all involved."

Maggie stared at her a moment. "Seems like none of us do, and yet, here we are, tangled up in Amanda Goran's murder investigation. I guess we were more connected to her than we realized."

"Maybe," Lucy agreed. The news of Amanda's death had been a greater shock than she could have ever guessed. And the event had stirred a curiosity in her that she'd never expected.

"I was talking to the yoga teacher after our class and it seems she and Amanda were friendly. She thought Amanda was having an affair with someone, meeting them in Boston a few times a month. Even before her separation from Peter," Lucy told Maggie in a rush.

"Whoa there . . . an affair? Amanda?"

"Yeah, pretty wild stuff, right?" Lucy replied.

"I'll say." Maggie shook her head. "You never know about someone, do you?"

"That's what I was thinking. We thought we knew Amanda, but we didn't really."

Maggie didn't answer for a moment, lost in her own thoughts. Then she suddenly looked up at Lucy.

"I was making some tea. Want some?" she offered, changing the subject.

"No thanks, I'm good." Lucy knew she'd surpassed the legal limit of caffeine for the day, sipping from the Schooner's bottomless cup.

Maggie disappeared into the kitchen and Lucy slipped off her jacket and took a seat in one of the overstuffed armchairs near the fireplace. She had to lift her butt to yank out some of Maggie's knitting, stuck under a cushion. She placed it on the coffee table, which was covered with pattern books and at least two other projects in progress: UFOs—unfinished objects, according to the official knitters' terminology.

Maggie's house was decorated in an eclectic mix of furniture, pulled together with colorful pillows and interesting fabric patterns and area rugs. Nothing really matched but somehow it all blended together in a warm, interesting style. Everywhere you turned, there was something eye-catching to look at. It was the kind of decorating that could never be duplicated: it was just so . . . Maggie.

The bay window in the living room was filled with plants and the top of the dark wood upright piano, covered with photographs, many of Maggie and her husband, Bill, looking tan and windblown on vacation, or like a couple from a magazine advertisement, dressed for a formal occasion. There was an abundance of family shots, most featuring their daughter, Julie, who was away at college in Vermont now. Lucy knew Maggie secretly missed Julie something fierce, but she wasn't at all the smothering type.

Maggie returned holding a mug that said "I'd Rather Be Knitting." She curled into the corner of the sofa. "So what did this intruder look like? You didn't say."

"I didn't get much of a look. It all happened in about ten seconds. And my face was full of snow as they were running away."

"Too bad . . . I don't have a very good alibi, either," Maggie added with a sigh. Lucy stared at her and noticed a smile.

"Maggie, please. I think you're all worked up over nothing. Did the detectives get in touch with you again?"

"No, I haven't heard another word. But it's only been a day," she reminded Lucy. "Do you think they let you knit in prison?" she asked suddenly. "Probably not, right? Since the needles are so sharp. The airlines hardly let you knit on a plane anymore. All those new security rules."

"Come on. I'm sure you're not the prime suspect. The police must be hot on some other trail by now. Now they have this intruder to consider. Maybe it wasn't just a petty thief who knew the shop was empty. Maybe it was someone connected to the murder and the police will have to start looking in a completely new direction."

"Maybe . . . but I'm not counting on it. Jack Haeger gave me the name of a good criminal attorney, just in case."

"Just in case of . . . what?"

"In case the police pursue this insanity any further. In case they really start to think I killed Amanda."

Maggie's hair looked very curly today. She'd either just washed it or had been working out. A chunk bounced into her face and she impatiently pushed it back with her hand.

Lucy didn't know what to say. She didn't think Maggie really needed an attorney, but the recommendation obviously made her feel better. Lucy didn't see how it could hurt.

Maggie moved to the end of the couch and picked up some knitting off a side table, a project that didn't look familiar. It must have been something Maggie had started over the weekend. Maggie was such a fast knitter, it was well under way.

"What you are making?" Lucy asked her.

"That big satchel from Cara's felting book. For Julie. If she doesn't like it, I'll keep it for myself."

"I think she'll like it. It's great for carrying books. Have you heard anything more about Amanda?" Lucy found it hard to say "about the murder," even hard to say Amanda's name.

"Peter is holding a service at that old cemetery on the road to the beach. It's set for Tuesday morning."

"Who told you that?"

"Edie Steiber called me. Amanda belonged to the chamber of commerce, though she wasn't at the meetings much. Edie was calling the members to make sure we knew about Peter's arrangements."

Maggie sat silently for a moment, her gaze fixed on her knitting, her fingers nimbly feeding the yarn and looping stitches. "I guess I'll go," she said finally.

"You will?" Lucy couldn't hide her surprise.

Maggie looked up at her. "Why not? I'd like to pay my last respects."

"Sure you want to do that? The murderer always shows up at the funeral in books and movies," Lucy teased her. "It might make the police suspect you more."

"Good thing I found that lawyer. They still give you one phone call, right?" Maggie flipped her knitting over.

Lucy was relieved to see she still had some sense of humor about the situation.

"I know it sounds insane," Maggie said after a moment, "but I'm going to miss Amanda. She was a royal pain, but she was part of my life. Whenever she got annoyed with me, it usually meant I was doing something really interesting at the shop. When you think about it, she gave me a lot of attention. She made me feel . . . important." Maggie picked her knitting up again and shook her head. "I don't know. Maybe in some ways, you miss your enemies when they go as much as you miss your friends."

Lucy didn't know what to say. Maggie's insight rang true, though Lucy had never thought of it that way. "I can go to the service with you," Lucy offered. "If you want."

"Would you? Gee, thanks. It will feel sort of strange there."

"I don't mind. I guess I'm curious."

Maybe it was purely lurid fascination, like being unable to look away when you pass a car accident. But Lucy guessed she wouldn't be the only person with no close ties to the deceased, who had just tagged along because they were curious.

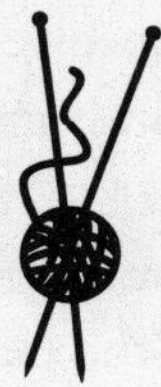

Chapter Four

Lucy fully expected the county detectives to get in touch with her about the police report she had filed. But it was still a surprise when Detectives Walsh and Reyes appeared at her front door early Monday morning.

Sneak attack, she decided, though it was nearly nine, an hour when most decent people were already showered, dressed, and out of the house. She'd been working late several nights in a row and had allowed herself an extra few minutes of sleep. So now they'd caught her in her bathrobe before she'd even had a chance to brush her teeth or down a cup of coffee.

"Are we catching you at a bad time, Ms. Binger?" Detective Reyes asked politely.

What do you think? Lucy nearly replied.

"Not at all, come right in," she said instead. She opened the door and tightened the belt on her robe. "I was working pretty late last night. I missed my alarm."

"What do you do for a living?" Detective Walsh asked. The way he was looking at her made her nervous. Did he think she was a pole dancer or something?

"I'm a graphic artist. I have my own business and I work at home."

"Lucky you." Detective Reyes smiled for a moment, then looked more serious. "We received a message from the Plum Harbor Police. You reported seeing an intruder at the Knitting Nest yesterday morning?"

Lucy nodded. "I went to a yoga class across the street, at the Nirvana Yoga Center. When the class was over, I was just standing on the sidewalk, talking with my friends—"

Detective Walsh had his pad out and looked down at it. "That would be Suzanne Cavanaugh and Dana Haeger?"

"That's right."

"Go on," Detective Reyes told her. "So you were standing there, talking?"

"Right. I happened to be looking at the Knitting Nest, thinking about Amanda Goran and what had happened to her. Then I thought I saw someone inside the shop. I told my friends, but they didn't believe me," she added. "So I decided to just take a look and find out if I'd been imagining it."

"Didn't you notice the crime-scene tape?" Detective Walsh asked. "That bright yellow stuff?"

His sarcastic tone made Lucy nervous again. "Yeah . . . but . . . I wasn't going inside, honestly. I just wanted a quick look through the window and then we were going to call the police."

He looked down at his pad again. "The report says you went to the north side of the building, is that correct?"

Lucy nodded, omitting that she'd felt the front was too obvious and she'd be more apt to be caught.

"It was dark inside. I couldn't see much. But finally, I did see someone in there . . . and a few moments later, whoever it was ran out the back door and into someone else's yard."

"And you couldn't say for sure if it was a man or a woman? And you didn't see the person's face." Detective Walsh's tone was challenging, as if he doubted what he read in the report.

"That's right. They just sort of dashed past. And I had slipped in the snow, facedown. So basically, while they were passing I was rubbing snow out of my eyes."

Detective Reyes seemed ready to say something, but when she looked at Walsh, she decided not to. Walsh rubbed his jaw. He looked genuinely annoyed, as if Lucy was purposely being obstreperous.

"Could you take a guess?" Detective Walsh coaxed her. "Was the person tall? Thin? Heavy? Did they have broad shoulders? Slim shoulders?"

"Not that tall," Lucy answered. "Maybe about my height? Or a little taller. They had on this baggy black sweatshirt and jeans. Pretty nondescript. Sneakers, maybe? That's all I saw, honestly."

Lucy was five feet seven, so that guess was probably not much help in determining whether the intruder was male or female.

"Why didn't you call the police from Hobson Street? Why did you wait and go into the village?" He tilted his head to the side, waiting for her to answer and looking as if he already doubted her explanation.

"Well . . . we thought about calling nine-one-one but it seemed silly. Whoever ran out of that building was long gone. We thought it would be a waste of time for the police to come there. And to tell you the truth, Detective," she added, "my clothes were all wet and I felt really cold."

He stared at her and let out a long noisy sigh.

"We've spoken to a few residents in the area," Detective Reyes said. "No one else saw this person in the neighborhood."

"Oh? Well . . . I guess it was early and a Sunday morning. And maybe the person who ran out of the shop had a car parked nearby?"

"Could be," Detective Reyes agreed. "We have a few more residents to speak to."

Lucy felt a funny nervous ripple in her stomach. Did they think she was lying? Making it all up? For what possible reason?

"Where was Ms. Messina?" Walsh asked suddenly. "How come she didn't go to the yoga class?"

"She wasn't interested. I'm pretty sure she was at home all morning. But you'd better check that with her."

"Yes, I will." Detective Walsh offered a tight smile.

Maggie had joked about it, but now Walsh was checking her alibi, wasn't he? Did he actually think Maggie was the intruder . . . or that her friends were covering for her in some way? Concocting this story to divert his attention?

Detective Walsh gave her a sour look and closed his pad. He seemed frustrated and, in a way, she didn't blame him. But she wasn't going to commit herself to specifics when she could barely recall what she'd seen.

Lucy now regretted giving into her snooping impulse. She hoped she didn't end up sitting in a witness box one day, still trying to explain how she'd flopped in the snow and really didn't have anything definitive to offer.

"Thanks for your help," Detective Reyes said politely. "We may have more questions for you at some point."

"Oh . . . okay. I'll be here." Lucy made an effort to sound extra cooperative.

"We'll be in touch, Ms. Binger," Detective Walsh said as he turned to go. His tone sounded ominous, Lucy thought. Did he suspect her of something now, too?

On Tuesday morning, low nickel-colored clouds filled the sky and a fitful wind tossed the bare branches of trees along the route to the old cemetery.

Perfect weather for a funeral, Lucy thought. She glanced at Maggie, who gripped the steering wheel, her gaze fixed on the winding road. As it turned out, Dana and Suzanne had also both been curious and wanted to attend the service. But at the last minute Suzanne was grounded with her twin boys, who were both home from school with a stomach virus. Dana had an emergency appointment with one of her clients, but promised to meet them at the knitting shop around noon for lunch and a full report of the funeral. Phoebe was content to remain at the Black Sheep, minding the store.

Maggie had offered to pick Lucy up, since her house was on the way. They didn't talk much during the short ride. The burial grounds, one of the oldest around, soon came into view. Surrounded by a stone wall, the entrance was marked with high wrought-iron gates that stood open today. Many grave markers and monuments dated back centuries, especially in the rows close to the gates.

The old headstones looked as if they were melting away, Lucy noticed as they drove past. Some were partially consumed by stains of green moss. The stone markers slanted in the ground at odd angles, as if they were too tired now to stand. As if even the careful deliberate efforts of the living to remember the dead were worn down by the passage of time.

It wasn't hard to find Amanda's memorial service, a small cluster of mourners at the edge of the property. Maggie parked her car as close as possible and they walked down a gravel path to the graveside. The group was larger than Lucy had expected and consisted mainly of women, she noticed. She recognized a few faces from town, store owners mostly whom she suspected were also chamber of commerce members. Edie Steiber was there, along with Fiona Seabold, who owned a hardware store with her husband. Lucy also recognized Alex and Judith Friess, who ran a bookshop on Main Street called Book Review.

She also noticed a cluster of women who were avid knitters,

regular faces at the Black Sheep, but obviously feeling some attachment to Amanda and the Knitting Nest, too.

Lucy hardly recognized Peter Goran, dressed today in a dark suit and long wool overcoat. He stood with his bare head bowed and hands loosely folded in front. A minister in a black frock and white collar stood next to him. Two or three small flower arrangements stood on the ground, next to the grave.

Maggie and Lucy had just found a place at the back of the group when the minister opened a prayer book and began reading a Scripture passage. Lucy's thoughts wandered as she glanced around at those gathered in a circle. Was Amanda's killer here to pay their last respects, maybe even standing nearby? Was he or she secretly gloating at their success? If it had not been a stranger, was it a random robbery gone bad, and if so who had done it? It certainly wasn't Maggie, that much she knew for sure. The others in the circle seemed highly unlikely, too.

Her gaze came to rest on the newly widowed Peter Goran. He looked appropriately bereaved, standing with his head bowed alongside a large pink-and-white floral wreath. A wide satin ribbon imprinted with gold letters read "Beloved Wife."

But Amanda hadn't been much beloved by him lately, had she?

The minister said a few words about the deceased, a generic epitaph Lucy thought captured none of Amanda's spirit, her sharp intelligence, her challenging, competitive edge. Or her creativity. Whatever you wanted to say about her, she had been very talented.

After another prayer, the mourners were invited to each take a flower and drop it on the headstone as they left.

Lucy and Maggie were among the last. They dropped their flowers and stopped to say a few words to Peter, who stood with the minister a short distance from the grave.

Lucy shook his hand first, offering her sympathy.

"Thank you for coming." He briefly met her glance. He wasn't bad-looking, she noticed, with pale blue eyes and fair hair going gray. She'd never seen him close up before, only from a distance as he rode around town in an old red pickup truck, his looks obscured by a baseball cap and a few days' growth of beard.

"I'm very sorry for your loss, Peter," Maggie said sincerely, stepping forward.

He took her hand and shook it. "I know you two weren't the best of friends. But Amanda looked up to you. In her way."

"Thank you for saying that." Lucy could tell Maggie was having trouble accepting the compliment. "I'm sure it's been an awful shock. I lost my husband suddenly, too," she explained.

"We had our problems. But who could ever imagine something like this? I mean, what kind of a person . . ." Peter's eyes turned glassy and he looked away. Lucy thought he might start crying. He pulled out a handkerchief and blew his nose.

"I know. It's very hard," Maggie said kindly. "If there's anything I can do for you, please let me know."

Peter sighed as he stuffed the hanky back in his coat pocket. "Now that you mention it, there is something I wanted to speak to you about. It's about Amanda's shop."

"Yes?" Maggie looked surprised and tilted her head to one side.

"I'm trying to sort out her affairs, the store and all. I have to clear out the Knitting Nest. Maybe you'd like to take a look, see if you want to buy anything in there?"

"The yarn, you mean?" Maggie asked.

"The yarn, the fixtures, whatever's in there. I'm not even sure myself and I know zip about that stuff."

Lucy could see Maggie was surprised by the offer and at

Amanda's graveside, no less. It seemed so odd, so . . . cold-blooded. Minutes ago, he'd been so mournful, practically weeping.

"I see. Well, I'll think about it." Maggie's tone was neutral.

"Just call if you're interested. I guess I can get some auction house to come by and take a look. But I'd rather not deal with a big company if I don't have to."

He was obviously in a hurry to get rid of everything, letting Maggie know if she wasn't interested he'd find someone else who was. Maybe he couldn't afford the rent on the store?

"I'll call you tomorrow and let you know one way or the other," Maggie said in a more definite tone.

"That would be fine." He nodded. It looked to Lucy like he wanted to smile, but realized it wasn't appropriate. "Thanks again for coming."

"You're welcome," Maggie turned. Lucy said good-bye to him and followed.

They didn't speak until they were seated in Maggie's car. Lucy yanked out her seat belt and clipped it. "So, that's that. Not much of a send-off."

"No frills, that's for sure." Maggie turned the key and started the engine. "I know they were in the middle of a divorce but I think he could have done a little better."

"Maybe he didn't know what to do. Men can be sort of inept."

"Some men," Maggie agreed. "Peter's the fumbling type, that's for sure. Which is why he was happy to let Amanda run the show."

"At first he seemed so broken up. Then he was all business, in a rush to clear out her store. That was . . . bizarre."

"Wasn't it? Still think he doesn't have a dark side?" Maggie prodded her.

"We all have one of those," Lucy conceded. Though some people get the deluxe version, with more twists and turns.

Lucy glanced out her window, watching the slow procession of headstones roll by. "But I still don't think he did it."

Maggie carefully steered the car down the narrow lane between the rows of graves. "I guess that's for the police to figure out."

"Speaking of law enforcement, isn't that our friends, Detective Walsh and Detective Reyes?"

"Where?" Maggie turned so quickly, Lucy was afraid she might drive right into a tree.

"Over there, parked near the gate."

Maggie slowed the car as they approached the high arched gates and they both checked out the passengers of a black Toyota Camry, parked a few car lengths back from the entrance, facing the flow of traffic.

Lucy saw them clearly. Detective Walsh was seated behind the wheel with a grim expression and Detective Reyes was in the front passenger seat, looking alert, but not quite as stressed out.

"Should we wave or something?" Lucy joked.

"Don't worry, I'm sure they recognize us." Maggie's tone was surprisingly serious.

When they returned to the Black Sheep, Dana had already arrived and was sitting with Phoebe at the oak pedestal table in the back of the shop. The table was set for lunch and they'd waited for Lucy and Maggie to begin.

Lucy noticed that they both had their knitting out and were making good use of the time, their needles clicking busily. She spotted three boxes of small gourmet pizza alongside a pile of paper plates and napkins. Her nose had actually alerted her to the surprising menu well before her eyesight caught up.

"Not exactly from the healthy choice aisle, Dana. What

happened to that big Greek salad idea?" Lucy prodded her friend.

"Phoebe talked me into pizza. She had a coupon. Buy two, get one free."

"We did get a big salad, see?" Phoebe added. The tiny stud in her nose caught the light, winking at Lucy. "You can have that if you don't want any pizza."

"Right." Lucy sat down and surveyed the tantalizing spread. She found a pie covered with roasted asparagus, artichokes, and goat cheese and selected a slice.

"It's amazing how walking around a cemetery works up an appetite," she acknowledged between bites. "Once you start thinking about your mortality, a few fat grams just don't seem that important."

"No, they don't, do they?" Maggie agreed, biting into her pizza.

"How did it go?" Dana tucked a napkin into the neckline of her fine-gauge V-neck sweater. "Did she have a decent turnout?"

"More than I expected," Lucy admitted.

Dana neatly cut into her slice of pizza with a plastic knife and fork. "How was Peter? Did he look upset?"

"He was all right during the service," Lucy told her. "Then he almost started crying when we walked over to say good-bye."

"He snapped out of it pretty quickly, though," Maggie added. "In the next breath, he was talking about selling out the inventory in the Knitting Nest."

"Fast work," Phoebe said.

"I thought so," Maggie agreed. "He said if I wasn't interested, he was going to call an auction house, or something like that."

"Sounds like he needs the money." Dana put a few spoonfuls of salad on her plate.

"Can he even sell all her stuff yet? I mean, legally?" Phoebe asked Maggie.

"Good question. I guess I'd better find out. It's odd enough to go picking through the Nest without creating more problems for myself. Now it's all falling in place for the police. I've killed Amanda to get the stock in her store."

"Maggie . . . don't even joke about that." Dana laughed around a mouthful.

"The police were at the funeral. Just sitting in their car, watching everyone coming and going," Lucy told Dana and Phoebe.

"Like two big spiders," Maggie added.

"One big spider, actually. I think of Detective Reyes more as a ladybug . . . or a firefly?" Lucy suggested.

"That's creepy." Phoebe shook her head.

"Yes, it was." A serious look dropped over Maggie's face. She put aside her plate and wiped her mouth with a paper napkin.

Lucy could tell she was nervous about something. Had a mere mention of Detective Walsh upset her again?

Dana noticed, too. She paused while working on the last few bites on her plate. "The police haven't bothered you again, Maggie, have they?"

"No, I haven't heard from them. But I've been thinking of calling Detective Walsh."

Lucy frowned. "Really? Why?"

Dana and Phoebe both stopped eating and looked to Maggie.

"What's going on, Maggie?" Phoebe asked quietly.

Maggie sat back in her seat and pushed back her hair with her hand. "Do you remember when Walsh was here and asked me about my car? He said a green Subaru was seen parked in front of the Knitting Nest the morning Amanda was killed?"

Maggie's friends nodded. Lucy did remember. Maggie had turned red in the face and snapped back defensively.

"Well . . . I lied to him." Maggie looked up at her friends, then looked away. "I did go to Amanda's shop on Friday morning. That was my car someone saw there."

Lucy took a sharp breath. "You did? Why?"

"I guess Amanda's visit Thursday night really threw me. Her behavior was so . . . off. I started to worry that she might have something up her sleeve and was planning to spoil Cara's signing."

"You had good reason, considering your history with her," Dana reminded Maggie.

"She did have a thing for embarrassing me in public. I decided I'd try to talk to her," Maggie explained. "Just to get an idea. I drove by the Knitting Nest and saw her car parked near the shop."

"Did you see her? Was she still alive?" Phoebe looked a little rattled by the revelation, Lucy noticed. She didn't blame her, she felt the same.

"I knocked on the shop door a few times. But no one answered." Maggie stared at Phoebe and looked down again. "I heard her dogs barking, so I knew she was in there."

Lucy cleared her throat. "She might have been. . . . It might have been over by then."

"Whoever killed Amanda might have still been inside," Maggie pointed out. "Listening while I knocked."

Lucy took a breath. She hadn't thought of that. "You need to tell the police, Maggie. The sooner the better."

Dana nodded. "Yes, she has to tell Walsh the full story."

"I know . . . I don't know why I just didn't tell the truth when he asked me. That was so stupid." Maggie shook her head, angry at herself. "I don't know why I lied. It's not like me at all."

"He intimidated you. Tried to shake you up with all those questions," Lucy reminded her. "He did the same thing yesterday morning, when he was asking me about the police report I filed.

He made me feel as if I had fabricated the whole thing and I was almost starting to wonder if I *had* made it up."

"If the police really want a confession, they do even worse than that," Dana told them.

"But I have nothing to confess," Maggie insisted. "Disliking someone, wishing they would just go away and leave you alone . . . that's not a crime."

"Fortunately. Or we'd all be wearing orange jumpsuits right now," Phoebe murmured.

"Just tell him what happened. Like you told us, " Lucy encouraged her. "You haven't done anything wrong. Not really."

Dana looked concerned, which wasn't a good sign. She knew more than any of them about the legal system.

"Look, the omission is understandable," Dana began in a careful tone, "but he's going to be pissed at you for holding back. You really should have an attorney present. Or at least speak to one beforehand. Did you ever call the attorney Jack recommended?"

"No, I didn't get around to it. But I have the number. I'll call her this afternoon."

Dana met Maggie's gaze. "Good. Then call Walsh. Before he calls you."

Lucy felt a hard knot in her stomach where the gourmet pizza had lodged. Dana really thought Maggie needed an attorney to see the detective. That made it seem serious.

The shop door opened and a young woman walked in. She carried a stylish knitting bag. Her jacket hung open, revealing a large pregnancy bump covered by a long fuchsia T-shirt that read "Baby on Board" in bold white print.

The customer smiled and waved hello. Maggie waved back. "Hi, Jen. Is it two o'clock already?"

"Not quite, I'm early. But I'm having a horrible problem with the booties. Could you take a look, Maggie?"

"Of course I will. We're meeting in the front room today. I'll be right there." Maggie jumped up from her seat and gathered up a few of the dirty plates and napkins. "The What to Knit When You're Expecting group." She checked her watch. "I almost forgot about them."

"I'll get this stuff," Phoebe offered, grabbing up more of the plates. "You'd better get in there. Those pregnant moms can be intense."

"It's the hormones . . . you'll see. One of these days," she added. "Thanks again for lunch," she said to both Phoebe and Dana.

"No problem," Dana replied. She rose along with Lucy and helped Phoebe clear the table while Maggie headed for the front of the store to help her expectant knitting student.

It was also time for Dana to return to her office. Lucy was walking home, so they left together and headed up Main Street.

Dana tied the belt on her long wool coat and flipped her scarf over her shoulder. Lucy remembered when Dana had made the scarf, back in the fall, working cream, brown, and yellow ribbon yarn into thick stripes. A matching hat was pulled down low over her brow, her pretty face framed by brown, shoulder-length hair.

"How's your work going, Lucy? At least I have appointments to keep me on track. Have you been able to get anything done in the past few days?"

"Just barely," Lucy admitted. "I'm mostly on the night shift these days."

"Sounds tough . . . and tough on your social life," Dana added.

Lucy shrugged. "No problem, since I don't have one. Though I did dodge a setup from my sister Ellen this weekend, thank goodness. One of her dinner parties. The last one was just about as much fun as Amanda's funeral. And the guy she made me meet—some investment banker or something like that—he was . . . well, not my type."

Dana smiled and shook her head. "Was he good-looking at least?"

"Ellen thought so. I thought he looked like a pro golfer." Lucy shrugged. "Just one woman's opinion."

"I think I remember that episode." Dana laughed. "At least you have a sense of humor about it."

"Barely," Lucy admitted.

They had reached the building where Dana had her office. It was an old building, made of brick, three stories high and painted white. A bookstore occupied the first floor, the large plate window shaded by a green-and-white–striped awning. Dana's office was on the second floor with a view of Main Street.

"Don't feel discouraged, Lucy. Every pot has its lid." Dana gently touched her arm and smiled.

"You forgot the rest: 'Even the bent one?'" Lucy finished the saying for her.

"I didn't forget. I just didn't want it to sound like I was giving you a diagnosis," her friend admitted.

Lucy laughed. "Well, gee, thanks . . . I guess."

"Even people who have loads of self-confidence feel knocked off course by a divorce. Give yourself time. It takes a while to get your balance back and figure out what you really want in a relationship. From everything. You're different now," Dana reminded her. "It takes a while to catch up with the changes. You'll know when you're ready."

Lucy nodded, touched by Dana's concern.

"And don't worry about Maggie," Dana added, as if she had read Lucy's thoughts back at the shop. "Christine Forbes, the attorney Jack found, is excellent. Maggie is in good hands."

Lucy appreciated hearing that, too.

After leaving Dana, Lucy picked up the pace, walking the rest of the way home under a heavy gray sky that threatened to rain, or maybe even snow again.

Dana's advice made good sense, Lucy thought, and put into words the way she'd felt for the past year or so. She did feel different inside—all the pieces tossed around and still settling. Maybe she just wasn't ready for a real relationship and when she was, it would happen, she reflected.

Dana saw the world with a clear calm vision and was usually correct in her predictions, but there was no getting away from the fact that Maggie's lie, innocent enough, had complicated her situation. Now, by her own admission, the police could place Maggie at the scene of Amanda's murder.

But Maggie didn't murder Amanda. Lucy knew that as well as she knew her own name. Someone else did. So there was really nothing to worry about, she reminded herself.

Nothing at all . . . right?

Lucy checked her e-mail to find that her client had reviewed the brochure designs and had some comments, most of them easy to remedy.

After a quick phone call with the Human Resources director and another manager in the Communications department, she set to work on the changes. She was eager to get the project completed and approved so that she could, of most importance, get paid.

She also needed to get cracking on her next job, designing a children's book for a local publisher, *The Big Book of Things That Creep and Crawl*. That one would be a bit more challenging and definitely more fun.

The gourmet pizza splurge had used up her calories and most of her appetite for the day. Lucy was content with a bowl of soup for dinner. She settled down to do some knitting, channel surfing each time she came to the end of a row, until it was clear that there was nothing worth watching on her three hundred channels of TV.

Finally, she shut off the set and concentrated on her brand-new knitting project, the first of two sock monkey hats. A rush order for her nieces, Sophie and Regina. The girls had seen some kid at school wearing one and taken a photo with Regina's cell phone, then e-mailed it to Lucy with their requests.

The fact that her nieces were eager to wear such seemingly outrageous counterculture headgear warmed Lucy's heart and gave her great hope. Luckily, she had the right wool and needles on hand to start one off right away.

Ellen was going to hate the hats. Even if they turned out true to the pattern . . . which Lucy already knew was highly unlikely. Her sister was going to hate mutant sock monkey hats even more, but picturing Ellen's reaction was a great motivator for her. Making these hats was a little like smuggling arms to guerrilla rebels in some fascist regime.

Puzzling over the instructions—which had promised to be "fast and easy," don't they all say that?—she was tempted to call Maggie for guidance.

So far, the only thing Lucy found easy and fast about knitting was finding all types of yarn she couldn't live without—but had no idea what she would do with. Buying it and hoarding it. At first, she'd thought she was alone in this compulsion and felt horribly guilty, then learned it was a common knitter's foible, called "building a stash."

She was also itching to find out if Maggie had connected with the criminal attorney and set up a meeting with Detective Walsh. But Lucy didn't want to bug her. The situation was hard enough. If anything important had happened, Maggie would call. It wouldn't help to seem anxious about it.

Lucy reminded herself of the same very sound reasoning

the next morning, as she considered calling Maggie again, but instead settled down at her computer. There was a knitting club meeting tomorrow night. She would bring the sock monkey hat in for consultation. If she had strayed too far from the pattern by then, she'd just have to rip away. Sophie and Regina didn't want to stand there and explain what the silly-looking faces on their heads were supposed to be. They wanted to just put them on and look cool.

Lucy sat puzzling over the brochure design, trying to figure out a new way to highlight certain sections of information without it taking up too much space. She'd come up with an attractive shadow box but the copy kept bouncing out of the frame.

The phone rang, interrupting her string of mild expletives. She looked up when she heard Maggie's greeting on the answering machine. "I just have a minute to say hello. I wanted to tell you, I went over to the police station this morning—"

Lucy leaned across her desk and grabbed up the receiver. "Hi, I'm here . . . you went to see Walsh?"

"Very early this morning. With Christine Forbes. She was great. She didn't let him needle me. Not like the first time."

That was some relief, but Lucy had expected the detective would handle Maggie differently with a lawyer present. "What did he say?"

"He was definitely annoyed that I'd lied to him, and interested to hear the whole story. That was clear. He kept making me go over the timing and little details, like where did I park, how long did I stand there knocking. That sort of thing. But he didn't really say much. He wanted to know if I had seen anything unusual, or noticed anyone on the street. He kept asking about that, too."

"Maybe that means he doesn't really suspect you," Lucy pointed out.

"Oh . . . I don't know what to think," Maggie said honestly.

"Did you see anyone there that morning?" Lucy realized she'd forgotten to ask Maggie that yesterday.

"Not a soul. And I've hardly been to the Knitting Nest enough times to know what would look out of the ordinary there."

"Well, at least it's over with. You must feel relieved."

"I do," Maggie agreed, though her voice still held a nervous edge. "You know how the police are. They never give you a real feeling of . . . closure. Not in a situation like this. But I'm glad I told him. I was worried someone had seen me and would report it. Then I would have really been stuck explaining."

That possibility had occurred to Lucy, too. "What does your attorney think?"

"She thinks I did the right thing."

"You did," Lucy assured her. "I'm sure Walsh knows you had nothing to do with it. Coming forward like this sort of proves that. I mean, you wouldn't go to see him if you'd done it. That wouldn't make sense."

"It depends on how you look at it. And how desperate the police are to find a suspect. So . . . what are you up to?" she asked, abruptly changing the subject.

"Working on extremely boring brochures about health benefits. Which would be a no-brainer, if the copy stopped jumping around the design," Lucy replied. "And I started a sock monkey hat last night. I got a confidential rush order for two of them."

"Sophie and Regina?" Maggie guessed. "Ellen's going to love that."

"That's what I'm hoping," Lucy said mischievously. "I got the first one going pretty well, but I'm having some trouble shaping it. Could you take a look? I feel sort of obsessed and if I wait until the meeting tomorrow night, it might be a mess."

"I'm giving classes today, back to back. And Phoebe just left for school. Can you stop by later, after four?"

"That would be fine. See you then."

Lucy knew she would have run into town if Maggie had been free, but it was just as well. She had to keep working on the pamphlets until the end of the day, or they'd never get done. The trip into town would be her reward. That and a stop at the grocery store. It didn't really take much to keep her happy, did it?

By the time the afternoon had passed, along with a few phone calls and e-mails with the copywriter on the project, Lucy had figured out an attractive solution to her problem, with an eye-catching two-color box and a few edits in the text. She still had to reduce some photos to fit the new design and change the typeface on the headings, but that would take no time at all. She considered the pamphlets basically finished and looked forward to sending in the revised files tomorrow, along with an invoice.

When Lucy entered the Black Sheep a short time later, she found Maggie ringing up a sale. The customer, a man in his thirties, was buying a pile of olive green yarn along with a few skeins of gray and black. The distinctly masculine color choices suggested to Lucy that he was making a sweater for himself or some other guy.

While growing up, she'd never met any men who knitted, though maybe they were doing it in secret. Judging from the traffic in the shop, there were a lot of men who knitted now. There was a wall full of photos in the shop, Maggie's gallery of celebrity knitters, both men and women, a display that included such unquestionably manly types as Brad Pitt, all-star hockey goalie Jacques Plante, Laurence Fishburne, and Russell Crowe. There was some debate about the latter being a true knitter, but Maggie thought the photos of the macho movie star wielding needles and yarn was too much to resist.

She'd read someplace that early knitters were mainly male.

Needle crafts and textile arts were part of most every culture in every part of the world. But in Western Europe, around the twelfth century, knitting in its present form emerged as a fine needle craft, practiced exclusively by men who were master craftsmen, well paid for their products. And later, by all-male knitting guilds.

But once knitting machines and later, knitting mills, came into the picture, hand knitting was no longer a lucrative or prestigious occupation. Knitting was taken over by women, especially those of the lower class, who often knitted out of necessity, to clothe their family.

Women like Lucy's mother, who struggled for equal treatment in the workplace and on the home front, looked down at domestic arts like sewing or knitting, and even cooking. But Lucy thought such views had leveled out these days. Men in her generation cooked and cleaned and were greatly involved in child care. Women pumped their own gas and unclogged drains. Nobody made a big deal about it.

Lucy considered her knitting another means of self-expression, of creating beautiful useful things. It was even a way of communicating her affection and admiration to those she knitted for. She didn't worry much about the gender issues.

A few months ago, she'd been invited to a singles knitting night, sort of a speed dating with knitting needles. But at the last minute, she'd backed out. Knitting was her sacred space. She didn't want to pollute that sanctuary with the low vibrations of a stressed-out crowd of desperately mingling singletons.

Finally, Maggie's transaction with the male knitter was complete. The satisfied customer gathered his bundles and left the store. Once the door was closed, Maggie cleared the counter of some extra skeins of green wool and sets of needles.

"He had good taste," Maggie said. "He bought a lot, too. Men are pretty easy customers. They don't stint when they're making a project."

"I noticed."

"Did you bring the hat?" Maggie walked over and sat down. "Let's take a look. You did a swatch to check the gauge, right?"

That question was the equivalent in Lucy's mind of the dental hygienist asking if you flossed regularly.

"No . . . but that's probably not the entire problem."

Lucy pulled out the hat and her pattern while Maggie slipped on her reading glasses.

Just as Maggie was turning the project inside out for a thorough examination, the phone rang. Maggie paused and listened to see who was calling.

"Maggie? It's Peter Goran. Good news. The police have let me back in the shop. I'm just calling to see if you're still interested in seeing the stock here . . ."

Maggie put the hat down, then headed over to the counter to pick up the call. "Let me get this. I'll be right back."

Lucy sat back and studied the hat pattern, but couldn't help overhearing the conversation.

"Oh, I see . . . well, I guess that would work out," Maggie told him. "I'll close up here around five and I'll come right over. Can you hold on a minute, please?"

Maggie covered the mouthpiece of the phone with her hand and turned to Lucy. "He says he wants me to go over to the Nest tonight, to look at the stock. Want to come?"

Maggie's tone was eager, as if this promised to be a fun outing. Lucy doubted that, but didn't need to be persuaded. She didn't like the idea of Maggie going there alone and quickly nodded.

Maggie turned back to the phone. "Okay, Peter. I'll see you in a little while."

Lucy soon heard her say good-bye and hang up. She returned

and sat down again. She picked up the hat, but Lucy could tell she was too distracted now to study it.

"I would have rather gone over there tomorrow. But he's really in a rush to move things along."

"Maybe he does have another buyer lined up. Or he just wants the money . . . or both," Lucy added.

"Yes, probably both. Thanks for coming. I'm sure I can use a second opinion," Maggie added.

"Not a problem. Though I'm pretty sure I can't tell alpaca from . . . Akita."

"You probably can't. But you have a good eye and great taste. By the way, you can't do much with dog hair. People have tried. I hear that some of it looks lovely spun and knit up, but once it gets wet . . ." Maggie made a face. "It stinks to high heaven and sort of melts in the rain."

Lucy found that bit of trivia a bit bizarre, but Maggie was perfectly serious.

"I'll try to remember that, if I'm ever tempted." Lucy paused. "Were you worried about being alone there with Peter?"

"Of course not." Maggie shook her head. "But as dear old Mom used to say, there's safety in numbers. Especially when it comes to men."

Especially a guy who may have murdered his wife, Lucy silently amended.

Chapter Five

At precisely 5:15, Lucy and Maggie stood side by side as Maggie knocked on the door of the Knitting Nest. Lucy heard a racket of barking inside and couldn't help but think of the last time Maggie had knocked on that door, the morning Amanda had been murdered.

Lucy had expected to feel odd coming here, especially after she'd spotted the intruder last Sunday, but she had definitely underestimated the creep factor. It was hard not to think about that shadowy figure—who was it and what were they after? And impossible not to think about Amanda and how she'd so recently been bludgeoned to death in this place.

The door opened a moment later and Peter Goran appeared. He looked his usual sloppy self again, wearing a worn flannel shirt over a T-shirt and jeans, a two- or three-day growth of sandy beard covering his face. He smiled and greeted Maggie, then looked surprised to see she wasn't alone.

"I brought a friend. To help me. I thought it would go faster that way," Maggie explained as she walked in. "I hope you don't mind."

Lucy thought he did mind. He looked annoyed.

"Of course not," he said. "Come right in, ladies."

Lucy followed Maggie and stood facing him. "We met at the funeral. I'm Lucy Binger."

"Sure. I remember you." Something in his tone and the way he looked her over gave Lucy more gooseflesh.

Was he coming on to her? Yuck . . .

Lucy made a blank face, her gaze darting away. She glanced around the shop. She'd only been inside once and her view from the window had been hazy, to say the least. Now she could see that the shop was L-shaped, narrow and dark, with a counter placed in the middle. It could have been furnished to lend a cozy feeling, with some armchairs and small tables, but Amanda hadn't done much of that. She had a flair for designing knitwear, but not much eye or interest in decorating.

A square table surrounded by folding chairs stood in front and wooden cubicles that held skeins of yarn covered the walls. A large spinning wheel stood in the back of the shop and a door stood open to what looked like a small office.

Three or even four dogs had been circling around them since they'd walked in, barking excitedly. One jumped up, trying to lick Lucy's chin.

"Oh my goodness . . ." Lucy stepped back and the dog jumped down again.

"Get out of here, Tink. Stupid mutt." Peter swatted at the offender but missed. The dog shrunk back, cowering.

Tink was a shaggy yellow creature with an impossibly long tail. Lucy felt bad for the poor thing. It looked starved for attention. Starved, period.

"Sorry . . . damn dogs. Amanda never trained them. She didn't believe in it." He laughed, but in a mean way.

"It's okay. I like dogs," Lucy told him.

Peter glanced at her. "Yeah, well, these dogs are pests. I'll lock them in the back if they bother you. I'm surprised they didn't chew up the whole damn place by now."

Lucy didn't answer. She wondered what he was going to do with his late wife's beloved pets. Probably dump them off at a shelter. She was surprised he hadn't done so already.

"Can we start in here?" Maggie asked, refocusing his attention.

Peter shrugged. "Go right ahead. There's more in that back room and a little storeroom near the office."

Lucy looked around and checked the store's layout. Now she could clearly see where the intruder had been when she'd been gazing through the window. Coming out of the office in back of the store, probably.

"Let's start on this wall. You take that side." Maggie's instructions interrupted Lucy's train of thought.

Lucy turned and followed her to the wall covered with wooden cubicles filled with yarn. They'd come prepared with index cards, tape, small scissors, and envelopes.

Back at the Black Sheep, Maggie had told her to just copy the label information of anything that looked interesting, try to estimate how many skeins there were, and take a little snip of the yarn. She would figure it all out later.

Lucy examined the yarns, jotted notes, and snipped away. She found bits of gray gritty stuff on the cubicles. Some of it had gotten into the yarn and she brushed if off with her fingers.

"What's this stuff all over the shelves? Do you see it on your side?"

Maggie glanced over her shoulder. "I think it's the dust police use to look for fingerprints. It's pretty much all over the place."

"It's gotten into some of the yarn," Lucy reported.

"Good . . . I can argue for a discount," Maggie whispered back.

Lucy smiled as she crouched down to check out the skeins in a lower bin. She didn't notice Tink sneaking up beside her until the dog sniffed her ear. Lucy turned and stroked the dog's head. Her fur was incredibly soft, like feathers.

"Hello, Tink," Lucy greeted her quietly. "You're a nice girl, aren't you? Yes, you are . . ."

Tink panted appreciatively and tried to lick Lucy's nose. She could swear the dog was smiling at her.

There was something a little goofy about this dog and her name seemed to fit her, too. "Tink" was a knitter's term, the word "knit" spelled backward, used to describe stitches that needed to be pulled out.

Lucy petted Tink some more and she was rewarded with a gentle lick on her hand. Then she glanced over her shoulder to see if Peter was watching. She was afraid if Peter saw her giving the dog attention, he might get annoyed again with the poor thing. The dog probably missed Amanda. She'd heard that dogs really mourn when they lost their owners or other animals in the house.

Peter had closed himself up in the small office. Lucy heard him talking on the phone and, from time to time, laughing loudly. Lucy couldn't help notice that he didn't seem saddened returning to this shop. Or unsettled at all by the thought that just days before, his wife had been murdered in one of these rooms, perhaps while sitting at her desk, in the same spot he now occupied.

Unless he was one of those men who automatically buried painful feelings. If that was the case, his grief had been buried deeper than Amanda's remains.

Lucy returned to her task and Tink settled down next to her with a sigh. The dog seemed content for a few moments, then as Lucy copied some information off a skein of red merino, she heard a hacking cough.

The dog stood up and tiptoed around in a circle, gagging as if it was about to choke. Lucy didn't know what to do. She looked around for Peter, but the office door remained shut.

Finally, the cough subsided. The dog went to a water bowl, took a long drink, then promptly spit up.

"Oh, geez . . ." Maggie had been watching the dog, too. She glanced back at Lucy. "I think that one's sick."

Lucy nodded. The dog did not seem right. She also walked with a slightly swaying gait. Lucy wondered if Peter had hurt her. He seemed to have a very short temper with the animals. He certainly had his grievances with his late wife. Maybe he saw the dogs as an extension of Amanda.

"I've finished my side. How are you doing?" Maggie asked, drawing Lucy's attention.

"I'm done, too. I found some wonderful yarns in there," she reported.

"It all looks good to me so far," Maggie whispered. "Let's check the back."

As Lucy might have guessed, the yarns at the back of the shop were cheaper and of lower quality than those displayed in the front.

"But useful for some types of projects," Maggie reminded her. "Hand-dyed organics and cashmere aren't for everyone's pocketbook, or skill level."

True enough. Lucy knew her own skills still didn't justify those purchases. Which didn't always stop her from buying them anyway, and stashing them away.

While checking the goods in that part of the store, Lucy also came across a few UFOs. Some were stored in a tapestry knitting bag, the old-fashioned stand-up kind. Lucy had a feeling it was Amanda's, especially when she checked the work, a section of a long coat with a pattern of several different complicated stitches.

"Look at this." Lucy held up the piece for Maggie to see.

"Wow. That's knitting. Looks like it was *hers*."

"I thought so, too." Lucy carefully placed the knitting back in the bag where she had found it, though she doubted the souvenir would have much sentimental value to Peter.

A wave of unease swept through her. Amanda was certainly not the first person to die suddenly and leave loose ends. But to handle something as personal as her knitting, which still seemed charged with her energy . . . Lucy found the experience unnerving.

Maggie looked through a rack of needles and Lucy checked a basket of buttons, sets of four sewed onto paper card stock. Mostly cheap and boring. The buttons in Maggie's shop were more upscale, with handmade glass and ceramics, finely painted enamel designs, interesting wood and leather fasteners.

They went into the small storeroom last, not much more than a glorified closet. Lucy was surprised to see the shelves practically bare. Nothing like the storeroom in Maggie's shop, which was brimming with stock.

But Amanda's business had been running on a shoestring, Lucy recalled. She didn't have the extra cash to invest in a deep inventory. Lucy suspected, though, that somewhere around here—maybe at her house?—Amanda had tucked away her very private stash; Lucy imagined that was the real mother lode.

What had the intruder been looking for, skulking around the shop on Sunday, she suddenly wondered. They probably hadn't snuck in to check Amanda's wool stock, that was for sure.

Was that mysterious person the murderer, who had come back to the shop looking for something they'd left behind? Some incriminating piece of evidence they'd hoped the police didn't find . . . or recognize?

Peter stuck his head in the storeroom, making Lucy jump.

"How's it going? See anything you like?"

"Some of it looks all right." Maggie's tone was low-key and "iffy," betraying none of the excitement Lucy had heard earlier. Maggie knew how to bargain. She strolled out of the storeroom and Lucy followed. "Amanda definitely knew her yarn," Maggie added.

"Yeah, that was one thing she knew." Peter's mouth turned down in a thin bitter smile. "So, what do you think?" he prodded Maggie. "Sounds like you're interested."

"I am. But I can't make an offer tonight. I need a little time to figure it out."

Lucy had a feeling Maggie had decided that even before she'd come. She was not the type to act impulsively, even under pressure. She liked to take time to think things over, especially a business deal like this one.

He crossed his arms over his chest and nodded. Lucy thought he looked disappointed. Perhaps he'd expected Maggie to just whip out a checkbook and settle it all here and now.

"Sure. I guess. How long do you think that will take?"

"Oh, a day or so. Not too long," Maggie clarified.

"That should be all right."

Tink had been resting on a dog bed in the front room, but now rose and began coughing again.

Lucy looked over at her, feeling alarmed. "One of the dogs got sick before. The yellow one," Lucy told Peter. "It was just a little water," she added, expecting he'd be annoyed.

"Yeah, she's not right. I called the vet, but I haven't had time to take her over."

Lucy heard a little buzzer sound in her brain, her bullshit detector going off. Peter was lying. He had not called a vet nor would he go to any trouble or expense for the dogs now that Amanda was gone. She was willing to bet on that.

"What are you going to do with the dogs?" Maggie asked. "Will you keep any of them?"

Lucy had noticed four dogs, including Tink. A large shepherd mix and two medium-size fluffy creatures that looked like a cross between a poodle and a miniature sheep.

"Nah . . . dogs aren't my thing. They're a lot to take care of and I'm not even sure of my own situation right now."

Lucy wondered what that meant. She glanced at Maggie. Were the police badgering Peter, too? Is that what he was hinting at?

He'd caught the look that had passed between the two women, Lucy felt sure of it. "I'm moving. I've been planning on it since Amanda and I started the divorce," he quickly clarified. "I'm not taking any dogs with me."

"Where are you moving to?" Maggie dropped her pad and scissors into her large handbag.

"South Carolina maybe. Or Arizona. I always wanted to get out of the cold, but Amanda wouldn't budge. She liked New England for some insane reason and she didn't want to start over with her business. Not much need for knitting shops in Arizona," he added with another strained smile.

"Oh, you'd be surprised," Maggie countered. "I hear they do very well out there."

"Could be. But not according to Amanda. Once she made up her mind, that was it. Case closed. You could get blue in the face trying to tell her otherwise."

Lucy felt uneasy hearing him speak so bluntly. Wasn't there some moratorium on surviving spouses criticizing their deceased partners?

But long-held marital frustrations were a little like roaches—they lived in a deep dark place and were fairly indestructible. You could tell he was still angry with her. Death hadn't made much difference.

"Well . . . I won't hold up your plans," Maggie promised. "I should be able to figure this out by tomorrow."

"I'll be around. I can't go anywhere until things are settled with the police."

Lucy wondered again if the police had been questioning him.

"Until they find Amanda's murderer, you mean?" she asked.

"Or give up trying," he replied. "I think they finally got tired of asking me questions." He met her gaze a moment and shook his head. "Hey, I know what people say. I've heard it all. But I didn't have anything to do with Amanda's murder. I practically pass out cold at the sight of blood. Anyone who knows me knows that."

He laughed weakly and looked at each of them in turn. "There's no big mystery here," Peter insisted. "It was a robbery gone bad. Plain and simple. The cops are trying to build this up into the crime of the century. They finally have something to investigate. I wish they'd get it over with already, call it for what it is and let me get on with my life."

"It must be hard for you, waiting to hear what they decide." Maggie's tone was sympathetic. Maybe she identified, since the police also held her in suspicion.

Or maybe it was her way of getting Peter to open up more?

"Damn right it's hard," he said quickly.

"What was stolen?" Lucy asked. She was curious. She didn't remember seeing that detail reported in the paper and while Dana had said the place had been ransacked, even she hadn't mentioned missing property.

"A laptop computer." Peter's tone was defensive. "An expensive one, too. She always had it with her. She worked on it night and day. I don't even know where she got the money to buy it. She bought that big spinning wheel, too. That didn't come cheap. She must have sold some of her knitting designs. We weren't talking very much lately."

Understandably. If Amanda had come into any extra funds in the middle of their divorce, she wasn't about to share the bounty with him.

"And they emptied out her wallet," he offered as further proof. "Turned this place upside down looking for more. Whoever broke in probably thought there was a cash box somewhere but Amanda always took that home." He had found a roll of paper towels in a cupboard and now crouched down to clean the floor where the dog had spit up.

Well, wiped it up more or less, Lucy noticed.

He stood up and tossed the wad of towel in a wastepaper basket. "I think it was kids who wanted money for drugs or were looking for anything they could carry out of here and sell," he added. "Amanda must have surprised them. Or maybe they came in without realizing she was here."

"You might be right." Maggie's tone was neutral, though Lucy knew better. She knew Maggie thought it could just have easily been Peter who surprised Amanda.

"Of course I'm right," he argued with her. He sounded angry now. "It's the only logical explanation. You know how Amanda was. She wouldn't have just let someone take what they wanted from her. She would have put up a fight."

He was right about that. Lucy could see the situation unfolding just that way. Amanda would not have given in easily to some nasty kid—even two nasty kids—who had violated her territory. She wouldn't have run away, either.

"What about the dogs? Wouldn't they have tried to protect her?" Lucy looked over at Tink and three others.

None were huge, but together, barking and growling, she imagined they'd scare off most intruders.

"Crooks know how to handle dogs. These dogs make a racket, but they're not exactly pit bulls."

That they were not. Lucy looked back at Tink again. She was curled on a dog bed, her head resting on her paws. She stared back at Lucy with sad brown eyes.

"Hey, what did you think of the spinning wheel?" Peter suddenly asked Maggie. "Practically brand-new. A big one like that costs a few hundred dollars. I'll move it for you, too."

"It is a nice one. But I already have a wheel in the shop. I'd take some fleece, though."

"I thought there were a few back here somewhere. You didn't see any?" Peter headed to the rear of the shop again and Maggie followed.

While they searched for fleece, Lucy walked over to Tink. She carefully sidestepped the wet spot on the floor, then crouched down and stroked the dog's head.

Tink looked up at her, licked her hand, then let out a long rattling breath, her eyes half closed. Lucy continued to stroke her soft fur.

"Ready, Lucy?" Lucy turned at the sound of Maggie's voice. She stood nearby with Peter.

Peter had his hands tucked in the front pockets of his jeans, watching her. "You like that dog? You can have her, if you want."

His tone was offhand, almost joking. But Lucy could tell he was serious.

She stared at him, but didn't answer.

"Go ahead. Take her. I'll throw in a leash and some dog food."

Lucy felt Maggie staring at her, but didn't meet her glance.

"She is sweet," Lucy said.

"Sure, she's sweet. The nicest of the lot. I don't want any of them." Peter raised his hands in a gesture of surrender. "They're all going to the pound."

"All right. In that case, I will take her."

He looked pleased. At least he'd made one sale today. "Great. I'll get the leash."

Before Lucy could change her mind, he walked to the back of the shop and disappeared into the office.

Maggie moved closer. "Are you sure? Dogs are a big responsibility."

"I know."

Lucy wasn't sure at all. Didn't she need to keep her options open? What if she met someone who had allergies? What if she wanted to go away for the weekend? Or just ended up staying over some guy's house unexpectedly?

Okay, she'd been in a dry spell dating-wise lately—the Sahara actually—but it was not beyond the range of possibilities, for heaven's sake.

Dana had said Amanda took in all these dogs as a substitute for children. Lucy wondered if this meant she'd given up herself and was going that route, too.

Somehow, she couldn't leave the dog here with Peter. The dog was sick and Peter could care less. Even if she didn't keep Tink forever, at least she could get that cough looked at.

She strolled over to Tink, who seemed to sense she was being talked about. She'd gotten up from her bed and sat at attention. She stared up at Lucy, in a very "good dog" pose.

Peter returned with the leash dangling from one hand and half a bag of dog food in the other. "Here you go. She eats one cup in the morning and one at night. Well, she hasn't been eating that much lately. I think she's missing Amanda."

He handed Lucy the leash and she bent over to clip it on the dog's collar. Tink jumped around, definitely delighted to be sprung from the Knitting Nest.

"Amanda brought the dogs to the vet down on Main Street," Peter added. "He'd have her records; shots and that sort of thing."

When Lucy stood up again, she found Maggie watching her. "She *is* very sweet. I hope she's housebroken."

"Me, too." Lucy hadn't even thought of that. It seemed too late now to ask.

Lucy and Maggie had driven over in separate cars and parted in front of the Knitting Nest. "Thanks again for coming with me," Maggie said. "I have no idea if he killed his wife. But something about that man gives me the shivers," she confided in a whisper.

"I hear you." Lucy glanced over her shoulder and looked back at the shop.

Peter had headed back to Amanda's office as they'd let themselves out. But Lucy kept glancing over her shoulder, feeling as if he might be watching from a window.

As Maggie drove off, Lucy opened the back door of her car and Tink boarded with a well-practiced hop. She headed for home, making a mental list of items she needed at the grocery store, many for the dog.

Just as she turned down Main Street, Tink hacked a few times and spit up in the back of the car. Lucy glanced over her shoulder at the mess, then back at the road.

Great. There is definitely something wrong with a person who adopts a sick dog, isn't there?

Lucy remembered Peter mentioning the vet at the end of Main Street. Lucy drove slowly, searching for the building. The sign came into view, "Harbor Animal Hospital," the words flanked by a silhouette of a dog and cat.

She saw lights on in the office and a few cars in the parking lot. Good sign. It was after six, but apparently, the office was still open.

She pulled into the lot and found a spot, then led Tink into the entrance. The dog suddenly recognized where she was and had to be dragged the last few steps through the door. As Lucy yanked her inside, a receptionist in an inner office peered out at her from a window.

"I don't have an appointment . . . but my dog is pretty sick. I think she's been here before."

The receptionist gave her a puzzled look. "Without you, you mean?"

It took a few minutes for Lucy to explain she had just adopted the dog from the Gorans and Tink's records would be found under that name. Finally, the receptionist turned to her computer and found Tink in the files. She asked Lucy a few questions to update the records, then told her to wait. She and Tink would be called in a little while.

Tink paced and strained on the leash, trying to sniff a cat hidden in a plastic crate on an older woman's lap. The crate bounced around, emitting a low growling sound. Tink jumped back, then wiggled between Lucy's legs. Lucy tried to calm her, patting the dog's head as Tink panted heavily.

The woman with the cat was called inside, but not before she gave Lucy a dirty look over her shoulder. Lucy pretended not to notice.

There was nothing to read, except a tattered magazine about horses and a large poster depicting the life cycle of the heartworm.

Lucy studied the poster, serving to remind her just how pitifully little she knew about dogs. Heartworms looked like pretty nasty customers. She'd never even heard of them before.

Lucy had always wanted a dog when she was a kid, but Ellen was allergic, or acted as if she was. Lucy thought now Ellen was just afraid of dogs. A dog would have been Lucy's first choice, but anything with fur would have filled the need. Instead, she had settled for a series of what she realized now had been pseudo-pets—hermit crabs, newts, an entire school of goldfish.

Now, at last, she had one. Did it matter that she hadn't the faintest idea how to train a dog, or take care of it? For goodness sakes, some people became parents knowing less about babies. She'd figure it out, Lucy assured herself.

She looked down at Tink, who had finally stretched out under the bench, her golden muzzle snuggled against Lucy's shoe.

A tall woman dressed in a nurse's pale green uniform came to the waiting door. "Tink?"

"Here we are," Lucy said, resting her hand for a moment on the dog's golden head.

Chapter Six

Lucy stood up and dragged the reluctant hound to the doorway and then to a small examining room, which was mostly filled by a bare metal table.

The nurse asked Lucy a few questions about the dog, and made notes on a chart. When she left, Lucy found herself studying more parasite posters, this time one that appeared to be the periodic table of ticks and fleas.

She turned to the other wall, which displayed an impressive collection of certificates and diplomas. It seemed Dr. McDougal had graduated from Cornell School of Veterinary Medicine. Lucy squinted to make out the date. Back in the . . . 1970s? Which would make him somewhere around her father's age, she calculated. That seemed reassuring.

She heard the door open again and turned. A man walked in dressed in jeans, a demim shirt, and a silk tie covered with cats and dogs. A stethoscope was slung around his neck.

"Matt McDougal. Nice to meet you." He smiled and held out his hand. Lucy automatically shook it. "Lucy Binger."

He was not what Lucy had expected. For one thing, he couldn't have graduated Cornell in 1972 since most likely, he was either in diapers or hadn't been born yet.

She snuck a peak at the certificate gallery again.

Ding.

The diplomas belonged to his father, Dr. *George* McDougal.

"So, you've adopted this dog from the Gorans?" He flipped through pages in the file as he spoke to her. "That was nice of you. I heard about Mrs. Goran. Was she a friend?"

Lucy shook her head. "Not really."

"Terrible, the way she died."

"Yes, it was . . . really awful," she agreed.

"Have the police caught anyone yet? I haven't heard much."

"They're still investigating. I think they have a few leads," she replied vaguely. She knew a lot about this topic, more than she wanted to admit.

"Well, that's something. Everyone in town is talking about it." He looked back at Tink's chart. "People don't think about making plans for their pets," he added. "But the animals are left and nobody wants them."

"That's what's happening to her dogs. Her husband said he was going to bring the rest to a shelter. So I took Tink. I think she's sick. I saw her coughing and she spit up. He said she hadn't eaten much the past few days, either."

"Let's take a look." The doctor crouched down next to Tink and took her face in his hands. The dog melted into a fur slushie at his touch. She flattened herself to the floor, doing a great imitation of a yellow bath mat, Lucy thought.

He patted the dog with one hand while checking her ears and mouth, then listened to her heartbeat with the stethoscope, the light blue shirt fabric pulling over his broad shoulders as he gently wrestled Tink to hold her still.

The vet's hand moved over Tink's stomach, and the dog suddenly jerked and whined. The doctor looked concerned. He examined the sore spot at closer range, pushing aside the fur.

"Looks like she has a bruise on her ribs. One or two might be broken."

That sounded painful. "How would she get hurt like that?" Lucy asked him.

"Hard to say." He glanced up at her quickly. "Someone could have kicked her."

Peter? He had a callous attitude toward the animals, but was he that cruel? Lucy wouldn't have thought so. But she'd seen a different side of him today. The more she knew of him, the less she liked him. Now she wasn't sure what to think.

"That situation wouldn't necessarily cause vomiting. There could be some obstruction in her stomach or intestinal tract. I need to take an X-ray and do a blood test before we can tell what's going on."

Lucy nodded. She felt terrible for Tink. But she'd had the dog for what . . . ten minutes? This was going to cost a small fortune.

The doctor looked up from the file and closed it. "Don't worry about the fee. We'll work something out. I treat a lot of shelter cases pro bono. This is almost the same thing."

"Thank you." Lucy felt relieved. Dr. McDougal the Second was a nice guy. With a dimple in his chin. She hadn't noticed that before.

He turned to a small sink and washed his hands. "I'd like to keep her overnight. Get some fluids into her. She's definitely dehydrated."

"Oh . . . all right. If you think that's necessary?"

"I do. But I guess you were looking forward to taking her home, right?"

"Yeah, I was," she admitted. "I never had a dog before."

He smiled at her and Lucy felt suddenly . . . inane. Why had she told him that? A few smiles from a guy wearing a dog and cat tie, and she regressed to adolescence.

Her sister was right. She had to get out more.

"It's about time, then. Something tells me you're a dog person." He smiled at her again and Lucy looked away, trying not to react to what seemed to be a compliment. "But I do need to keep her."

Lucy nodded. "Whatever you say. I don't want her to get any worse."

Tink had wandered back to her side. Lucy bent over and stroked the dog's head, then impulsively leaned over and kissed her on the ear. Tink answered with a quick lick on Lucy's chin.

"Good-bye, Tink." Lucy felt sad, giving her up so quickly. "Can I visit?" she asked the vet. "I mean, if you need to keep her longer than just one night?"

"Sure, you can visit her if she has to stay. Which I hope won't be the case."

Lucy handed him Tink's leash. Then he opened the door, then politely stepped aside so Lucy could walk ahead while he followed with Tink.

They stood together in a narrow corridor, Tink panting and straining toward the next door, the one that led back into the waiting room and out to the parking lot.

"I'm going to x-ray her tonight. I'll keep you posted," Dr. McDougal promised.

"Good. I'd like to know what's going on."

When she met his glance again, Lucy felt a wave of . . . something. Something that didn't have anything to do with the dog.

She opened the door to the waiting room while the vet tugged Tink in the opposite direction. Once outside, she waited awhile for the chart to be returned, then was called up to consult with the receptionist again.

"No charge for this visit," the woman said, looking at the chart.

"Um . . . thank you." Lucy grabbed a few flyers on dog care and headed for her car.

Dr. McDougal the Second had been a pleasant surprise. A bright spot in an otherwise challenging day.

She had a feeling he liked her . . . but she doubted he was single. That would be too easy. He hadn't been wearing a ring but that didn't mean anything. Lucy sighed. She'd be smart not to make too much of this.

Veterinarians did well with women, she guessed. It was the whole doctor thing. Vets were probably right up there with real doctors, cops, and firemen, of course . . . and professional athletes. Though she'd always heard carpenters, and handy guys in general, ranked pretty high in sex appeal surveys.

But this was about Tink, she reminded herself. She hoped there was nothing seriously wrong with the dog and just to keep on a positive track, she set off for the turnpike where she knew the warehouse-sized Pet Planet, the pet supply megastore, would still be open. She would buy the dog a cozy bed, a set of bowls, some chew toys, and other necessities for her homecoming.

Considering her feelings about Amanda, it did seem a little odd to Lucy that she'd so willingly taken in one of the woman's beloved companions.

But life had a way of taking strange, completely unpredictable turns. And wouldn't it be deadly boring otherwise?

Lucy didn't get home until nearly eleven. She dumped her assorted pet store purchases in the living room and kitchen, then checked her machine to find she'd missed a call from Dr. McDougal.

The irony of it. One of the first men she'd met in a while who had promised to call her, and then actually did.

He hadn't left much of a message. Lucy was left to wonder if he'd made any progress diagnosing the dog.

After fixing some tea and kicking off her shoes, Lucy sat at the computer and checked e-mails. She meant to open the brochures she'd been working on, to review what she had to finish tomorrow, but instead, impulsively pulled up Google and typed the words "Amanda Goran" into the search window.

Several postings came up. The first few were connected with the Knitting Nest. One was for a beginners class Amanda had taught at adult education courses in the school district. There was also a posting of her name as an attendee at a conference in Boston and another as the runner-up in a design contest.

Second place. Wasn't that the story of the poor woman's life?

Lucy had expected to find some mention of knitting designs and she was curious to see them. Peter thought she'd been selling her designs recently. Doing well enough to buy a laptop and the big spinning wheel. Maybe even to afford her super makeover?

But Lucy didn't find any posting of that type. None at all.

She thought of doing a different search but she was tired and it was already late. She had a lot to do tomorrow and answering this question wasn't exactly an emergency.

She just let it go and headed for bed.

Lucy loved Suzanne's house, a big rambling old colonial, always in the process of some home improvement project. Like many others who worked in real estate, Suzanne had fallen in love with a house she was assigned to sell—definitely in the "just needs TLC" category, but large enough to keep up with her growing family. She'd been pregnant with her twins at the time and now, eight years later, the place was still a work in progress. Suzanne's husband, Kevin, was a contractor, which should have made the renovations easier, you would think. But just like the shoemaker whose kids are going barefoot, Kevin's own home was always last on his list.

Lucy was the first to arrive. Suzanne's oldest, a thirteen-year-old daughter, Alexis, answered the doorbell wearing an iPod.

Lucy tried to say hello. Alexis smiled and waved. Lucy wasn't sure the girl actually heard her.

"Mom? Lucy's here," Alexis called out, then ran back upstairs.

Lucy heard a blender whirring. "Come on back," Suzanne shouted over the noise from the kitchen.

Lucy knew the way and followed the appetizing aromas wafting through the rooms.

The group usually met in the great room, aptly named, which adjoined a drop-dead-gorgeous kitchen. This part of the house had been Suzanne's home improvement priority and she'd gone the distance—top-of-the-line stainless-steel appliances, shiny black granite countertops, and walls of cherrywood cabinets.

Suzanne's three children kept the area down to earth with school papers, sports schedules, and artwork plastered to the refrigerator and assorted miscellaneous evidence of their presence: sneakers, books, backpacks, and musical instruments.

"What did you make? It smells great," Lucy said as she walked in.

Suzanne was busy at the sink, loading up the dishwasher. She glanced at Lucy over her shoulder. "Just Mexican. Guacamole and quesadillas. And some margaritas. Sort of a Cinco de Mayo in March theme? I am so flippin' tired of winter, I can't take it anymore. Here, have one . . ."

Suzanne poured Lucy a margarita from the blender, then filled a glass for herself. She had even coated the edges of the special glasses with coarse salt.

"Here's to knitting," Suzanne toasted. They clinked glasses and Lucy took a sip.

It was sweet, tart, salty, and cold all at once and when she closed her eyes a second, it did almost feel like summer.

Lucy wasn't sure margaritas and knitting needles were the best combination, though a sip or two couldn't hurt, she thought, and might even help her improvise when she misread her patterns. Unlike real life, knitting could be ripped back and started over the morning after. No explanations necessary.

Suzanne set a basket of chips and some chunky-looking guacamole in the center of a low wooden table in the great room. Lucy followed and sat on the big sectional that was dotted with large boldly colored pillows.

"You didn't have to make all this food, Suzanne," Lucy told her. "You spoil it for the rest of us. I can barely serve coffee and cake."

"Oh, I don't mind. I like to cook for you guys. You actually sit, take your time, chew the food. Taste it. My kids inhale it and Kevin is usually watching the news, or he's home so late the stuff has been sitting in the oven a few hours and the thrill is totally gone."

Kevin's contracting business was one of the busiest in town. Sometimes he bought low-end houses, renovated them, and Suzanne handled the sales end. They'd done well flipping a few times, though that market had gone pretty flat lately.

"I just don't know how you pull it off, with the kids and your job and all."

Suzanne laughed. "It's like spinning plates, Lucy. You get one going, then start the next. Make sure the spinning ones don't crash on the floor."

Lucy liked that paradigm. If she ever had to juggle a job with child raising, she'd have to remember it. She scooped up some guacamole on a chip and popped it into her mouth.

"How did you make this? It's awesome."

"Secret recipe . . . I'll write it down for you later."

Suzanne's twins ran into the room, Jamie and Ryan, who were eight years old. They both wore pajamas that looked like football uniforms, the New England Patriots, of course. Their hair was still wet from a shower, spiking up in spots.

They seemed to somehow be simultaneously wrestling while running side by side. They came to a stop, hurtling into Suzanne as if she were a human trampoline.

"Hey . . . what's the story, guys? Did you finish your homework?"

The boys had finished their homework, they claimed, but were in a hot dispute over a handheld video game. Lucy could see now that Ryan, who was slightly larger, held it in one hand and waved it over his brother's head.

Suzanne stood up, took the game, then took one boy by each arm, leading them out of the room.

"Okay, that's it. I warned you about fighting over that game. You're going to bed. Say good night to Lucy . . ."

"Good night, guys." Lucy tried to smile at them, but they looked pretty unhappy. Jamie was red faced, about to cry, and Ryan was pleading his appeal.

"But, Mom . . . Jamie started it . . . it's not even eight thirty . . ."

Suzanne placidly ignored him.

"I'll be right back," she told Lucy.

The doorbell rang just as Suzanne reached the foyer with her captives. Lucy heard Maggie come in, along with Phoebe. Dana arrived a few moments later. Suzanne called Alexis to escort the boys upstairs and they all returned together.

As margaritas were poured all around, Suzanne took two kinds of quesadillas out of the oven, sliced them up, and served them in the sitting area. Everyone found a place on the couches and pulled out their projects, then took turns complaining about what was going wrong.

Luckily, Lucy had been too busy to go further with the sock monkey hat and was afraid to inflict more damage. She took it out along with the pattern and a picture of the finished product that she'd printed off the Internet.

Phoebe was instantly fascinated. "You have to finish these, Lucy. They're brilliant."

"Yes, I'm definitely going to finish. I promised Sophie and Regina."

And one of her New Year's resolutions had been "no more knitting UFOs."

She did have a habit of starting things, getting frustrated, and jumping ship when only halfway done, especially if some new yarn or pattern caught her eye. Maggie had told her not to feel guilty, every true knitter hopped around. It didn't mean she was fickle or slutty. It was more of a joie de knitting thing. So many patterns and yarns, so little time?

Not too many knitters were like Dana, who stitched away as steadily as a plough horse, straight ahead, row by row. She never started anything new until she'd finished the project she was working on. Lucy noticed tonight that she was about to complete the shawl-collared cardigan she'd begun about two weeks ago.

As the margaritas and tasty Mexican dishes disappeared, the conversation turned to Peter Goran and Maggie's visit to the Knitting Nest.

"He called yesterday afternoon, around half past four, I guess," Maggie explained. "He wanted me to run right over. Lucy was in the shop, so she came, too. Thank goodness. It was sort of creepy," Maggie admitted.

"I'll bet." Dana glanced at Lucy. "How did he seem? Did he mention the murder?"

"He wasn't exactly paralyzed with grief." Lucy recalled the way he had been laughing on the telephone. "He did say he knew people were gossiping and saying he killed his wife. But he claims it's ridiculous. And impossible. He says he couldn't have murdered her, he faints at the sight of blood."

Suzanne switched her knitting for her dish of quesadillas. "He came right out and said that? Wow, that was nervy."

Dana shrugged. "He knows people are talking. He wants to get his side of the story out."

"He wants to get out of town," Maggie clarified. "He told us he's moving down south or to Arizona. Someplace warm. That's been his plan all along, while he and Amanda were getting divorced. But now the police are holding him up."

"He kept going on about Amanda's murder being a simple robbery but the police are making too much of it," Lucy added. "He said a few things were stolen and the shop had been ransacked."

"That doesn't prove anything." Phoebe shook her head. "Anybody—including Peter—could have done all that to make it look like a robbery."

Dana put her dish aside and wiped her hands on a dark blue cloth napkin. "The police say there was no forced entry. No locks or windows were broken. Someone would have had to enter with a key."

"Or Amanda could have let them in," Lucy added.

Maggie dipped a chip in the guacamole. "Good point. I guess he still had the most to gain by her death."

"There was insurance money, too. I hear he's going to get a nice check." Suzanne leaned over and tested the quesadillas. "I can heat these up again if anyone wants?"

"Who told you about the insurance claim?" Dana looked

surprised, Lucy thought. She usually had the inside scoop on these things and wasn't used to being trumped.

"We use the same agent as the Gorans and I had to sign off on a change in our homeowners' policy, so I stopped in there on Wednesday. The secretary was talking to Peter on the phone and I had to wait. I couldn't help hearing at least one side of the conversation. Sounded like he was pushing hard to move the paperwork along on Amanda's life insurance policy. Good thing the divorce wasn't final or his name wouldn't even be on it, I bet. It's a pretty big number, too," Suzanne added. "I guess I shouldn't have eavesdropped," she shrugged, "but I couldn't help it."

"And Jack heard Peter's alibi is weak," Dana tossed in, not to be upstaged. "He told the police he was home alone on the morning of the murder and didn't speak to anyone on the phone or see anyone before he left his house and found her body."

"No wonder the police told him to stick around." Suzanne added a dollop of sour cream to her dish. "I'm surprised they didn't arrest him by now."

"They need more evidence." Dana was looking down at a piece of her knitting, smoothing it over her lap. "Solid evidence. So far, it's all circumstantial."

"Yes, it is," Maggie pointed out. "So his wife had an insurance policy and he's collecting on it. You can't assume he killed her just because of that."

Perhaps feeling unfairly suspected herself, Maggie spoke up to defend him. Lucy thought she made a good point. So far, it was all just gossip and guesswork.

Okay, maybe Jack Haeger's connections to the police force lent them a little more inside information than most people in town. But what did they really know about who may have killed Amanda?

"You can't assume but things do add up," Dana argued as she

examined the piece she was working on. "They add up and reach a critical mass. Unless there's some big breakthrough, that's how the police figure it out."

Maggie glanced at Dana over the edge of her reading glasses but didn't argue the point further, just stretched out a length of yarn and kept knitting. Maggie was still working on the tote bag for Julie, Lucy noticed. Some wide stripes showed now and it looked like it was almost done.

"Peter never mentioned that someone had broken into the shop on Sunday morning," Lucy noted. "I think the police must have told him, don't you?" she asked Dana.

"Yes, I think they had to. After all, the shop is his now." Dana looked down at her knitting, counting out stitches. "Maybe he didn't have any reason to mention that situation to you and Maggie. He probably didn't know you were the one who reported it."

Lucy had considered that possibility. She still thought it was an odd omission. He'd spilled his guts about nearly everything else. "It just seemed odd to me, unless he didn't want us to know someone had been spotted sneaking into the building. Looking for something, maybe?"

Dana nodded. "That's possible, too. It does cloud his random robbery theory."

"What about the stock in the Knitting Nest?" Suzanne asked Maggie. "Are you taking any of it?"

"It's pretty good stuff. I'm going to take all of it." Maggie looked up and paused, knowing they were surprised to hear her decision. "I called Peter today and made what I thought was a low offer, figuring he'd make a counteroffer. He said he'd found more yarn at the house—that was probably her real stash—and I could have the whole lot for just a little more. So I made a deal with him," Maggie explained. "It's about what I expected to pay just for what I saw in the shop."

"That sounds like a good bargain," Dana said.

"You ought to work in real estate, Maggie," Suzanne added. "You're a real closer."

"Don't be silly. I would have even gone higher, but he isn't a very good negotiator. He has no idea of the value of the stock. But he didn't pay for it, either, so it's all profit for him." She shrugged and snapped a thread of yarn with her fingers. "I feel a little strange," she admitted, "but it's too good a bargain to pass up. I really can't resist."

"Well, that's a surprise ending to the story of you and Amanda." Dana had come to the end of a row. She pulled out the needle, then began binding off the edge. "Who could have imagined that twist, you winding up with Amanda's stash?"

"I guess it is an ironic ending. If the story is finally over," Maggie murmured.

When nobody answered, she added, "It's not like I feel some great victory by taking it. She would have wanted it to pass on to someone who knows the value of what she had in there, don't you think? Not some big anonymous estate auction place." Maggie turned to Lucy. "It's a little like Lucy taking one of the dogs."

"You ended up with one of Amanda's dogs?" Suzanne turned to Lucy, her brown eyes wide.

Dana looked over at her, too. "Really? How did that happen?"

"I don't know. I felt sorry for the dog. Peter told us he's just going to dump them all at a shelter. Her name is Tink and she's very sweet. Sort of a golden retriever-ish mix . . . but not too big."

Phoebe took a handful of chips and crunched down loudly. "Goldens are great. Can you bring her to the shop tomorrow?"

"She's at the vet. She didn't seem well and I brought her in to see what was going on. He decided to keep her there overnight."

"I bring Charlie to Dr. Newton. He's pretty good but he's

gotten expensive." Suzanne patted the huge chocolate Lab who was stretched out at her feet.

"I went to McDougal, on Main Street. Peter said Amanda brought her dogs there and the office had all the records."

"I take Arabelle there." Dana was very proud of her purebred Maine coon cat. Lucy was terrified of the beast.

Arabelle would perch on top of a bookcase in the family room and hiss at everyone below. Once she took a flying leap and attacked Lucy's knitting. Dana claimed it was just hunting instinct but Lucy thought dear Arabelle was psychotic and needed drugs. Dana seemed in denial about the cat's social problems.

"Did you get the father or the son?" Dana asked. "The son just joined the practice."

"I got . . . Matt. The son, I guess."

"He's doesn't look like a pro golfer, does he?" Dana gave her a knowing look.

"Absolutely not," Lucy agreed, trying to keep a straight face. She felt the others staring at her, especially Phoebe.

"Some private joke going on here?" Phoebe looked at Lucy, then at Dana. "Share the mirth, girls."

"Nothing really," Lucy said, moving on. "It looks like the dog ate something nasty and it's stuck in her digestive tract. She's getting medication so she can expel it. If that doesn't work, she'll need an operation."

"Whoa . . . I'm not done eating yet, if you don't mind." Suzanne made a face. "But I hope your dog gets better, Lucy."

"Me, too. It was nice of you to take her in." Dana smiled at Lucy, then reached into her knitting bag and took out several pieces of her long cardigan. She spread them out on the coffee table, like parts of a puzzle.

"Okay, I just finished. What do you think? All I have to do is sew it together and block."

Maggie leaned over and picked up a sleeve. "Nice work. You've got a very even gauge."

"High praise coming from you. Thanks. It has a belt, too," she said, showing the long knitted strip. "I was looking through Cara's book and thought I could really do something interesting with those felted flowers she used on her jacket."

Dana had brought the book with her and flipped it open to the section that showed the three-quarter-length jacket Cara had been wearing and the felted flower detail.

"Oh, right. Those would look great on that sweater," Suzanne agreed. "Maybe a few down the front?"

Phoebe leaned over and looked down at the photograph. "It looks sort of complicated. Then you have to shrink them down . . . does she give good directions?"

"Good question." Dana slipped on her reading glasses and tucked a few strands of hair behind her ear. "The directions aren't wonderful," she reported after a moment. "And there aren't any great pictures, either. No step by step you can study. Once I have pictures I can usually figure things out."

"Bad book design. I would have thought of that," Lucy said.

"Maybe the graphic designer doesn't knit?" Phoebe teased her.

"Maybe . . . but Cara does," Lucy replied.

"I took pictures that day. But they're still in my camera." Maggie fished around her knitting bag and pulled out a slim digital camera. "I'm not great at getting these things in the computer, either. Why don't you call Cara and ask her how to make the flowers? I'm sure she won't mind."

"I don't want to bother her, she seems so busy. I'll just muddle along, see what I come up with," Dana said, looking back at the book again.

"Give me the camera." Lucy reached over and took it off the table. "I'll make prints and enlarge the flowers, if I find any."

"Super. Thank you." Dana nodded appreciatively. "I can't start the flowers until I find the yarn. It seems tricky enough without improvising."

"Let's see, what does the pattern ask for?" Maggie pulled the book over and checked. "I don't think I have any of that in stock . . ." She looked up and frowned, then her eyes lit up. "I'm pretty sure I saw some at the Knitting Nest today. I should have it soon."

"No rush," Dana replied. "I still have to put this together and block it."

Knowing how efficiently Dana worked, Lucy guessed that phase would be done by tomorrow.

Suzanne stood up and gathered a few dirty plates. "Who wants dessert and coffee?"

Maggie shook her head. "I'd love some coffee. But I can't eat another bite. Everything was too good. As usual."

A chorus of similar replies rose up from the rest of the women.

"I made flan . . . light as a feather," Suzanne said, tempting them.

No one answered for a moment . . . then they all gave in.

Suzanne's flan was a rare treat. And, afer all, Lucy rationalized, it was Cinco de Mayo in March.

Chapter Seven

Lucy checked in with the Harbor Animal Hospital on Friday morning at about 11:00. It was not good news. Tink's digestive tract was still in a state of gridlock.

"I'd rather not operate if I can help it. She's a little weak from not eating any solids," Matt McDougal told Lucy. "Let's give it another twelve hours. She's on an IV and seems comfortable."

He had a nice voice, deep and relaxed sounding. It was not the first time Lucy had noticed. She gave herself a mental shake.

"That sounds reasonable . . . I think I'll come by later and say hello."

"Fine with me. But I'm booked with appointments until five thirty."

Very amusing. "I meant the dog," Lucy replied.

"I know." She could hear the laughter in his voice but didn't really mind it.

After her flirting break, Lucy worked steadily until 4:00. She had sent the revised brochures on Thursday, as she'd planned, but of course, there was always one person signing off on these projects who had to rattle your cage, just to show they could.

Lucy had worked in plenty of offices. She should have

remembered. It was never over until the fat lady sang. But not before she called to complain about—for instance—changing the photos they had all been looking at for weeks. Lucy had received those very instructions during her last phone call with the company.

"And the little boy sitting on his mom's lap, blowing bubbles? Well, we all thought he had a really funny expression. And he was squinting."

Did you ever see a kid blow bubbles who didn't have a funny expression?

Of course, Lucy did not reply with that question.

She simply hung up the phone, took a deep breath, and charged into the dangerous depths of Internet image banks. Hours later—hungry, thirsty, and feeling as if her butt had gone numb—she emerged with one photo that fit the budget and satisfied the critique.

In fact, it was just what they deserved, she decided, showing a child with pop eyes and cheeks puffed out like Titan, god of the sea, about to whip up a typhoon.

But definitely not squinting.

She honestly had not meant to head over to the animal hospital so close to 5:30 that it might appear to Matt McDougal she'd purposely timed her visit with Tink so she could see him. It was just the way the day had worked out.

She had to shower and wash her hair, didn't she? It was Friday night. Maybe she'd go out for a drink with Maggie, or catch a movie . . . or something.

After a brief chat with the receptionist, Lucy was led to a back room by a vet tech. A chorus of barking grew louder as the door was opened and Lucy was led inside. It was a bare clinical-looking room with another metal table in the middle. The walls were lined with cages like cubicles, most of them occupied by dogs or cats, though she did spot a large lop-eared rabbit hunkered down in the corner of one cage.

She saw Tink right away in a cubby near the door, on the upper level.

"Hey, Tink. How are you, sweetie?"

The dog lay on her side. She stared at Lucy and beat her big tail but didn't respond much otherwise. Lucy felt a wave of concern.

"She's a little groggy. We sedated her so she doesn't pull out the IV," the veterinary technician explained.

Lucy saw the line attached to the dog's front leg. She nodded, her gaze fixed on Tink. She still didn't like to see the sweet hound looking so weak.

The vet tech checked a few of the cages and made notes on a clipboard, then left the room. There didn't seem to be anything she could do for the dog, but Lucy didn't want to leave her so quickly. She stayed close to the cage and spoke in a soft comforting tone. She poked her finger through the wire door and stroked Tink's paw.

"I know you don't feel well right now, but you're going to be just fine in a day or two . . ."

The dog wiggled her head close to the grate and Lucy touched her fur through the openings. She was probably confused and lonely here after hanging out in Amanda's dog pack. She was probably scared, Lucy realized.

Lucy heard the door open again and looked up to see Matt McDougal. He'd exchanged his denim shirt and animal pattern tie for a surgical green scrub top and was looking very doctor-ish. A patch of dark chest hair showed at the top of the V-neck and Lucy vainly fought off a wave of some medicinal-scented aphrodisia that filled the air.

He smiled at her, then peered into the cage. "How's Tink doing?"

"I'm not sure. I know she's on sedatives, but she looks so listless. Is that all right?"

"She's stable. But she can't stay like this for too much longer."

He grabbed a stethoscope off the metal countertop, then opened the cage and listened to Tink's heartbeat.

When he was done, he held the cage door open for Lucy. "Want to pet her?"

Lucy nodded, surprised by the offer. "Just watch the IV," he warned.

She quickly stepped over and reached inside the cage. She gently pet Tink on her head and chest. Matt stood close, watching her, but she tried not to notice. Tink lifted her head and licked Lucy's hand. Lucy wondered if the dog remembered her.

Finally, she drew back and let him lock the crate again.

"She's been through so many changes the last week or so. I hope she doesn't just give up and fade away on me," Lucy confided.

"Don't worry, she's hanging in there. Dogs are pretty resilient and flexible. Unlike most people." He put the stethoscope aside, his expression more serious. "But the blockage isn't moving or breaking down, as I'd hoped. We need to talk about an operation."

"I remember you said that was a possibility."

"I can take care of her tomorrow morning. It shouldn't take long. We'll put her under, of course. You'll need to sign some forms at the front desk. If everything goes well, we can send her home on Monday. How does that sound?"

"It sounds like a good plan. I mean, there's really no other choice at this point, right? She can't stay like that forever."

"No, she can't. There's danger of infection and blood poisoning."

That sounded pretty awful to Lucy. She wished he could operate right away. The alarming thought must have showed in her expression.

Had she rescued Amanda's dog just to see the poor creature waste away? Lucy felt a pang of guilt, feeling sure that Amanda was out there somewhere, watching this situation unfold, no doubt none too pleased.

The poor woman was murdered, her head bashed in, her killer still on the loose, and Lucy couldn't even offer a little peace to Amanda's restless soul by saving one of her beloved dogs.

"Don't worry." Matt lightly touched her arm. "Tink isn't at that stage yet and we have her on antibiotics, as a precaution."

Lucy nodded. She glanced at her watch, even though she didn't have anywhere particular to be. "I guess I'd better go. Should I call at any special time to see how the operation went?"

"I'll call you when it's over. Can I reach you at the home number?"

The question was logical. Why did she feel he was poking around to see if there was some reason she wouldn't be home early on a Saturday morning? Or wouldn't be home *yet*.

"Um, sure. I'll be around. I think I also gave the receptionist my cell number."

"Okay."

Lucy hitched her purse strap over her shoulder. "Okay, well . . . good luck tomorrow." Lucy smiled briefly.

"Don't worry, it will go fine. I guess I'm curious to see what she swallowed. You can't tell from the X-rays, unless they've swallowed something solid, like a coin or a rock. All I can see is the gas patterns. We don't have a clue."

"I'd rather not go there, if you don't mind," she warned him.

He laughed and smiled as she slipped out the door.

He seemed to find her amusing, even when she wasn't

especially trying to be. That was encouraging. Her ex-husband rarely seemed to get her jokes. Though that was really the least of their problems.

Lucy stopped at the front desk on her way out and was given a few forms to sign, giving permission for Tink's operation.

As she handed the sheets back, she started to worry again about the dog. Silly, she hadn't even taken the dog home yet but she still felt attached.

Dr. Matt McDougal must do this procedure all the time, she assured herself. So on Saturday mornings he was in here, bright and early, eager to dissect dog bowels. Did that mean he wasn't in a relationship, either? Probably a good sign, Lucy thought, holding her battered optimism in check.

Lucy drove down Main Street and parked near the Black Sheep. The shop usually stayed open on Friday nights fairly late, especially if Maggie held a class, which usually started at 8:00 and went until 10:00 or even later. Lucy remembered that there was going to be a class on intarsia knitting tonight, a fancy name for using two or more colors, knitting an argyle or Fair Isle pattern, for instance.

Lucy had not been tempted to take the challenge and was content right now to take on one strand at a time.

The shop door was open and she walked in to find most of the front rooms filled with boxes. She looked inside an open carton and saw skeins of yarn. Phoebe was carrying a box into the storeroom. Maggie was at the oak table, writing on a box top with a thick black marker. She paused and waved as Lucy walked back.

"Stock from the Knitting Nest. The first wave, anyway. Peter wanted me to get it out ASAP," she explained. "Phoebe and I packed up all we could this afternoon and he brought it over in his truck. That was nice of him, I thought." She straightened up and snapped the top back on the marker. "He's bringing some more this weekend and throwing in some shelving, too. I'm going to put it up in the storeroom."

"Murdered my wife . . . everything must go . . ." Phoebe sang out from the storeroom.

"You're a very twisted young woman . . . but amusing," Lucy called back. She heard Phoebe snicker, then turned to Maggie. "I think you got the best of that deal. Look at all this. It didn't seem like half as much in the store."

"It wasn't. He found more boxes of yarn at home and upped the price a bit," Maggie reminded her.

Lucy remembered now Maggie had mentioned that last night. "Right . . . her private, private stash . . ."

"Some of that is primo," Maggie confided. She sighed, perhaps feeling a wave of guilt or conflict at the strange turn that had placed this bounty at her doorstep.

"Oh . . . and Peter gave me a box for you, too." Maggie stepped around some cartons, then chose one and put it down near Lucy's feet.

Lucy lifted the flaps and saw that it was filled with small knitted garments. She reached in and pulled one up. She thought it was a baby sweater at first, a bright pink turtleneck covered with small hearts. Then she realized by the shape and armholes it was for a dog.

"These are . . . dog sweaters?"

Maggie nodded. "Looks like it. I think Amanda sold a ton of them. Guess he figured you could use them for Tink."

Lucy crouched down and dug around in the box. "She'll have a bigger wardrobe than I do."

Most of the sweaters wouldn't fit Tink. They were either too large or too small. Lucy figured she'd pull out one or two and then donate the rest. Maybe to the Harbor Animal Hospital? So far Dr. McDougal hadn't charged her a cent.

Phoebe had returned. "How's your dog doing?"

"Oh . . . not so well. The vet is going to operate tomorrow, to remove the blockage in her stomach. I just went to see her," Lucy added. "She looked weak."

"That's too bad. I hope the operation goes well. . . . You look nice," Maggie noticed. "Do you have plans?"

Maggie's diplomatic way of asking if Lucy had a date.

Lucy shook her head. "Nope, just thought I'd take a shower and wash my hair. Basic hygiene."

Okay, she'd done a little more grooming than that.

"You clean up well," Phoebe teased. Phoebe gave her a look. Lucy figured Phoebe had guessed something might be going on, but she hesitated to tell her friends about her interest in Matt.

"Josh and I are going to Newburyport. His band has a gig at Gunther's. Want to come?" Phoebe's boyfriend, Josh, played bass guitar in a band called Error Messages, which pretty aptly described their music, in Lucy's opinion.

"Thanks, but I think I'll pass. I'm just going to stick around town."

"Not a problem. Except that I'm getting this feeling you're holding out on us. . . . Are you sure you're not going out tonight? Doing one of those speed date things again?"

"I am not. And that was speed dating for single knitters . . . and I didn't even go," Lucy corrected her.

"Well . . . something's up," Phoebe countered. "Hair product, perfume," she added, moving close enough to sniff. "And the icing on the cake, a push-up bra."

"I am not wearing a push-up bra. I don't even own one."

Lucy realized Phoebe was just not used to seeing her in a real bra. Most of her lingerie—comfort fit from Target—looked like an Ace bandage wrapped around her breasts.

"Okay, if you say so," Phoebe tartly conceded. "I still say something's up . . . besides your chest, Lucy."

"Phoebe, give the poor woman a break," Maggie interrupted. "Can't she put on some perfume without getting the third degree?"

Now she was looking at Lucy, too.

"Does it smell too strong?" Lucy tried to smell herself, which was fairly impossible.

Had she seemed this obvious to Matt? Maybe he'd thought she was going out on a date after visiting Tink?

"I get it." Phoebe nodded, the lock of magenta in her dark hair bobbing up and down. "It's the veterinarian. The one taking care of your dog. Right?"

Maggie looked at Lucy with interest. She and Phoebe were both staring at her now and Lucy just nodded.

"Okay. I'm busted. It's the vet."

"I knew it. I could tell when you mentioned him the other night. Dana said he was cute and you didn't say anything. I just knew from the look on your face," Phoebe said.

"Pretty good, maybe you should be helping the police with their murder investigation," Lucy granted her. She sat down in an armchair, feeling found out. It was actually a relief. "Do I really have on too much perfume? I hate that."

"After what he smells all day, I don't think you need to worry about it," Maggie told her.

Phoebe drew closer. She wanted all the details, Lucy could tell. "So? What's he like? Did he ask you out yet?"

"Oh . . . it's just a lot of . . . meaningful looks so far. Or maybe they're actually meaningless looks and I'm reading into all this stuff?" she amended. "I don't even know if he's single."

"Ever think of asking him?" Phoebe suggested.

"What fun would that be? He doesn't wear a ring," she added as a hopeful note.

Maggie met her gaze. She knew what she was thinking—that didn't mean anything. "How old is he?"

"Oh, in his midthirties. Around my age."

"Why don't you just ask him out? Next time you see him, just do it," Phoebe encouraged her. "You'll find out pretty fast if he's interested in you."

Lucy didn't answer right away.

"I guess I could," she finally said.

Lucy glanced at Maggie, expecting some backup. But Maggie just cast her a wistful smile.

Lucy noticed Maggie wasn't offering any advice or strategy. Maggie did date from time to time, but it was usually some man she met totally by chance, who liked her more than she liked him. And it never went very far.

She seemed pretty content without a long-term relationship. Bill had been the love of her life and Lucy knew Maggie didn't expect to meet anyone again who would come close to replacing him.

Lucy sighed. "It's just a real change to meet someone really attractive who I actually like. It's nice to feel some . . . connection, you know? I don't know that anything is going to happen, though."

Phoebe gave her a blank stare. "Get a grip, Lucy. That is such a defeatist attitude."

Maggie turned to Phoebe. "Lucy knows what to do. I think she can figure it out."

Phoebe didn't say anything for a moment. "Sorry to be so annoying. I had to ask Josh out the first time. He would have never made a move on me otherwise. He said I intimidated him, can you believe that?"

Lucy and Maggie glanced at each other. Lucy didn't say anything.

"Men are like timid woodland creatures, Lucy," Phoebe told her. "Live large, okay? Take no prisoners."

"Uh, okay." Lucy smiled at Phoebe, who she knew meant well. But life had seemed simple to her, too, when she was Phoebe's age. Oh, to be so young and bold, so sure of yourself. Hanging out in bars and listening to bad music. Writing papers about Kant.

Phoebe fluffed her hair. "Time to tart myself up. Later, guys."

Once Phoebe left, Maggie pushed a box aside with her foot. "Enough talk about men. How's your knitting going? How are those hats coming along?"

"I'm getting there." Lucy had made some progress last night at Suzanne's. "That reminds me, I have something for you." Lucy sat down and pulled out a manila envelope from her big purse. "The photos from the book signing. I printed them out today. And here's your camera back."

"Oh . . . thank you." Maggie quickly pulled open the envelope and sat down to go through the pictures. "Some of these aren't bad, considering I was so rattled after the news about Amanda. My hands were shaking so much I'm surprised everything isn't a big blur." She looked through a few more and started to separate out the ones she liked. "Guess I'll hang some on the bulletin board . . . and send a few to Cara."

"How is she doing? Is she out on the book tour?"

"I really don't know. I haven't heard from her. I don't think the book tour has started yet. She's probably still in Boston. She's really a very busy girl."

So I've heard, Lucy wanted to say. The Knit-Purl Princess couldn't be bothered to give Maggie a call after the book signing. But she caught herself just in time. It had only been a week ago. That wasn't very long.

"I found a few pictures of the flowers on Cara's jacket and enlarged them for Dana," Lucy told Maggie.

Lucy opened her purse and pulled out another envelope, filled with shots showing the felted flowers. She'd thought the blowups should definitely help Dana figure out the pattern.

"Dana is coming for the class. She should be here any minute. I found the yarn she needs. It's in one of these boxes. I forgot which . . ." Maggie jumped up and started poking through the boxes again.

Lucy wrote Dana's name on the envelope and left it in the middle of the tea table. Then she stood up and slipped on her jacket.

"You're not staying?" Maggie asked. She stood up, two dark red skeins of fine-gauge wool in her hands.

"I'll pass, thanks. I have enough trouble working with one strand. I don't want to be traumatized."

"You never know. My mother's very first project was argyle socks. She knit them for my father, before they were married."

"Premartial socks in that generation? Pretty wild stuff."

"It was fine. They were engaged by then." Maggie smiled and winked, not missing a beat.

"Maggie? Are you here?" a voice called from the front of the shop. Lucy and Maggie turned to see Edie Steiber moving as fast as her big body would allow. Dressed in a long lavender down coat and large white sneakers with Velcro tabs, she looked practically pneumatic, Lucy thought. She also looked flushed and out of breath.

"Edie . . . what's the matter? Are you okay?" Maggie rushed to the front of the shop to greet her old friend.

Edie nodded but was too winded to speak. She landed squarely on the seat nearest the door, an antique armchair with a carved mahogany frame. Lucy knew it was one of Maggie's favorites and hoped it held up under Edie's considerable bulk.

"Did you come for the class? We don't start until eight," Maggie told her.

"Didn't you hear? Someone tried to break into Seabold's Hardware. Just a little while ago."

Maggie's gentle expression grew alarmed. "Oh my goodness. Did they get inside? Was anyone hurt?"

"Nope, luckily. George sometimes stays there alone to check the stock. But he and Fiona were having dinner at their daughter's house in Gloucester so they left at five on the dot. The break-in happened around six thirty, just after it got dark. The crook was pretty bold, if you ask me. But that end of the street gets quiet once the post office and auto repair place closes."

Seabold's Hardware, owned by George Seabold and his wife, Fiona, stood at the end of the street one block in from Main. It was on the same street as the post office and Harbor Auto Repair but there wasn't much else around there, Lucy recalled. Just houses.

"Just like the Knitting Nest," Maggie said quietly. "That shop is on a quiet street, also."

Edie nodded. "That's just what I was thinking. They busted a window in the back. But George just had a new alarm system installed. Went off like a charm and scared the bugger away." Edie laughed. "George was griping that he overpaid but I'll bet he's not complaining now."

Lucy quickly recalled the enterprising salesman from Gladiator Security and expected to see him back in the neighborhood very soon.

"That's serious news. I'm so glad the store was empty." Maggie looked concerned, Lucy noticed, and even a bit worried.

"The Seabolds were lucky," Edie agreed.

Lucy felt the same. They were all thinking of Amanda, who had not been so fortunate.

"You know I always hang around the Schooner alone at night,

catching up on the books and nosing around the kitchen. I never gave it a thought." She shrugged. "But I'll be damned if I'll stay alone in that place one minute until the police catch this maniac."

Edie had automatically assumed the same person who had robbed the Knitting Nest and killed Amanda had tried to break into the hardware store, Lucy noticed. It seemed a logical conclusion but this latest event could be entirely unrelated to Amanda's murder.

"It does make you worry," Maggie agreed.

"Damn right it does." Edie shook her head. "I know you stay alone in here all hours and I'm telling you right now, Maggie, you're taking a big chance. You don't want to join Amanda's new knitting group, do you?"

Maggie shook her head. "Of course not."

"Well . . . wise up. That's all I'm saying." Edie glanced at Lucy. "You're her friend. Knock some sense into her. She's the stubborn type."

Lucy nodded, ignoring Maggie's look. "She is."

Having spoken her piece, Edie seemed satisfied. She hoisted her big body out of the little chair, seemingly unaware of how the frame groaned and creaked. For a moment, Lucy thought she might be stuck. But finally, she emerged and stood upright.

"Sure you don't want to stay for the class? Intarsia," Maggie told her.

Edie waved her hand. "I've got to get home to my quiz shows. Maybe some other time."

"Sure. Thanks for coming, Edie."

"See you, Edie," Lucy added.

"So long, ladies. Take care of yourselves." Edie waved again and let herself out.

Maggie looked at Lucy. "What do you think of that?"

"Edie is right. This burglar is bold. She was also right about you staying here alone at night. You can't do that anymore, Maggie. It's not smart or safe."

"Yes . . . I know. I start to straighten things out and rearrange a bit, and I lose track of time."

"You'll have to come earlier in the morning, then," Lucy suggested.

"But that's when Amanda was killed, in the morning," Maggie reminded her. "I hardly see that as a solution."

Lucy sighed. "You know what I mean. At least you have Phoebe right upstairs."

"When she's not with Josh," Maggie added.

Like tonight, for instance. Lucy had forgotten about Josh. "Just be careful, " Lucy urged her friend. "No one in town is safe until the police catch Amanda's killer. Especially shopkeepers, seems to me."

"I'm probably the least likely victim. After all, the police still suspect me of killing Amanda."

"They might suspect you a lot less after this episode," Lucy pointed out.

"Good point . . . unless Walsh comes marching in here, checking on my whereabouts between five thirty and six."

"Highly unlikely. And you have an airtight alibi, this time," Lucy reminded her. "You were hanging out with me and Phoebe, discussing male psychology and push-up bras."

"Right. Detective Walsh will love that one." Maggie nodded, finally smiling again.

Lucy left the Black Sheep a short time later, as Maggie's intarsia students strolled in. She drove down Main Street, not sure what she wanted to do. She felt hungry, but didn't know what she wanted to eat. She considered stopping at the Main Street Tavern, a comfortable place, but it looked crowded and she didn't like dining out alone, especially on a Friday night.

It was easier to go to a movie solo, though she still found herself slumping down in her seat until the lights went off. When she passed the theater in town, there was a movie showing that she wanted to see, a foreign film about two sisters in Afghanistan. She had missed the early showing and the next one was starting very late.

Finally, she headed home, planning a favorite emergency meal of scrambled eggs with melted cheese and toast and more work on the sock monkey hats. Another wild night in Plum Harbor.

Most of the time, Lucy didn't mind being unattached. Living alone had its pluses and she sometimes wondered if she could easily adapt again to sharing her space and accommodating someone else's schedule and moods.

Being single—even the low points—definitely beat a life of quiet desperation, stuck in an unhappy relationship.

There were times just like tonight when it got to her and she felt so completely solitary, the empty space around her seemed to be closing in, bending her a bit out of shape. Maybe she was turning into a bent lid, like the saying goes.

Most of all, sometimes she wished she had someone waiting at home to talk to. That's one of the things she missed most about marriage. Tonight, for instance, she would relate the late-breaking news about the attempted break-in at Seabold's Hardware. Had Amanda's murderer struck again? Or was this latest crime—attempted crime, actually—unrelated?

It seemed to support Peter Goran's claim that his wife had been killed in a robbery. Unless Peter himself had caused the mischief, setting off the alarm to create the impression that there was some desperate culprit on the loose. That would be an interesting twist, she thought.

And what about the intruder she'd seen in Amanda's store? The police had never figured that one out to her knowledge. For all she knew, they believed she and her friends had made the story up for some odd reason. To distract them from looking at Maggie as a suspect?

Lucy sighed and brought her empty plate to the sink. She sometimes got tired of having these debates with herself, all in her own head. It started to make her feel a little looney.

Matt McDougal was easy to talk to. She felt relaxed and so much herself around him, which didn't happen to her very often.

But she'd seen this game play out before. She really couldn't count on anything evolving there. Not at this point. Maybe she would take Phoebe's advice and ask him out next time she saw him. That would answer a few questions.

Don't worry, you've already found the perfect companion, Lucy reminded herself. She listens intently to everything you say. She won't monopolize the remote, complain about your cooking or your wardrobe, and she'll never leave you for a younger sexier owner.

Saturday morning, Lucy woke up bright and early, then puttered around the cottage, performing her usual weekend cleanup. She went through the motions on autopilot, feeling distracted and jumpy. Finally, the phone rang. She heard it over the sound of the vacuum and ran to pick it up.

"Lucy? It's Matt McDougal." Of course it was. She recognized his voice instantly.

"How's Tink? Did everything go all right?"

"The operation went fine. We got right in, took out the obstruction, and sewed her back up. No problems."

"Thanks, that's great."

"It looks like she ate something fibrous . . . fabric maybe. It just wouldn't break down."

Lucy didn't really care to hear the gory details. "As long as you got it out. That's the main thing."

"She's definitely a chewer. We'll have to watch that."

She liked the way he said "we," as if they had some sort of future—him, her . . . Tink?

"She's still groggy from the anesthesia. I think she'll be sleeping for a while. But you can come by to see her this afternoon, if you want."

Yes, she definitely would. And she'd go easy on the perfume this time.

When she hung up, she felt light and happy inside and, for once, didn't stop and analyze why.

Lucy arrived at the hospital at 3:00 and told the receptionist she was there to visit her dog. She waited in the outer office, expecting the vet tech, but Matt came out instead and led her to the kennel room.

Tink was in the same type of cubicle she'd been in the day before, but she did look better, Lucy thought. She was lying down, but not flat to the floor. She started panting and seemed to smile as Lucy came closer. Matt stood a few steps back as she went close to the crate and talked to Tink.

"She looks better already," Lucy said, turning to him.

"She's coming around. We're watching to make sure there's no infection. Then she can go home. Hey, I want to show you something." He stepped over to the metal counter on the other side of the room and picked up a small glass vial.

"This is what I took out." He showed Lucy the clear bottle with a gross-looking orange-reddish lump inside.

Matt seemed very excited and even proud about the disgusting discovery.

"Wow . . . look at that." Lucy tried hard to feign interest, but possibly the way she shrunk back, stifling a scream of "Get that disgusting thing away from me!" gave her away.

He laughed at her reaction and put the bottle down on the table.

"Do you expect me to take that home as a souvenir?"

"You don't want it?" He looked shocked—and pretty darn cute—his blue eyes wide and clear. "Man, that's the first thing people ask me about. I don't know what they do with them, sell them on eBay?"

"If it came out of Angelina Jolie's stomach, maybe."

"Actually, I took a closer look before you came. I think it's just a wad of yarn. Something knitted. Maybe that's why it didn't dissolve in her stomach acids."

Not a big surprise, considering the dog had spent most of her time hanging around a knitting shop. Maybe Amanda didn't feed her enough. Tink did look awfully skinny. Lucy could hardly look at the ugly glob, so she turned back to Tink and pressed her hand to the cage. Tink eagerly leaned over and licked her fingers.

"Do you think she remembers me? I mean, I only had her for what . . . an hour?"

When she turned, Matt was looking at her in a way that sort of made her toes curl. "I think she remembers you . . . you make a strong impression."

"Well . . . thanks." Lucy smiled back at him and looked away.

Should she ask him out? It didn't seem as if she was going to find out if he was available otherwise. Maybe it was time to have that conversation before she got all carried away with this . . . this crush situation.

Crushing on a veterinarian . . . how corny was that?

"Come in my office a minute. I have something for you."

Well . . . this was getting interesting.

Lucy followed him through a door on the far side of the

boarding room and found herself in a small office, three of the four walls lined with tall bookcases.

A large heavy desk held a computer and phone, buried in piles of file folders, journals, and books that spilled onto the floor. A large window framed the view of an enclosed yard with a tree in the middle, decked with several bird feeders.

Matt picked up a pile of books from his desk and handed them over to her. "This should get you started. Tink seems calm but I don't think she's had much training. I'm not sure if she even knows how to walk on a leash."

Lucy remembered Peter mentioning that Amanda didn't believe in training the dogs.

She hoped Tink wasn't difficult. That was one reason she'd been wary of motherhood, she didn't think she'd be very good at asserting her will over another creature. Even a baby. A dog would probably be good practice.

As Matt pulled another book off the shelf, a small framed photograph flew off and dropped on the floor. Lucy picked it up and placed it on his desk, but not before taking a look at it. The photo showed Matt and a little girl at the beach. Matt held her up in the waves. They were both drenched and smiling madly. Yes, he had the terrific body she suspected.

"Sweet . . . is that your daughter?"

Well, this was it. No more living in blissful ignorance.

Matt nodded, suppressing a smile. "Dara. This photo is pretty old. She's seven now."

"She looks just like you . . . she's adorable." That was true. Lucy didn't know what more to say.

"She's great. I don't get to see her nearly as much as I'd like to."

There was an opening for you. "Because of work, you mean?"

"I'm here too much. That's for sure. But mostly because of

her mother." No mistaking the sour note in his tone. "We're in the middle of splitting up and Elaine knows how to get to me."

"That's too bad." Lucy really did sympathize with him yet, somewhere deep inside, her own inner seven-year-old was doing a cartwheel. "My divorce got pretty nasty at the end. But at least there were no children involved."

He met her gaze but didn't say anything. So now he knew she was divorced, too. If he'd been wondering. So now should she ask him out? Maybe ask if he'd seen that foreign film that was showing in town?

Lucy took a deep breath, rallying her nerve . . . then chickened out. She looked down at the stack of books he'd chosen for her. "Guess I have some reading to do before Monday."

"Yeah, guess you do. Hope you don't have any big plans for the weekend."

Was he trying to figure out if she was available, and was this not a perfect opening for her to ask if he had plans for the weekend . . . and if he wanted to see a movie with her? Did she have to be hit over the head with one of these dog-care manuals? If she didn't live large now and take no prisoners, Phoebe would never forgive her.

The phone rang.

Matt glanced at it, then hit a button and picked up. "Yes? Oh . . . right. Better put her on." He covered the receiver with his hand. "Sorry, I have to take this."

Lucy nodded. "That's all right. I've got to run. Thanks for the books."

"You're very welcome. See you." He smiled briefly, then turned his attention back to the phone call. Lucy slipped out of the office and closed the door.

Well, she'd definitely made some progress. At least she knew he wasn't married . . . and he knew she wasn't, either. Lucy knew she made it too complicated. She'd do better next time. If he didn't ask her out when she came back to pick up Tink, she would ask him.

Then she could go from worrying about if he was single to worrying about being his first relationship after a divorce—the kiss of death. Everyone knows that's the transitional relationship and it never works out.

Either way, it was definitely time to take this situation out of the kennel room.

Chapter Eight

On Saturday night, Lucy was content to stay home, watching an old movie and feverishly knitting the sock monkey hats. She was not a huge fan of Bette Davis. Her favorite actress of that era had always been Katharine Hepburn, who seemed so witty and capable, and as if she'd be a good friend. Lucy could not say the same about Bette. She'd love to hang out with Bette, but wouldn't trust her alone for very long with a boyfriend. Bette and Katharine had both been avid knitters, however, so on that score at least they remained tied.

Lucy could rarely resist a showing of *All About Eve* on the classic film channel. The story did not show women in the best light, she realized, with the fawning unassuming Eve Baxter pretending to worship Margo Channing, while all the time scheming to ruin her. But it was believable, Lucy thought. Ambition and a hunger for public acclaim was a powerful motivator and could drive a person to all kinds of desperate acts.

At one point in her life, Lucy had practiced Margo Channing's peerless line so many times, her throat had gone hoarse from imitating Bette's famous low notes.

When the famed screen moment arrived, Lucy put her

knitting down, sat up straight, and delivered the dialogue aloud along with the television, as if participating in some bizarre religious ceremony.

"*Fasten* your seat belts . . . it's going to be a *bumpy* night . . ."

At least the hazy lavender fog of loneliness that had swirled around her last night had mysteriously burned away, most likely due to the anticipation of picking up Tink . . . and seeing Matt again on Monday.

Her knitting was going well and that always improved her brain chemistry, Lucy reflected. Maggie had managed to coach her over the phone through a rough patch or two and Lucy was now clicking along, finished with the first hat and well into the second.

Progress was a good thing, since Sophie and Regina had just sent a diplomatically worded e-mail, asking when the hats might be done. These trendy apparel items had a short shelf life and besides, it was almost spring. But Aunt Lucy had reassured them, the hats were nearing completion and, as Yves St. Laurent once said, "Fashion fades, style is eternal."

These hats had real style.

On Sunday night, in the middle of *60 Minutes*, the hat project hit a snag. Lucy found herself short of the correct weight cream-colored wool for the second monkey's face. She decided she'd stop at the Black Sheep on Monday, before she picked up Tink. She could also pick up the dog sweaters. The impromptu life-coaching session with Phoebe had made her forget the carton.

On Monday morning, Lucy got the all-clear sign from the vet tech, Amy, to come in. Tink had done well over the weekend. She was active and eating "and passing waste appropriately." She was ready and eager to go home.

Lucy drove into town at 9:00. Although the Black Sheep

wasn't open for another hour, she saw Maggie's car out front and knocked on the door. Phoebe answered.

"So, how'd it work out with Dr. Doolittle? Did you ask him?"

"Hey, Phoebe. What's up? How was your weekend?" Lucy backtracked over the usual niceties.

"You wimped out, right?"

Lucy jammed her hands in the pockets of her down vest. "I was just about to ask him when he got a phone call and I had to go."

Phoebe's expression showed no sympathy. She wasn't buying it.

"I definitely made progress. He told me he's divorced. Or almost. And he has a daughter who's seven. Her name is Dara."

"I don't like the 'almost' part," Phoebe said wisely. "If you're almost divorced, you're almost married, right? Does that sound good?"

Lucy wasn't wild about the almost part, either. But hey, nobody's perfect.

"Phoebe, marriage is like a refrigerator. You have to rock it back and forth a few times before it tips over," Lucy said in his defense.

"Whatever." Phoebe sighed and checked her nail polish, an unusual shade of purple that reminded Lucy of Halloween. "So what about the dog? Did you get her yet?" Phoebe was definitely eager to meet Tink. Lucy secretly eyed her as a potential pet sitter. She suddenly knew how new mothers felt, meeting responsible teenagers who liked children.

"I'm just on my way to pick her up. But I forgot the pet sweaters. I thought I'd give them to the animal hospital."

Phoebe nodded, looking impressed. "Nice touch."

"I thought I heard your voice." Maggie came out of the storeroom. "Aren't you picking up the dog this morning?"

"I'm on my way. But I forgot the box with the pet sweaters."

"Oh . . . right." Maggie frowned. "I know I saw it someplace. Peter brought over the rest of the stock yesterday. It's just a huge mess in here. It'll take me weeks to sort it all out."

"God, I hope not." Phoebe moaned.

The shop's usual tidy appearance had given way to some disorder, Lucy noticed, with cartons stacked against the walls in all the rooms and bags of yarn tucked into random nooks and corners. Lucy could only imagine what the storeroom looked like right now.

"I can get it another time, Maggie."

"Let's take a fast look. It should be right on top. Come on back with me," she beckoned.

The storeroom was even more crowded with cartons than the front of the shop. "I think I marked the outside of the carton, but I'm not sure."

While Maggie started on one side of the room, Lucy checked the other. They'd barely begun when Phoebe poked her head in the room. "Maggie, Cara's here."

Maggie looked surprised but pleased. "She is? I'll be out in a second."

She turned to Lucy. "I'll be right back."

"Don't worry, I can handle it."

Lucy kept searching. Some of the cartons were marked and some were not. She thought she remembered what the box looked like, but faced with an entire roomful, she couldn't be sure.

Phoebe poked her head in the room. Lucy thought she'd come to help but was sadly mistaken. "I'm heading out. Got an early class but I'll be back here later. Let me know how it goes with the dog, and Doolittle."

So Matt's nickname around here was going to be Doolittle? Darn it. Lucy hoped that wouldn't catch on.

Lucy glanced at her watch. The vet tech had told her to come at 9:30. They needed to clean Tink up and check her stitches. Lucy had ten minutes more. She didn't want to miss Matt if he'd made time to see her.

She heard Maggie's and Cara's voices out in the shop but couldn't discern their conversation. Suddenly, Maggie appeared in the doorway carrying a big bouquet, Cara standing behind her.

" . . . and there's even more in here." Maggie walked into the storeroom and headed for the sink with her armful of flowers.

Cara stood in the doorway and gazed around in awe. "Whoa . . . you'd never think Amanda had so much stock in that tiny shop. Look at all this. You won't have to buy any yarn for a year."

"That's what I'm hoping . . . Lucy, look at these beautiful flowers Cara gave me." Maggie ran some water into a tall blue vase.

Lucy stood up. "Very nice . . . Hi, Cara," she said finally.

Cara smiled and waved. "Hey, Lucy. I didn't even see you back there. How's it going?"

"Oh, can't complain . . ."

Before she could say more, Maggie cut in. "You didn't find the box yet, I guess?"

"Not yet, but I've narrowed it down to this corner."

"Let me help you." Maggie snipped the ends off the flower stems and placed them in the water. "All the buttons are in the drawers by the table," she told Cara. "Just help yourself. I'll be right out."

"Don't rush." Cara disappeared back into the shop and Maggie came over to help Lucy.

"Cara stopped by to thank me for the book signing. She brought these flowers, isn't that sweet?"

"Very thoughtful," Lucy agreed. "Have you heard anything more about Seabold's Hardware?"

Maggie shook her head. "Not much more than what Edie told us. But a few other store owners got in touch with me over the weekend. They want the police to get in gear and catch this person. I agree. I can't understand why it's taking so long. Probably because they are looking in all the wrong places."

Maggie met Lucy's gaze. Because their detectives seriously consider people like me suspects, Lucy knew she meant to say.

"What can the business owners do?" Lucy asked.

"Not much," Maggie admitted. "The chamber of commerce has written a letter to the mayor and police chief. A woman's been murdered in cold blood, for goodness sake. And now another store has nearly been broken into. It's really the county that's handling the investigation but we've decided to start at the village level. All of the members have signed."

Lucy wondered if it was wise for Maggie to sign a letter of complaint, all things considered. But she had every right; she owned a business and was rightfully concerned.

"Not that these bureaucrats pay much attention to our complaints," she added.

"It's good to get it out there. Maybe the newspaper will pick up on it and do a story about your protest," Lucy suggested. "Then they'd have to pay attention."

"That would light a fire under them," Maggie agreed. "The police have to catch this creep. Before he or she strikes again."

The image was chilling but very possible, Lucy thought. She didn't want to imagine who might be next.

Lucy had finished her side of boxes and Maggie swiftly checked the last few. "I don't know, I thought the box of sweaters was back here. Maybe they're in one of the boxes in the shop."

"All right. I'll just take a quick look outside before I go."

The two women left the storeroom and Lucy headed for the

closest stack of boxes, in a corner of the back room. Cara stood at the big oak table nearby, sorting through a pile of buttons.

"Looks like I came to the right place. You have an amazing selection."

"I try to keep it interesting." Maggie sat at the table and picked up a card with burnished metal disks. "I took a lot from the Knitting Nest, but nothing special."

"I don't want anything wooden or stamped metal."

"Of course not. Too obvious," Maggie agreed. "Did you look in that bottom drawer? There are some big ceramics. I think they would go well."

Cara picked up a big shopping bag that was on the floor near her feet. She put it on the table and pulled out a long coat sweater made of brownish wool with a hood and bell sleeves.

Lucy thought it looked like a monk's habit but what did she know?

"Here's the sweater, let's see how some of these match up," Cara murmured. She smoothed out the front of the sweater and placed a button on the placket.

"How did the audition turn out? You never said," Maggie reminded her.

"It went pretty well. I'm still waiting for the final word but it looks like a go." She turned to Maggie. "You can be my guest sometime."

Maggie looked embarrassed but complimented. "Me? What would I do on TV?"

"The same thing you do here. You could do a lesson. Argyle or maybe some spinning?"

"Oh . . . maybe. That reminds me, do you need a wheel? That's about the only thing left at the Knitting Nest. It was a big one, nearly new. Peter Goran said he'd deliver it, too."

"Really? Maybe I'll call him about it," Cara said. "We could use it on the show. I am serious about you coming on as a guest, Maggie. It would mean a lot to me."

Lucy could tell by Maggie's tone that she was flattered. "Oh . . . we'll see. You get the job first. Then my people will call your people."

Cara laughed. She paused in her button search and smiled down at Maggie, resting her hand on the older woman's shoulder. "I really have you to thank, Maggie. For all the encouragement you gave me back in high school. I loved art, but I never thought I had much talent or could really get anywhere. My mother's a great person, but she always focused so much on my looks. All she ever wanted for me was to nab a rich husband."

Which still wasn't out of the question, Lucy wanted to remind her. Cara stood an excellent chance of having it all, if anybody did.

"Oh . . . don't be silly." Maggie patted Cara's hand. "I didn't have much to do with it. You've worked hard and anybody could see you have talent. I just knew you when, that's all."

Lucy felt a bit uncomfortable, being privy to the private scene. She focused on the cartons, knowing she had time for just this pile.

Flipping open the flaps on the box on the very bottom, she finally found the sweaters.

"Here they are." Lucy stood up and held up a sweater for Maggie to see.

"Thank goodness. I thought I was losing my mind. I could have sworn it was back in the storeroom. I'm sorry I made you look through all that stuff back there."

"That's all right. I'd better get going."

"Lucy's getting a dog. She rescued one of Amanda Goran's pack. Amanda's husband is giving them all away."

"Oh, how nice of you to do that. I love dogs," Cara said kindly. "Did the police catch anybody yet?"

"Not yet," Maggie reported. "Amanda's husband doubts they'll ever find the person who did it. He thinks it was a robbery but the police keep questioning him about it," Maggie added. She glanced at Cara but didn't say more.

Maggie had neglected to add that the police were questioning her also, Lucy noticed. But maybe she was embarrassed to tell Cara about that situation?

"Do they really think it's her husband? Oh . . . that's awful."

"Yes, it is, if it's true. Now this other break-in—attempted break-in, actually—at the hardware store seems to support Peter Goran's argument that there's some cold-blooded killer on the loose, and the police are too busy trying to prove him guilty to catch the real criminal."

"Another break-in? When did that happen?" Cara asked.

"Friday night. At Seabold's Hardware. The store was closed and someone broke a window in the back but the alarm went off and apparently scared them away," Maggie explained.

"Really? I didn't hear about that." Cara seemed concerned. "Guess I haven't been keeping up with the local paper."

Lucy zipped up her down vest, grabbed the carton, and slipped out the door, leaving Maggie and Cara to sort through the puzzling events surrounding Amanda's murder and the piles of button possibilities. She expected both conversations would take some time. Maggie hadn't even opened the drawer that held the toggles yet.

Cara wasn't so bad, she reminded herself as she headed for her car. I'm just jealous of her success. Maybe even a little jealous of the way Maggie makes such a fuss over her.

Lucy knew she and Maggie were much closer friends and would always be. But the former star student obviously held some special place in Maggie's heart. Cara seemed somehow charmed in Maggie's eyes in a way that Lucy, with all her endearing ticks and insecurities, knew she'd never be.

• • •

It was nearly a quarter to ten by the time Lucy reached the animal hospital and announced herself to the receptionist.

"I'm here to pick up Tink Binger?" she said, as if talking about a child to the school nurse.

"She's ready. You can go on back."

Lucy nervously touched her hair as she walked down the narrow corridor to the kennel room. She'd skipped the perfume and earrings entirely but had swiped on some lip gloss and had used a little hair product. After Phoebe's analysis, she hadn't wanted to look too overdressed, just better than normal.

She knocked on the kennel room door and it quickly opened. The vet tech she'd spoken to on the phone that morning was there, a tall thin woman named Amy.

"You're here for Tink, right? She's all ready for you."

Lucy saw Tink standing up in her cage. She barked and wagged her tail. The dog looked as good as new, Lucy thought . . . except for a big swatch of fur that had been shaved off around her middle and a white, funnel-shaped collar, which Lucy knew would prevent Tink from getting at her stitches.

"Hey, Tink, how are you? Ready to come with me? I bought you a lot of chew toys."

"Those should come in handy. She's a strong girl," the vet tech said. "She really needs a nice long walk after being stuck in that crate all weekend," Amy pointed out.

Lucy planned to get into a good dog-walking routine, just as the dog books advised. It would give her exercise every day, too.

She handed Lucy a big manila envelope and gave her instructions about Tink's medications. "It's all written down. Everything is in there."

"And the bill?" Lucy asked.

"Oh . . . the doctor made a note." Amy plucked a yellow sticky off the envelope. "Says you can settle that later."

Where is the doctor? Lucy was about to ask her. But Amy rushed on. "Do you have a leash?"

"Right here." Lucy pulled the leash out of her pocket, hot pink with white paw prints.

"Here she comes." Amy opened the crate and Tink sprung out like a wild thing. Amy held Tink's collar while Lucy clipped on the leash, which was no small feat.

"She's up to date on all her shots, so you shouldn't have to come back for a while," Amy said brightly.

"Right . . ." Lucy nodded. Not what she wanted to hear. "How about her stitches? Don't I need to come back to have them taken out?"

"Nope, they just melt away," Amy said cheerfully. "It will take about three days. Then you can remove her collar. Easy, right?"

Too easy, Lucy thought.

Tink jumped and hopped around Lucy's legs, biting her leash and pulling toward the door.

"Gee, she really wants to get out of here, doesn't she?" Amy observed with a laugh.

Lucy didn't answer. So, that was it? She wasn't going to even catch a quick glimpse of Matt?

She stared at the door that led to his office, trying to summon her X-ray vision, but it was impossible to tell if he was in there.

"Is Dr. McDougal around? Matt McDougal, I mean?"

Tink pulled her from side to side, panting so hard her tongue dragged on the floor. It was difficult for Lucy to maintain an air of nonchalance while hanging on to the crazed beast.

"He's in surgery. An emergency came in. Do you have a question? You can ask me."

Lucy smiled quickly. Would you like to catch a movie with me sometime, Amy?

"That's okay . . . it's not important," Lucy mumbled.

She grabbed the big envelope with the medicine and quickly turned her attention to Tink. "Come on, pal. I think we're done here."

As the dog books advised, Lucy kept Tink confined to a limited space, the kitchen and her office, which Lucy had set up in a closed-in porch that adjoined the kitchen. As she proved herself worthy, the dog's territory would expand. So far, Tink seemed content, mainly watching out the kitchen door at birds and squirrels in the backyard, as if glued to the Nature channel.

When Lucy finally checked inside the manila envelope, she found a sheet of postoperative care instructions and two bottles of pills. She felt very proud giving Tink her medicine, hidden in chunks of peanut butter, a dog-care tip she'd found in one of the books.

The envelope also contained the vial containing the stomach obstruction. She had thought it was a third bottle of pills, until she pulled it out. She took one look, shrieked, and the vial went flying.

The dog stared up at her, looking concerned, then ran to find the bottle, obviously thinking her wonderful new owner was playing "let's fetch the lab specimen."

Lucy raced the dog to the vial, which had rolled under the drawing table. She squatted down and quickly snatched it from Tink's eager jaws. She ended up nose to nose with the shaggy yellow hound. "That's all we need. You eating this darn thing twice. What are the odds of that happening?"

Lucy didn't even know why Matt had included the gross souvenir in the packet. Maybe it was just protocol? The way car mechanics give you the old parts to prove they fixed something?

Or maybe, seeing her reaction the first time, it was some slightly twisted Doctor Doolittle prank?

Cripes. She had to stop calling him that. Even in her private thoughts. She was just thankful the bottle had not broken open. Who wanted to clean up that mess? Holding her face away so she didn't even have to look at it, she slipped it back in the empty envelope and tossed the whole thing into the garbage.

Even though she'd started her workday hours later than usual, Lucy decided to finish up at around half past four so she could take Tink into town before dark. The poor dog had been held hostage for days and Lucy had read more than once that exercise was the key to good behavior. "A tired dog is a good dog." Given the choice, Lucy wanted a good dog rather than a bad dog and she was eager to introduce Tink to her pals at the Black Sheep.

She and Tink had made it less than two blocks from the cottage when Lucy realized this dog-walking business was harder than it looked. Tink was either pulling Lucy's arm out its socket or so engrossed in sniffing something on the sidewalk they would stall out.

By the time the pair reached Main Street, Lucy was exhausted. She'd taken a shortcut and instead of coming into town at the harbor, she'd walked down a side street that intersected Main about a half block from Maggie's store. She rounded the corner, panting as heavily as the dog, then pulled up short.

One . . . two . . . three police cars were parked in front of the Black Sheep. The lights on top slowly turned and radios crackled. A group of onlookers were gathered on the sidewalk in front of the building and some cops in uniform stood around on the sidewalk, keeping them back.

Lucy ran up to the crowd with Tink. The shop door stood

open, and she could see a lot of activity within. Lucy saw more men, some in uniform, some not, walking in and out. She pushed through the gathering, ran up the path and up the porch steps before anyone could stop her, dragging the dog behind her without thought.

"Hey . . . whoa there." A uniformed policeman held out his hand and stopped her at the top of the steps. "You can't come up here. The store is closed, miss. Sorry."

"What's going on? Is anyone hurt?"

"Police business. Nothing to worry about."

"My best friend owns this place. Is she here? Can I speak to her, just for a minute?"

Lucy strained to see inside the shop, the policeman doing his best to block her view with his broad body. "You can't go any farther. This is a closed area."

A closed area . . . what the hell did that mean?

Lucy ignored him, weaving from side to side. She finally caught a glimpse of Maggie in the back room standing with Detective Walsh. Lucy could tell by her gestures that she was upset, very upset. She was arguing with Detective Walsh.

She heard Maggie's voice rising, though she couldn't tell what she was saying. Not a good sign.

"Hey, did you hear what I just said?" The policeman got into her face again. "You have to get down on the sidewalk. Right now."

He stepped forward and Lucy stepped back. She stood her ground for a moment, then turned and pulled Tink down the few steps to the stone walk, then down to the sidewalk.

Meanwhile a swarm of blue uniforms carried cardboard cartons out of the Black Sheep, all the boxes of yarn that had come from the Knitting Nest. What in the world was going on?

Even more people were gathered on the sidewalk by now and

she stood at the front of the group, waiting for another glimpse of Maggie.

Maggie was in trouble, that much was clear. But what in the world was going on here?

Lucy pulled out her cell phone and called Dana's office, hoping to catch her in between appointments. The message tape played and Lucy waited for the beep. "Dana? The police are at the Black Sheep. They're taking a lot of stuff out of the shop . . ."

"Lucy, what's going on? You sound hysterical."

"Thank goodness you picked up. I'm sorry, but it's really bad. There are a ton of cops here. They won't let me talk to Maggie. They won't even let me inside—"

"Hang on, I'll be right there," Dana said quickly. "I'm going to call Christine Forbes," she added. "Maggie needs her."

They said good-bye and Lucy hung up. She turned to see Phoebe's little red VW Bug pull up, parking down the block since the patrol cars took up the spaces near the shop. Phoebe got out and ran toward the shop. Lucy saw her stop to talk to a policeman who stood by a cruiser, probably to ask him what was happening. Lucy ran to meet her.

"I'm sorry, miss. You can't go in the building for a few hours. Until they've finished the search," Lucy heard him say.

"A few hours? I live in there. That totally sucks," Phoebe told him.

Lucy tugged at her sleeve, pulling her away before she had two friends arrested tonight. Phoebe turned to face her and gripped her arm. "Oh my God, Lucy! The police are going to arrest Maggie! What should we do?"

Phoebe looked about to cry and hopped up and down. Her black eyeliner was already smudged and about to drip down her face. Lucy let out a long slow breath. She felt exactly the same way but was too old and self-conscious to act out so dramatically.

"Hang on, Phoebe. Maggie is in there talking to Detective Walsh and they're taking the boxes from the Knitting Nest out. That's all we know."

Phoebe nodded, her chin trembling. "But we have to help her. We know she didn't do anything wrong. It's just not right . . ."

It wasn't right. And she was positive Maggie had done absolutely nothing wrong. But there was no use trying to argue that point right now.

"Dana called Maggie's lawyer. I hope she can get over here soon. That's all we can do right now. They won't even let me up on the porch."

"Yeah . . . I know. That cop said I couldn't even go up to my apartment. Doesn't that stink? What about a person's constitutional rights. This is turning into, like, a police state . . ."

Lucy nodded. The whole situation stunk. What in the world did they hope to find? The police had already searched the Knitting Nest for several days. There was nothing new here, except for the extra boxes that had come from Amanda's house, Lucy recalled. But she'd just looked through practically every carton today, searching for the dog sweaters. It was yarn, yarn, and more yarn, with maybe a few boxes of knitting needles or crochet hooks thrown in.

She was starting to think Peter Goran was right. The police around here so rarely investigated a murder, they didn't know what they were doing. They were making a mess of it, creating some big mystery when it had simply been a random robbery. Now poor Maggie was taking the brunt of their ineptitude and inexperience.

"Oh, is this your dog?" Phoebe sounded all weepy as she leaned over to pet Tink. "Oh, Lucy, she's beautiful."

Grateful that someone had noticed her, Tink lifted her head and softly licked Phoebe's hands, exposed by fingerless gloves.

Lucy didn't answer, just looked down at Tink. All the excitement seemed to have made the dog wary and she sat calmly at Lucy's feet, leaning against her legs. The feeling of her warm body was comforting.

With their gazes fixed on the front door of the shop and the porch swarming with cops, they hadn't even noticed Dana coming down the street until she stood right beside them.

"Anything happening? Did they take Maggie out yet?"

"Take her out?" Lucy spun around to look at Dana. "God, I hope not. She's still in there, talking to Walsh. Maybe he just wants the boxes."

Dana pursed her lips a moment, her expression grim. "I think we'd better prepare ourselves. Looks like they're going to arrest Maggie for Amanda's murder."

Lucy felt stunned. "They can't . . . she didn't do anything. Dana, how can they do something like that? She's completely innocent!"

Now it was Dana's turn to calm Lucy. She rested a hand on her shoulder and spoke in a slow soft tone. What you would call a very therapeutic tone . . . and for good reason, Lucy realized. She was about to totally lose it.

"*We* know she's completely innocent. But they must be looking for something that will tie her to the murder. Something that's come into the shop by accident probably, along with the stock from the Knitting Nest." Lucy had already figured out that much, though she couldn't imagine what that something could be.

"Even if they don't arrest her, I'd say it's one hundred to one they're taking her to the station for questioning tonight. Don't worry, it will all be sorted out," Dana added. "Christine is very good. She won't let them hold Maggie a minute longer than necessary."

"Oh my God . . . look! It's Maggie, she's coming out." Phoebe gasped. Lucy drew close and put her arm around Phoebe's slim shoulder. She thought the poor kid was going to faint.

Maggie walked between Detective Walsh and a uniformed policeman. She wasn't in handcuffs, thank goodness, Lucy noticed, but she did look more or less trapped between the two large men. She certainly wasn't happy about going with them. Her coat was open, flapping in the breeze. She looked down as she walked, obviously embarrassed to be seen by the group of looky-loos that had gathered on the sidewalk.

How awful for her, Lucy thought. Maggie had worked so hard to build such a great reputation in town. She must be mortified. How will she ever live this down? Lucy's heart went out to her. What a nightmare.

"Maggie!" Lucy drew closer and waved. Maggie looked up, a flash of hope in her features.

Her friends waved in unison. "Don't worry, we called Christine," Dana called out to her. "She's going to meet you at the police station."

A wave of relief washed over Maggie's features. "Thank God"—Lucy saw Maggie mouth the words, though she couldn't hear her.

They had reached the police cruiser. Walsh stepped aside to let Maggie get in. Lucy saw her hesitate a moment, then with resolve, climbed in the back of the police car.

The doors slammed and the patrol car pulled away from the curb.

The three watched, dumbstruck. The remaining policemen dispersed the crowd. "That's it, folks. Nothing to see here . . . time to move on," they murmured.

Lucy thought there was something to see. The Black Sheep was surrounded by yellow tape that read "Caution—Police Line—Do Not Cross."

She turned to Dana. "Should we go down to the police station and wait for her?"

"It might take hours," Dana said. "I don't know if it would be that helpful, either." Dana's cell phone buzzed. She pulled it out of her pocket and checked the number. "It's Jack. I called him before I left the office. He was going to try to find out what's going on."

Lucy waited as Dana spoke to her husband. She hated to eavesdrop but couldn't help herself. Not that it helped. Dana's side of the conversation was a lot of "uh-huh"s and "oh, I see"s. There was one "gee, that's not good," causing an instant knot in Lucy's stomach.

Dana clicked off and looked back at them.

"What did he say?" Phoebe asked eagerly. "Has he heard anything?"

"He nosed around a little. It seems someone called in a tip and the police got a warrant to search for the murder weapon."

"That doesn't sound good," Lucy said quietly.

"No . . . it doesn't," Dana agreed. "But let's not get carried away. We don't even know if they found anything."

"Let's just hope they didn't. Then they really have no grounds to hold Maggie very long, right?" Lucy asked her.

"No grounds at all," Dana replied.

Phoebe looked bleak and bit her fingernail. "Did anyone call Suzanne? She's going to be extremely pissed if she's left out of this."

"Yeah, you're right. I'll call her," Lucy offered, but before she took out her phone, Dana touched her arm.

"Listen, it might be a long night. Why don't you come back to my house and hang out for a while? Christine said she would call me once she knew what was going on."

That was enough to persuade Lucy. "Thanks, Dana. I just have to drop the dog off."

"I'm there," Phoebe said. "I can't get into my own apartment yet anyway, and Josh has a gig somewhere."

"Great. Let's meet back at my house. I'll fix something to eat," Dana said. "Let's not panic. Even if the police find something incriminating in all those boxes, there are a million reasons why it might be in Maggie's shop."

A million reasons other than Maggie being the murderer, Dana meant. Reasonable doubt. Wasn't that what they always said on lawyer shows? "So why do I feel so panic-stricken?" Lucy wondered.

Phoebe gave Lucy and Tink a lift back to the cottage, so Lucy could drop the dog off. She hated to leave Tink alone her first night home, but the dog did seem tired out from the long walk and all the excitement. Tink inhaled her kibble, then curled up on her new bed. She looked pretty much done for the day.

Lucy patted her head. "I'll be back in a while. Be a good girl."

She headed for the door, then ran back to the sitting room and grabbed her knitting bag. Dana said it could be a long night. What else would they do all that time?

Though it would hardly be the same to sit and knit all night without Maggie.

Chapter Nine

"They haven't formally charged Maggie with anything, but she's been brought in for questioning." Dana's voice, which was normally so clear and confident, had trailed off so quietly Lucy could hardly hear her. She had just finished talking to Maggie's attorney, Christine Forbes, and put the phone down on the slate coffee table in her living room. The circle of friends sat in stunned silence. How many times had that ever happened? Lucy couldn't remember.

As Dana had predicted, it had turned into a long grueling wait. Stationed in the Haegers' spacious living room, they ate, drank, knit, and commiserated about Maggie's unjust incarceration. Dana put together a platter of fruit, cheese, and French bread, along with a bottle of cabernet.

Mostly, they waited for updates from Maggie's lawyer in order to learn what was going on. Dana took a deep breath and picked up her knitting. Lucy watched as she settled her troubled expression into something more resigned and controlled.

"How can they hold her for questioning about anything? They don't have any proof," Phoebe insisted.

"Christine just told me that the police say they've found the murder weapon," Dana reported. "They say they took it out of the shop, in one of the boxes."

"A weapon? What was it?" Lucy could hardly imagine. She'd looked through all the stock in Amanda's store and then had looked in most of the boxes again this morning, searching for the dog sweaters. There was nothing even vaguely resembling a weapon. Not that she'd noticed.

Dana tugged on the ball of yarn she was using. "The police believe Amanda was struck on the head with a heavy blunt object. They've found a wooden hat block in the shop, at the bottom of a box of yarn. The bloodstains match Amanda's blood type," she added. "That's about as much as they can know for sure right now. Except checking it for fingerprints. They've sent it to a lab for DNA tests. But that will take a while."

"Okay, so they found this hat block that someone probably used to kill Amanda. The killer left it in the Knitting Nest and Maggie comes along, buys all the stock, and ends up with it in her shop. Even if it has her fingerprints on it, how does that in any way prove Maggie is the murderer?" Suzanne argued angrily.

"Detective Walsh is totally desperate and pathetic. How could this ever hold up in a courtroom?" Phoebe agreed.

"I never saw a hat block." Lucy had been thinking about it and knew she'd remember something like that. "I was with Maggie last week, when she went through the stock in the Knitting Nest. It's not something you'd miss seeing or not remember. If it was in the Nest all this time, why didn't the police see it when they searched after Amanda's murder?"

"They couldn't find it if it wasn't there," Dana pointed out. "Whoever used it on Amanda—Peter, most likely—must have taken it with them and hid it somewhere," Dana pointed out. "Didn't Maggie say Peter brought over more boxes from his house?"

Lucy frowned. So Dana thought Peter had killed Amanda,

took the hat block home with him, and then planted it in a box when he delivered the stock? That seemed logical. But why hadn't anyone seen it sooner?

"I looked through most of those today. I never saw it."

"I didn't see it, either," Phoebe added. "But there were about a zillion boxes and even a bunch of shopping bags. We probably just missed it."

"Anybody notice that we're back to Peter Goran again?" Suzanne's smile was tight and disdainful. "It's very obvious. Peter's trying to frame Maggie for the murder. That's why he was so pushy about her buying the stock and rushing her to take it out of the shop."

"Maybe that's why he didn't bargain with her," Dana pointed out. "Didn't Maggie say her offer was ridiculously low and he just took it, no questions asked?"

Lucy sipped her wine and nibbled on an apple slice. She remembered Maggie saying that a few times and that she'd even felt guilty about cheating him.

"Nobody does business like that," Suzanne said knowingly. "He's desperate for money, too. I was at the office today and this agent I'm friendly with told me she went over to appraise the Gorans' house this week. Peter wants to put it on the market and wanted to know what he can get. He said he was waiting for the police to close Amanda's case. Of course, he gave her that bull about the murder being a robbery and all that." Suzanne shook her head. "Get this, the agent says there was a woman there, you know, living in the house. A girlfriend. Who knows how long that's been going on?"

"Dana's yoga teacher, Wanda, told me that she thought Amanda was having an affair," Lucy recalled. "So maybe they both had extramarital activities, hidden from the other," Lucy said. "Now Peter is free to do as he likes."

"Right. Maybe he *freed* himself of Amanda to do as he likes," Suzanne said. "But aside from the girlfriend, he starts asking the real-estate agent how fast he could close the deal so he can leave town. He told the agent he has some debt to pay off. Some serious debt. Not just a few credit cards . . . now what does that mean?"

Dana looked down in her lap and fiddled with her knitting. "Peter has a gambling problem. The attorney who was handling the divorce told Jack. I wasn't supposed to tell anybody but . . . since you seemed to already know most of it . . . well, don't ever say you heard the rest from me," Dana added. "That was the big issues in their divorce. Amanda wouldn't agree on sharing his debt."

"Maybe that's why he went to talk to her the morning she was murdered?" Lucy recalled. "Maybe he hadn't even found out about her affair. Maybe, when she kept saying she wouldn't help him with his debt, he got so angry that he went over the edge."

"Does it really matter what they argued about? For once, he got the last word," Phoebe finished for her.

Lucy felt her skin crawl. She could picture it now . . . Peter and Amanda. The way they had argued. The hat block in Peter's hand, striking her on the head. . . .

"So why is poor Maggie sitting in the police station, being browbeaten for the past three hours?" Suzanne demanded to know. "What's wrong with this picture, ladies?"

"How long can they keep her there?" Phoebe asked Dana.

Dana shrugged. "I don't know. I guess it depends if they can tie the hat block to her somehow. If they have enough evidence to charge her, she can still get out on bail. But she'll have to go before a judge. Probably tomorrow, at this rate."

The thought of Maggie going through that ordeal made Lucy feel sick to her stomach. And angry. At the police, Peter Goran . . . at whoever had done this to her.

"Fingerprints would be pretty flimsy, don't you think?" Lucy asked Dana. "Considering the block was in the shop and she could have handled it by accident?"

Dana nodded. "I'm sure Christine will be able to talk them out of something that weak. Christine is smart and tough. She can put two and two together. She knows Peter Goran probably did it and he passed all that stuff to Maggie. I'm sure she's going to argue that scenario to Detective Walsh."

"Just in case, next time you speak to her, please relate the highlights of this conversation?" Lucy asked.

"Of course I will." Dana reached over and touched Lucy's hand. "Jack says the police are really tiptoeing around this case. They want to make the charges stick. This is an election year for the county DA and he doesn't want to be embarrassed."

"I guess that's something in Maggie's favor. I just wish it wasn't taking so long to get her out of there." Lucy sighed.

"The wheels of justice grind slowly." Dana's tone was solemn.

"And the wheels of injustice seem to grind even slower," Lucy countered.

"Doesn't the American Civil Liberties Union have a hotline or something?" Phoebe asked mournfully.

Suzanne was the first to go and very reluctantly, a few minutes after midnight. She wanted to stay longer, but she had a full day to look forward to, getting her kids up and off to school in the morning and then holding an open house in town.

The big sectional sofa was comfortable and Dana had started a fire in the hearth. The leaping yellow flames made a hypnotizing contrast to the smooth granite mantel. Lucy watched the fire, struggling to keep her eyes open. She wondered if Tink was all right being by herself, but she didn't want to leave without hearing from Maggie. The platter of fruit and cheese was picked over and just about empty, the same for the wine bottle.

Dana sat on the other end of the sofa, still steadily knitting. But

Phoebe had fallen asleep, curled into a ball in one of the leather chairs, her long legs tucked up to her chin, her knitting dangling off her lap. More crazy-looking socks for Josh, it appeared to Lucy. Her features had relaxed in sleep, making her look much younger.

Dana had noticed it, too. "She looks like a little girl," she whispered.

"Yeah, one that's allowed to get piercings and tattoos," Lucy whispered back.

Dana laughed but luckily Phoebe didn't wake up.

They did wake her up, though, when Christine Forbes called again at about half past one. It was good news. Maggie was being released. The police were not charging her, for lack of evidence, her lawyer told Dana. They couldn't find a fingerprint match on the hat block, which was good news. The bad news was they were still trying to link it to her someway.

"Did you speak to Maggie?" Phoebe asked with a groggy yawn.

"No, I didn't get to speak with her. Only with her lawyer." Dana sat back and sighed. "Looks like we'll have to wait until tomorrow to hear the whole story."

Lucy rose and stretched her legs. She picked up her knitting and stuck it back in her tote. She was still working on the second hat. It seemed to have stalled out in all the excitement.

"This is the first time we've ever met and knitted without Maggie," she said to Dana and Phoebe.

Dana was also putting her knitting away, including one of the flowers she planned to felt and use to embellish her new sweater. "I was thinking the same thing," she admitted. "Let's hope it's the only time."

Maggie and the Black Sheep knitting shop had made the local newspaper again, the second time in less than two weeks. Finally on the front page, though hardly the way Maggie had hoped, Lucy thought with a cringe.

A half-page article with a photograph covered the surprise police search and Maggie's night of questioning at the station, "in connection with the recent murder of Amanda Goran, Plum Harbor resident and former owner of the Knitting Nest."

"In connection with the recent murder of . . ." The phrase made Lucy shudder. At least they hadn't called her a "suspect." That would have been too much to endure.

Lucy could only imagine how Maggie felt reading any of it. Or how she felt trying not to read it.

As Tuesday wore on, she could only imagine it, since Maggie would not speak to anyone all day. Lucy called around to her friends—Dana, Suzanne, and Phoebe. They were getting the same silent treatment. Maggie just wouldn't talk to anyone.

"This has been a real shock for her. A real blow to her self-esteem. She needs some time to process," Dana told her. "We can't take it personally."

No, they couldn't. Lucy wanted to be there for Maggie but it seemed the only way to do that right now was to give her some space. Lucy understood that.

When Lucy went out to the supermarket at 5:00, she drove past Maggie's house. The curtains were drawn and the windows dark. She decided not to stop after all.

When Lucy got home she found a message on the machine. "Hi, Lucy, it's me. I'm sorry I didn't pick up when you called. I'm all right. I was exhausted from being up all night and slept most of the day. We'll talk tomorrow, okay?" Maggie hadn't said whether or not she would open the shop tomorrow, Lucy noticed. Maybe she didn't know herself.

There was another message after Maggie's. This one was from Matt McDougal. Lucy had almost forgotten about him.

Almost . . . not quite, she admitted to herself. She did feel a tiny ping of victory, hearing his voice. "Hi, Lucy, it's Matt McDougal. I'm just calling to see how Tink is doing. Give me a call at the office if you have a chance . . . I'd really like to say hello."

Pretty much a standard doctor-patient follow-up call. Except for the closing. He'd like to say hello? Really like to? Well, that was something. She had to agree with Phoebe. Men were timid woodland creatures and this was moving so slowly they were practically going backward.

The next morning, Lucy had just come in from giving Tink her morning walk when she heard the phone ring and then Phoebe's voice on the machine. "Lucy? It's Phoebe. Maggie just called—"

Lucy picked it up. "Hey, what's up?"

Phoebe sounded upset. Lucy hoped it wasn't more trouble with the police. "Maggie's not opening up today, either. Bummer, right? She says she's still too tired. But I think she's just afraid to show her face on Main Street after that story in the newspaper and all. It's really so unfair. The police are fascist pigs—"

When Phoebe got nervous she just kept talking. Lucy had to interrupt her. "I think she's embarrassed, too. I'm not sure what we can do," she added, remembering what Dana had said. "She probably needs more time, Phoebe."

"Yeah . . . I know. I just hate to see her in lockdown mode, acting as if she really did clip Amanda on the head, when it's not her fault at all. Know what I mean?"

Lucy did know what she meant. It wasn't like Maggie to crawl into a hole like this. She was more the type that came back out swinging.

"I don't think it's a good idea for her to be alone right now, either," Phoebe added.

"I thought of that, too." Not that there was even a remote chance of Maggie harming herself. But it wouldn't make her outlook any lighter to skulk around alone in her dark house.

"Why don't we just go over there?" Lucy said suddenly. "I'll call Dana and Suzanne. If she really doesn't want to see us, we'll go away but at least she knows we're thinking of her."

"An intervention. I like it." Phoebe sounded relieved.

"Can you meet at her house in fifteen minutes?"

"I'm there," Phoebe promised.

Dana and Suzanne were upset to hear that Maggie planned to stay barricaded in her house today and both liked the girlfriend intervention plan. They dropped what they were doing and jumped in their cars to meet Lucy and Phoebe. Suzanne had just bought bagels and cream cheese for a morning meeting at her office but offered to donate them to the cause.

When they finally gathered at Maggie's front door and stood shoulder to shoulder, Phoebe rang the bell. Lucy was glad she was not alone. It would have been a simple matter for Maggie just to talk to her through a crack in the door, claiming she was still just too tired to see anyone, though she appreciated Lucy's concern. Lucy knew she wouldn't have been persuasive or pushy enough to force her way in.

But it was pretty darned near impossible for Maggie to face down all four of her stalwart friends at once. It reminded Lucy of her days on the high school soccer team, when the opponent was taking a corner kick at the goal and the coach would shout, "Make the wall! Make the wall!"

They were making the wall, and Maggie might give it her best shot, but she would not get the ball past their loyalty and deep concern.

They heard the bell ring inside and a few moments later, they saw Maggie peek out the living room curtain. They waited. But she didn't come to open the door.

"What if she doesn't answer?" Phoebe whispered.

"She's got to answer," Lucy said.

"Not necessarily. She didn't ask us to come here. She specifically told us not to. She has a perfect right not to let us in," Dana reminded them.

"If she doesn't answer, you're all taking bagels," Suzanne mumbled.

Finally the door opened. Maggie looked pale and flustered. Her hand clung to the open top of her long cardigan sweater. She wore a T-shirt and velour sweatpants, but was barefoot, which led Lucy to suspect Maggie had still been in her bathrobe when she heard the bell and had run upstairs to quickly pull some clothes on.

"Oh . . . this is very sweet. But I'm really not up for company right now," Maggie said quietly.

"We aren't company, Maggie. We're your best friends," Dana replied in an even quiet tone.

"Your homegirls? Your posse?" Lucy offered, trying to interject a light note.

"We're a flippin' intervention, Maggie. You don't have a choice." Phoebe's high thin voice was stern.

Maggie turned to her, looking surprised. But she hardly budged or opened the door any wider. "Do you really want to socialize with a murder suspect? Word gets around. You might regret it. Bad for business, I'll tell you that much."

It was hard for Lucy to tell if Maggie was joking. She sounded so serious. And sad.

"If you don't let us in this instant, you'll definitely regret it. That much I can say for sure." Suzanne leaned forward and nudged the door open with her shoulder, like a linebacker heading for the end zone, the bag of bagels tucked under her arm.

Once she'd clear the way, Maggie had no choice but to step aside.

"Please come in. Nice of you to drop by . . ." she said as they traipsed past her into the foyer.

They filed into the living room, then chose places to sit. Lucy and Dana sat on the camelback chintz sofa. Phoebe sat in a wingback chair. Suzanne pulled over the rocker from its spot near the fireplace.

"You sit down here, Maggie. I'll make some coffee."

"There's a full pot. Hardly touched it," Maggie murmured.

They all sat looking at her, waiting for her to speak. Lucy thought Maggie looked lost in her private thoughts, hardly aware they were even in the room.

"Maggie . . . tell us what you are thinking," Dana coaxed her. "We want to help."

"Yes, we want to help," Lucy repeated. She sat forward, waiting for Maggie to reply.

"I'm ruined. What else could I be thinking?" Maggie's voice trembled. "Who will come to the store now? Especially after that awful article in the newspaper. Everyone is talking about me. I'm sure of it." She looked down at her hands twisting in her lap. Lucy could rarely remember seeing her sit in that chair without some knitting in her hands.

"But you're innocent, Maggie," Dana reminded her. "It doesn't matter what other people think. In time, they'll see that they were wrong."

"In time, of course. But I don't have that much time. A little shop like the Black Sheep can go out of business quickly. And I didn't look innocent when I was dragged off by the police Tuesday night. Did you see the crowd on the sidewalk? Oh . . . it was awful.

I've never been through anything like it. Not even when Bill died," she added. She took a deep breath and composed herself. "No, I can't survive this. The shop . . . everything I've worked so hard to build there . . . it's all been taken away from me. Like that." She snapped her fingers in the air. "I guess Amanda Goran has had her revenge on me after all, hasn't she?" she asked bitterly.

"Maggie, you can't be serious," Lucy implored her.

"We know you feel terrible, Maggie. Anybody would," Dana said quietly. "Violated and accused of something horrific that you didn't do. But give yourself some time. Don't make any big decisions right now. You aren't thinking clearly."

"Oh, yes I am. I might as well just close up shop. Quick and painless. Instead of sitting there every day, hemorrhaging money. Waiting for customers who never come. Waiting for the police to come back and take me away for good this time."

Her last line shut them all up, Lucy noticed. For a long moment, nobody even dared to breathe.

Dana was the first to find her voice. "This is not like you, Maggie. You know people will still come to the shop. The police will find the person who killed Amanda and everyone will forget that you were ever involved."

"People have, like, very short attention spans, know what I mean?" Phoebe said. "They're talking about this now, then next week, it's something else. Global warming . . . bad tomatoes."

Maggie glanced at her but didn't say anything. She pulled an afghan around her shoulders and curled into the chair, staring into space again.

Lucy understood now. In that last gesture, Maggie was trying to tell them that she didn't feel safe in the Black Sheep anymore. She felt vulnerable, exposed. Under attack by the small-town gossip she was sure had already begun. And that was the saddest thought of all.

"Maybe you should close for just a week or so, see how that goes," Dana suggested gently. "Just until the police tie up this case and it all blows over."

Dana glanced at the others, silently soliciting support. Lucy thought that was a good compromise. She did think Maggie was acting rashly. Maybe closing for a few weeks would be the best thing, considering Maggie's frame of mind. No use trying to force her to go back if she really didn't want to.

But closing the Black Sheep, even for a little while, would be a great loss to all of them. Lucy didn't even want to think about the doors shutting forever. But if that's what Maggie needed, how could they argue?

Suzanne bustled back in with a tray that held cups, the coffeepot, cream cheese, and a stack of bagels on a platter.

"That idea sucks," she said bluntly. She set down the tray and turned to Maggie. "If you close the shop, even for the rest of the week, that's like hanging out a big banner that says, 'Hey Everybody. You're Right. I Did It!' Are you going to let them take it all away from you? Are you going to let Amanda win, from beyond the grave, for Christmas sake?"

Maggie stared up at her, a curious light in her eye, her mouth hanging open.

Lucy couldn't tell if Suzanne's outburst had made her angry. It had definitely caught her attention.

"Oh, easy for you to say. Try sitting in an interrogation room for three hours. And being fingerprinted like a common crook. . . ." She held her hands out, spreading her fingers. "See? I still can't get all the ink off. It's horrible . . . then tell me that I'm giving in too easily."

"I'll tell you that I'm disappointed in you," Suzanne continued. Dana turned to look at her, shaking her head, trying to signal she was going too far. Suzanne ignored her.

"I never expected you to turn tail and run like this, Maggie," Suzanne continued. "I always thought you were a fighter. You always said you didn't care if people gossiped about you. You didn't care what they said. Why start now?"

Maggie squared her shoulders. Her mouth twisted but she didn't say anything. Lucy felt a glimmer of hope that Suzanne's tough love approach was working.

"Why start now . . . Suzanne has a point," Dana jumped in.

"Hey, the way we all hang out there all the time, the place always looks crowded. No one's going to think you lost business," Phoebe pointed out. She reached over for a cup of coffee and a cinnamon-raisin bagel.

"We're your best customers," Suzanne reminded her. "And we're not going anyplace."

"We certainly buy enough yarn every month to cover the rent," Dana added in a lighter tone.

"And probably the utilities, too." Lucy glanced at Maggie. Her rigid expression was relaxing a bit, wasn't it?

"Not with the discounts I give you, ladies . . . and all the freebies I hand over."

"Exactly. That's why we can't let you close. We need that free yarn," Phoebe told her. "Hey, I've got it. If Maggie gives up the shop, we take over. Is that brilliant, or what? I can't put up any cash right now, but you'll get my management experience. I totally know how to run the place."

Maggie made a snorting sound. "You do not."

Dana laughed. "Brilliant . . . I think we should do it. What do you say, Maggie? Is the Black Sheep up for grabs?"

Maggie turned her head to the side. She sighed. "No . . . it is not."

She didn't say anything more. Everyone waited.

Lucy wondered if she was angry and didn't appreciate being

cajoled out of her black mood. Maybe she thought they weren't taking her crisis seriously enough?

"I will tell you all that if you need any yarn, the shop will be open tomorrow, the usual hours," she said slowly. "Suzanne, you're wasting time with real estate. You ought to get a job for Detective Walsh. In the interrogation room. But you're right. No use acting as if I have something to hide when I don't. No use letting people who want to believe the worst about me win. That really isn't my style."

"That's all I wanted to hear." Suzanne picked up a bagel and slathered it with cream cheese.

The bagels look good but Lucy stuck to her coffee. She'd skipped breakfast in her rush to get over here but was trying to watch her carbs. She had to lose ten pounds by the weekend. Just in case she ended up going out with Matt.

Dana sighed. "Now that we settled that problem, can you tell us about last night?"

Maggie shrugged. "There's not too much to tell. There was a lot of waiting. Like a horrible long layover in an airport except much more agonizing. That's how they try to wear you down. Get you on edge. Walsh asked me the questions along with Detective Reyes and another detective. Gardener, I think his name was. They must have asked a million times if I'd ever seen that hat block before, how it got into the shop. They made me tell them all over again about my relationship with Amanda. Everything I'd told them that first time."

"But you must have told them that the block came in the boxes from the Knitting Nest, right?" Lucy asked eagerly.

"Oh, I did. About a thousand times. I also told Walsh and Reyes I hadn't seen it at the Knitting Nest when we looked through the shop that first time. And I really didn't remember if it had been in the boxes of yarn Peter brought over from his house.

It might have been there . . ." She looked at Lucy. "You went through those boxes on Monday. Did you see it?"

Was that only two mornings ago? It seems like ages ago now.

"I didn't," Lucy told her. "But I didn't look in all the boxes. Mainly the ones in the storeroom."

"They didn't find it in the storeroom. They found it out in the front room. At the bottom of a carton. Someone called Walsh and said the murder weapon was in my shop. So they ran right over. Can you believe that?" Maggie shook her head, her eyes bright. She was angry. "It had to be Peter Goran. But it's so transparent, it's practically unbelievable anyone would try a move that lame."

"I'm sure the police are questioning him again today," Dana said. "I wonder if they'll get anywhere, though. If they can't tie him to the block in some way, either, we're just going around in circles."

"For goodness sakes. Let's wake up and smell the coffee. He was trying to frame Maggie," Suzanne insisted. "In a village idiot way, I agree. But what else could it be?"

Lucy almost agreed with her, but it did seem too simple, even for Peter.

"Well . . . we know Peter showed Maggie the inventory of the store and he acted as if she was the only one he'd asked to look at it. But he could have been lying to her. There could have been people in and out of the Knitting Nest last week for a lot of reasons, and one of them could have found out you were taking the stock and planted the hat block."

"Possibly. Except that Phoebe and I packed the first set of boxes ourselves. Then we carried them out to his truck. He was the only other person who touched them. But he did bring part of the other load from his house," Maggie added. "My attorney raised that point with Walsh, as well. It didn't have to be Peter," she conceded, "though he seems the most likely. It does seems too obvious, even for him."

Dana took a sip of her coffee and shook her head. "I keep getting this feeling we're missing something. It's right in front of us but we don't see it."

"Me, too. Like trying to find a dropped stitch. Sometimes you see the hole . . . but you can't figure out how it got there." Phoebe sighed and turned to Maggie. "We missed you last night, Maggie. We kept messing up our projects and we didn't have anyone to fix them for us. "

"You were knitting while you waited to hear about me?"

Suzanne smiled. "Of course we were. What else would we do?"

"I guess that makes sense. I don't know why . . . it just really gets me." She sniffed and blew her nose in a tissue. She'd been under so much pressure, she was just very emotional right now, Lucy realized.

"Well . . . tomorrow is Thursday . . . already," Maggie reminded them. "We're still having knitting night, right?. Bring your messes to me then," she told them.

"Where are we meeting? I forgot." Suzanne's BlackBerry started to buzz. She pulled it out of her purse to check the message.

"At the shop. It's my turn," Phoebe said. Phoebe's apartment was too small to host the group so when her turn came around, they met at the Black Sheep. "I have a real treat planned for you guys. I'm going to show you how to hand-dye with Jell-O. Is that cool or what?"

"That does sound cool," Lucy said. "I think I read about it somewhere."

"I think I read about it, too. The question is . . . why?" Suzanne had entered the meeting info into the BlackBerry, then stood up and gathered her things.

"Because of the awesome colors you can't get with regular dye," Phoebe explained patiently. "And it smells really good. It really gets you in the mood to eat Jell-O. I'm going to bring some, so you won't be tempted to stick your fingers in the dye baths."

"My mother used to make amazing Jell-O molds. Remember those things?" Dana smiled, remembering. "They were about a foot high and had ten different layers."

"There's a real art to a good Jell-O mold," Maggie agreed.

"A lost art," Lucy said.

"Right . . . and it can stay lost, if you ask me." Suzanne rolled her eyes and waved good-bye. "Time to show a house. What a barn. Seller has to drop his price seriously. He'll figure it out. . . . See you tomorrow at the Black Sheep?" She looked at Maggie.

Maggie nodded. "Definitely. See you then."

Chapter Ten

Lucy woke up Thursday thinking about Maggie, wondering if she really would open the shop today, as she had promised. It would be hard for her, no question about that. No one could blame her if she decided to keep the door locked and stayed home again. But Lucy hoped Maggie hadn't slipped out of the spirited frame of mind they'd left her in yesterday—the Maggie that everyone was used to, the one who would always pull up her skirt and plough on.

Lucy showered, made coffee, and kept looking at the phone. It was too early to call Maggie, even if she was home. Lucy didn't know what she could say that wouldn't sound condescending, as if she was watching her, like a patient in a ward.

While Lucy considered the possibilities, Tink caught her eye, hopping up and down near the kitchen door. Lucy felt like a bad mother. Thank goodness the dog had a strong bladder.

She pulled on her jacket, leashed the dog, and headed into town. Tink provided the perfect cover for stopping by the Black Sheep so early. Hopefully, this time, she wouldn't find any police raids or major upsets.

When they reached the shop, Lucy was relieved to see activity inside. She tied Tink's leash to the porch railing in a spot near the large front window and promised to be back quickly. Lucy knew Maggie wouldn't mind having the dog inside, but considering Tink's weakness for eating yarn and all the snout-level baskets, it seemed best to keep her out of temptation's path.

She walked into the shop to find Maggie sitting at the oak table in back. A coffee mug sat to her right and the newspaper was spread out on the other side. Meanwhile, her wooden umbrella swift was clamped to the table as she read, sipped, and furiously wound away. The swift was whirring around so quickly, she didn't even notice Lucy until she stood nearby.

Then again, maybe she did. Before Lucy could say hello, Maggie lifted her head and looked at her over her reading glasses.

"Good morning, Lucy. You're out early."

"I had to take Tink for a walk. My new routine. I thought I'd stop by." Not entirely a lie, though she knew darn well Maggie saw through her easier than a lace poncho. She glanced at the front of the shop. Tink had gotten up on her hind legs and was staring through the window.

"You can bring her in. At least until customers come."

So, she expected customers after all? That was a good sign.

"Thanks, but I'd rather not. I'm trying to cut back on the yarn in her diet."

"I get it. How's it going with the dog? I never got a chance to ask."

"Pretty good." Lucy nodded and took a seat at the table. She couldn't help smiling. "She did chew a sock. That was my fault, I shouldn't have left it on the floor. But she's not much trouble, so far. And I don't feel like I'm walking around the house talking to myself anymore."

"That's a plus," Maggie agreed. "And how's it going with the veterinarian?"

Lucy was surprised Maggie remembered the vet with everything she had on her mind. But she had a feeling Maggie was trying hard to normalize today and talk about anything but that horrible night and the murder investigation.

"Not bad on that front, either," Lucy reported. "He called to see how Tink was doing and when I caught up with him yesterday, he asked me out."

Now Lucy couldn't help smiling.

Maggie glanced at her. "So he asked you. Just as well. Men say they like women to make the first move but I don't think they really do. I think it scares them."

Lucy mostly agreed with that observation.

"Maybe they like it, but it also scares them," Dana offered. Nobody noticed that she'd walked in and was already close enough to hear their conversation.

Dana set her large coffee cup on the table and slipped off her coat. "So, which of you is planning on scaring a man—and who is he?"

"Lucy was invited on a date. She was going to ask him, but he asked her first."

Dana sipped her coffee. Her eyes widened over the edge of the cup. "Uh-huh," she said as she put the cup down. "Let me guess . . . Dr. McDougal?"

"Am I that obvious?"

Maggie and Dana glanced at each other.

"In a good way," Dana offered. "You're very . . . sincere."

"When are you seeing him?" Maggie stopped the swift a moment to untangle a strand.

"Friday night. Dinner and a movie."

"Time to talk and get to know each other. But the movie takes the pressure off," Dana noted with an approving smile.

"Tomorrow is soon," Maggie said abruptly.

"Last time I checked. . . . Has there been some change I didn't hear about?" Lucy glanced at her.

"It's soon, that's all I mean." She shrugged.

Lucy had a feeling she was about to say something more.

Ask Lucy what she was wearing or suggest she get a haircut. But then she stopped herself, because she didn't want to sound like Lucy's mother.

Actually, that was her sister Ellen's territory. Lucy's mother never asked those kinds of questions, instead she'd want to know where the man had gone to college and what were his politics.

"I might get a haircut. Just a trim," Lucy revealed. She tugged a clump of her hair and checked the ragged ends.

"You're gorgeous just the way you are. Just be yourself," Dana insisted. "But a good haircut does give your self-confidence a boost."

"You should have seen her the other night . . . and she was just going to visit the dog at the animal hospital." Maggie glanced at Lucy. "If she really works on herself, this guy's in trouble."

Was that a compliment, or was Maggie suggesting she should "work on herself" more?

"Thanks for the vote of confidence in my bombshell potential, guys. But I don't think he's looking for a Malibu Barbie."

"They're all looking for Malibu Barbie," Dana whispered. "Don't kid yourself."

"She's getting coached by Phoebe on this one," Maggie murmured. "Heaven help us . . ."

The last bit of yarn flew off the swift with a flourish and the little machine kept spinning.

"Where is Phoebe? Isn't she working today?" Lucy wanted to share the small victory with her dating coach, though Phoebe would probably suggest that she get her nails done neon green, or antimatter black, and a faux nose ring might be a nice touch.

"She's around," Maggie nodded. "She told me her class was canceled and she'll be here all day."

Lucy wondered if the class really had been canceled or if Phoebe didn't want to leave Maggie alone in the shop this afternoon, easily falling prey to unhappy thoughts if there were no customers. Or if some customer or fellow shopkeeper came in and said something nasty.

Phoebe seemed to be a space cadet most of the time, but was surprisingly aware of other people's needs and feelings. And she did give fairly good advice, despite what Maggie thought.

"She came down when I opened up," Maggie added, "but I let her go back upstairs for a while. To work on her Jell-O project."

"Oh, right. Tonight is the Jell-O and fiber fest. That concept could catch on with knitters in a big way," Dana pointed out.

It was a scary thought, but true.

Lucy stood up and glanced out the window. Tink had found a sunny spot and finally lay down, looking out through the railings at the world passing by. Pretty good, she thought, though she wouldn't take her chances and leave her out there much longer. She wasn't sure how well the leash was tied and if a cat or squirrel caught her eye, she might turn into Houdini dog.

Just before she turned away from the street view, she saw Suzanne's SUV pull up. So they'd all had the same idea: coming here to check on Maggie this morning.

"Suzanne's here," Lucy said, turning back to the others.

"We might as well have the meeting this morning," Maggie said drily.

Of course they couldn't stay and knit. They all needed to head off for work in a few minutes, Maggie was just being sarcastic.

Lucy was sure she knew why they'd all dropped by this morning, she just didn't want to talk about it.

Suzanne entered the shop at a swift no-nonsense pace. She was either in a hurry to get to her next appointment or had some news.

"Good . . . you're all here. Guess what I just heard? Peter Goran was taken to the police station this morning. Now he's being questioned. It's about time, wouldn't you say?"

"I expected them to bring him back in," Dana said. "But why do I feel like the police are just spinning in circles? I'm not sure they're making any progress."

"I heard the police have linked him to the incident at Seabold's Hardware, too. That's progress," Suzanne insisted.

"He fakes a break-in attempt at another shop to throw the police off his trail and make it look as if there is some berserk burglar on the loose. When that didn't work, he planted the hat block in Maggie's shop. He's been desperate to create some diversion, to keep the police from zeroing in on him."

"Maybe," Dana replied. She still didn't seem convinced.

Maggie suddenly looked upset. She tugged on the swift, winding the ball of wool even faster. Lucy knew that wasn't the best way to do it. She was pulling too hard and would stretch the yarn—a tip she'd learned from Maggie herself—but didn't say anything to stop her.

"Did they search his house or anything like that?" Lucy asked.

"Not that I heard," Suzanne said.

"You ought to call Christine later and see if she's heard anything," Dana suggested to Maggie.

"Yes, I plan to. I have to speak to her anyway."

Suzanne dropped her voluminous leather bag on the table but didn't sit down. She pulled out a thick datebook and flipped it open to check something. "Maybe by tonight we'll have good news. Maybe the police will finally arrest Peter Goran and Maggie won't have to worry anymore."

Lucy was never one to be cheered by anyone else's misfortune, even when that person seemed to deserve it. But for all the easy banter and good humor between her friends this morning, there was no getting around it—a cloud of unease hung over the Black Sheep.

The police had already come here once without warning and taken Maggie away. They all knew that until someone else was arrested for Amanda's murder, it could easily happen again.

When Lucy got home a short time later, she was relieved to find an e-mail from her client. The health benefits brochures were finally accepted and the last set of initials, signed off. The big boss had actually liked the new photo, where the kid blowing bubbles looked like Titan.

As Oscar Wilde said, "In matters of taste, there can be no argument." Lucy wasn't going to argue, as long as she was getting paid.

On to her next adventure, a children's book. The project was nonfiction, an oversize, chockful-of-facts volume called *The Big Book of Things That Creep and Crawl.* Arranging the photos, illustrations, sidebars, and text was definitely a design challenge . . . or nightmare, depending on how you looked at it. The book was the first in a series and she wanted to do a good job so she'd be called back for the others.

The project was way more interesting than dull insurance-benefit pamphlets and paid better, too. Lucy was excited about it, at least for now.

That was the upside of having her own business. If one job was torture, you could always look to the next for relief.

Sometimes that worked out and sometimes the next one was just as torturous—but in a different way.

Lucy opened the first file of the book. Slimey and wiggly-legged creatures filled her oversize computer screen. Fortunately, she wasn't squeamish about bugs.

Immersed in the new project, Lucy stared at her computer the whole day, taking short breaks to stretch her legs, make tea, and let Tink out for quickies in the backyard. She'd faced the fact that she wasn't going to lose five pounds—or even two pounds—in time for her date tomorrow night. But she dutifully ate salad for dinner and decided she would wear lots of black. Easy. Beyond that, it was pretty much a take-it-or-leave-it proposition for the good doctor.

It was dark outside by the time she shut down and got ready to leave for the knitting club meeting. She needed to get an early start in order to make a stop beforehand at the big discount drug mart on the turnpike. Lucy had a long shopping list of items that were crucially needed before tomorrow night. The winter had gone on forever and Lucy felt like a she-bear emerging from a cave.

She wondered how Maggie's day had gone. She'd thought about making some excuse to call the shop today, but that seemed too transparent.

If there had been a problem with customers today, Lucy doubted Maggie would even tell her. She'd seemed very subdued this morning, not her usual self, and resigned not to talking about her situation—being a suspect in a murder investigation.

The news about Peter Goran being taken in for questioning again and being linked to Seabold's Hardware store should have cheered Maggie, Lucy thought. But she didn't seem particularly happy or even relieved.

The truth was, until someone was actually arrested, Maggie was still under suspicion and that had to be an awful feeling.

When Lucy finally pulled up at the Black Sheep later that night, she could tell from the cars outside that she was the last to arrive. She entered the shop but didn't see anyone at first. Then she heard voices, coming from the storeroom, and walked back to find that Phoebe had already begun her demonstration.

Phoebe had set up her wool dyeing operation on the counter near the microwave and the rest of the group stood in a tight circle around her.

"Hi, everyone. How's the Jell-O experiment going?"

Suzanne turned to her first. "I know I was skeptical but look at what Phoebe made so far." She pointed to the small table where there were several skeins of yarn, some bright colors, some muted, but all very interesting and definitely unique.

Lucy couldn't get close to the counter so she picked up the Jell-O-dyed samples and looked them over. She'd only tried dyeing her own wool once or twice, with formulas she'd ordered online. She'd never quite gotten the colors she expected and had nearly ended up dyeing the entire kitchen and some of her best cookware. The experimentation and playing with the colors, hand painting different colors on the same skein, still appealed, so she wasn't quite ready to give up the idea. Jell-O could be the answer.

"This one turned out great, Phoebe. I love the blue."

"Jell-O Berry Blue." Phoebe glanced over her shoulder a moment to clarify.

"There are a few ways to do this," Phoebe explained. "You can heat it on the stove or pour hot water into a dye bath. I'm going to mix everything up and zap it in the microwave a few minutes."

Phoebe had some written instructions on a pad that she referred to and used to explain as she went along. "First, I need to put a few cups of water in the bowl . . ." She measured about four or five cups of tap water and poured it into a big plastic bowl. "Then some salt," she said, using a measuring spoon. "Then one pack of your favorite color Jell-O . . . I'm going to use cherry for this batch." She opened the Jell-O and poured it in.

"It's so pretty. And I love the smell," Maggie remarked.

"Well, this part smells bad. You might want to pinch your nose," Phoebe warned. "You always need to add some vinegar. To make the color stick or something." She measured a cup of white vinegar and poured it into the mix.

"Like dyeing Easter eggs," Suzanne said.

Phoebe mixed the ingredients with a wooden spoon until all the clumps of Jell-O had dissolved. "Now, for the wool." She took a skein of white yarn she had on hand and dumped in it. "I like to make the color come out uneven, so I let some of it stick up but if you're a neat freak," she paused and glanced at Dana, "you can soak it more evenly."

Phoebe carried the bowl to the microwave and popped it in, then shut the door and set the timer. "I'm going to zap this for about three minutes and then check."

Phoebe set the timer and they all waited quietly. Amazingly quiet for their group, Lucy thought. Jell-O dyeing had them enthralled.

The microwave beeped and Phoebe took the bowl out. "Hmmm . . . it's not soup yet," she said. She showed it around and they all agreed. She checked her pad and nodded to herself. "I need to let it rest a minute or so before I put it back in. You don't want it to get too hot."

"That makes sense," Maggie said. "This is certainly easier than the stove-top method. If it works."

"Oh, it works. Don't worry," Phoebe promised.

She needed to zap the bowl and let it rest two more times,

but true to her word, the skein of yarn finally emerged a scintillating shade of cherry red. Phoebe lifted it from the mixture with the spoon for all to see.

"Wow. That's beautiful," Suzanne said.

"Great color," Lucy agreed.

"The article I read online said you can get some great effects, mooshing the Jell-O directly into the yarn and using different colors on the same skein. But I thought I'd give you just the basics first," Phoebe said.

"For our next lesson," Maggie said.

"Okay, next time. I'll study up," Phoebe replied. "This needs to cool, then I can hang it to dry." She put the bowl aside and turned to face the group, wearing a big satisfied grin, Lucy noticed.

"Okay. My work is done here. You guys go inside," Phoebe told them. "I have to run upstairs a minute."

Phoebe quickly wiped her hands on some paper towels. She had a splash of red Jell-O on her cheek, Lucy noticed, but it looked sweet. "I have sort of a surprise for you. You can like, wait out in the shop, okay?"

"I think I can *like* guess what's coming . . . but I won't ruin it." Maggie led the group into the back room.

They dutifully traipsed into the back room, took their usual spots at the oak table, and pulled out their projects. Suzanne was the first to nab Maggie. She pulled out a vest she was making for her husband. Suzanne had abandoned the chulo hat, Lucy noticed, or maybe set it aside for a while. Lucy didn't blame her. Working in three colors did look challenging. The vest was a much simpler design, slate blue with a darker blue stripe.

Matt looked good in blue, Lucy mused. She could make him a great scarf in that color. Or a sweater . . . or try spending an evening together first, she reminded herself, before you start planning all the knitting projects you're going to make him.

"Is it my imagination or are the stripes slanting to one side? Can I fix it when I block it?" Suzanne asked hurriedly, not even waiting for an answer to the first question.

Maggie took the piece and stretched it flat on the table. "It is slanting. Look at that. I think you'd better rip back. Otherwise it's not going to meet the back section right."

Suzanne sighed and took her knitting back. "Maybe I'll just ask Kevin to lean to one side when he wears it. Or it can go in the bottom drawer of his chest, with the rest of my handcrafted presents."

"Jack wears a few things that I make for him," Dana said. "It's hit or miss. I don't take it personally. I'm sure it's the same for him, on the nights when he does the cooking."

"At least he does some cooking. I swear, in my house they'd starve to death if they didn't call for takeout. I don't think Kevin even knows how to turn the stove on," Suzanne complained. They continued to trade complaints about their spouses. Lucy just smiled. That's why they call it stitch 'n' bitch, she thought.

There had been some major distractions from stitching this week, for all of them but Lucy was surprised to see Dana had not gotten very far with her flowers. She was the most methodical, efficient, steady-going knitter of the group but tonight she seemed totally frustrated.

"When you're done straightening her out, Maggie, I really need some help with these freaking flowers. They're starting to look like . . . brussels sprouts," Dana moaned.

Maggie got up and came over to Dana's side of the table. "Let me see . . . you've got the right gauge yarn, we know that. You're the only one who got anything out of the Knitting Nest stock," she added.

"Yes, lucky me." Dana's tone was dubious. "I've got the right stuff, so that's no excuse."

Lucy didn't understand what Maggie was talking about at first, then remembered. Maggie did have the yarn Dana needed for the flowers on hand at the Black Sheep, but had found some in the Nest stock and given it to Dana before the police took everything else away.

Dana took out her copy of *Felting Fever* and opened to the flower instructions. The photos of the event that Lucy had passed to her flew out on the table and Lucy grabbed them.

"Were the photos any help?" she asked Dana.

"They helped some." Dana glanced at her. "Thanks for printing them out for me."

Maggie had been reading the pattern and examining Dana's efforts. "I think it's hard to tell until you felt and everything tightens up and shrinks down."

"I did try one." Dana dug into her knitting bag. "I was embarrassed to show you, but now that you ask . . ." She pulled out a small gnarled glob of reddish-orange wool and tossed it on the table. "Look at this gorgeous specimen. Looks like the dog's breakfast, right?"

Suzanne started laughing. "I'm sorry, Dana. But you said it."

Lucy could see that Maggie was trying hard to withhold comment. She picked up the felted bud and turned it around in her hand. "Something's gone wrong here," she said in a serious tone. Then a small smile broke through for the first time all night. "Terribly, terribly wrong."

"I know," Dana agreed. "Look at the flowers on Cara's coat. I don't think they started off like this."

Lucy flipped through the enlargements of Cara's sweater coat before handing them back, looking closely at the felted button covers. She noticed the jacket was missing a flower, at the bottom. Maybe that one had turned out like Dana's and Cara plucked it off, Lucy thought.

She passed the pictures over to Dana and Maggie, who were now both studying the project instructions and the photos in the book.

"I think you goofed up when you felted it," Maggie decided. "Maybe it was in the washer too long . . . or the action was too strong? Why don't you finish one more flower and we'll felt it here, by hand. It will be good practice for me. I want to do a class this spring with the flowers. Handbags and things."

Dana sighed. "Okay, I'll give it one more try."

Lucy picked up the mishapen flower, Dana's discard. She turned it around in her hand. It looked like something familiar to her . . . she wasn't sure what, the image hovering at the edge of her brain.

"Ta-da! Hold your applause, please, until the end of the program." Phoebe stood in the doorway, carefully carrying what had to be the largest, tallest, multilayered, multicolored Jell-O mold in modern history.

It jiggled and vibrated, threatening to self-combust with Phoebe's every step. It looked like something the Cat in the Hat might serve for dessert, after green eggs and ham.

It was clearly the ninth wonder of the world, defying every law of engineering. It appeared that Phoebe had ambitiously, and optimistically, used the biggest pot she owned for her mold, one that could comfortably boil three pounds of spaghetti. Or boil a few lobsters. Only someone who had no knowledge of cooking could have put the thing together and expected it to stand upright.

"Sorry I was up there so long. It was stuck in the mold and I didn't want to break it."

"Whoa, that's amazing. I never saw one that high." Dana stared at it, wide-eyed.

"That must have taken days to make," Maggie observed.

"A week," Phoebe confessed. "Two layers a day. One in the morning, one at night."

"I know I was trash-talking Jell-O molds, but I'm totally impressed." Suzanne checked the massive dessert from different angles. "I didn't even know you could cook."

"I wouldn't exactly call this cooking. I did mix in some stuff, though. Pineapple chunks. Mini marshmallows. The blue layer has kiwi slices. Don't they look beautiful? Sort of just floating in outer space or something. I should have put them on top."

"None of the yarn you were dyeing got in there, I hope," Maggie teased, pretending to check the layers.

"No . . . but I did toss in a little plastic baby. You know, like a Mardi Gras king cake? If you find it, you get a wish."

Maggie pulled up close to the table. "I could use a wish. Give me a big scoop, please."

Phoebe had brought bowls, teaspoons, a large serving spoon, a tub of low-fat whipped topping, and a squirt can of whipped cream. She served everyone and then herself.

"This is super, Phoebe, thank you." Lucy took her second bite, savoring the mixture of sweet and tart flavors and surprising ingredients.

"Retro food. It's making a comeback." Phoebe took the can of whipped cream and shook it with vigor before covering her entire dish. How did she stay so stalk thin, Lucy wondered. Then she realized this was probably Phoebe's main meal for the day.

"I used to love this stuff when I was a kid." Phoebe passed the can to Suzanne. "My brother and I would have whipped cream fights with it in the kitchen."

"We did that at our house," Suzanne confessed. "Now I squirt it on Kevin."

Dana started laughing and ended up coughing up some Jell-O. She covered her mouth with a napkin. "In the kitchen, or the bedroom?"

Suzanne shrugged. "Hey, after three children and seventeen years of marriage, you have to mix it up a little." She took the can, shook it, and squirted a swirl into her bowl. "They sell this stuff in chocolate now, too. Why did it take so long to figure that out?"

"Jack likes Cool Whip better. He thinks the can is too noisy—ruins the mood." Dana glanced up quickly, then looked down at her dessert dish again, smiling to herself.

Maggie looked about to reply, then made a funny face. Her mouth twisted and she spit something out in a napkin.

"Look . . . Maggie got the baby!" Phoebe practically jumped out of her seat. "We have a winner."

"For goodness sake, I nearly cracked a tooth . . ." Maggie shook her head, staring at the little rubber toy.

"That a good sign, Maggie," Suzanne said decisively, though Lucy wondered if Phoebe had fixed the contest.

"Make a wish. Don't tell us," Dana added, "or it won't come true."

Maggie glanced around at her friends, then carefully placed the little pink plastic baby in the middle of a clean napkin.

"All right, here goes." She closed her eyes a moment, then opened them and sighed.

Her friends glanced at one another, then continued to finish their Jell-O and whipped topping in silence.

As if by some unspoken pact, no one had mentioned the murder investigation tonight. Bless Phoebe's pointed little head, Lucy thought, she had successfully distracted them with her zany dyeing technique and her flamboyant dessert.

But they all knew what Maggie's wish would be. That the police would close the case quickly and her good name in town would be cleared.

Lucy wasn't sure how other people looked for a relationship and had a full-time job, too. It seemed to her that dating was a job and left little time or mental energy for anything else.

Her new book design project—that crept crawled and squirmed—beckoned. But Lucy had to quit work early on Friday afternoon or she'd never be ready in time for her date with Matt.

As ridiculous as that seemed, it was true.

She had a haircut appointment in town at 4:00 and she required a complete overhaul—from her head down—by then.

It had been a long solitary winter.

Swooping by the value drug mart on the way to the Black Sheep last night, she'd quickly filled a shopping cart with beauty and hygiene products of all descriptions—exfoliators, depilatories, pore cleansers, eye cream that claimed to erase dark circles and lift sagging lids, moisturizer with seaweed extract, teeth-brightening rinse, cover stick, lip gloss, a three-toned pack of eye shadow, and a set of surgical-steel eyebrow tweezers, industrial strength.

Dana had her eyebrows "threaded," whatever that meant.

And her favorite purchase of all, an overpriced pink plastic razor that excreted soothing lotion as you shaved your legs and promised "to bring out your inner goddess."

Was she ready for her inner goddess to be outed? That was a good question.

Not that she planned on exposing any significant body parts tonight. But smoothness was important, a psychological edge. Could she really feel sexy, witty, and irresistible knowing she looked like Sasquatch in her underwear? Of course not.

It was like having condoms in the night table drawer. Not that she planned on tearing into any foil packets tonight, but it was something you needed on hand, just in case. Like a box of baking soda next to the stove. Did you plan on having a kitchen fire? Of course not. But if that grill pan flared up, you were ready.

The woman at the register in the drug mart was old. Lucy felt sorry for her. She looked like she came to work every day in an ambulette. She scanned Lucy's purchases with care and curiosity as if she'd never seen the stuff before, which, of course, was impossible, Lucy realized. She hummed to herself. It sounded like "That Old Black Magic."

When she came to the pack of condoms she stared at it, turned it over in her hand a few times, and waved it over the scanner without success. Then, to Lucy's horror, she picked up a microphone. Her slow reedy voice blasted through the empty aisles.

"Price check, register five . . . Strider extra-durable condoms . . . economy pack?"

Lucy cringed and stoically faced forward, hearing snickers in the long line behind her.

Being a grown-up was not easy.

Nobody said it would be.

That afternoon, as a mint julep purifying clay face mask set her features into rigor mortis, Lucy found an e-mail from her nieces:

Dear Aunt Lucy,

We know you are a very busy person but are our hats done yet?

Tomorrow is the first day of spring. Remember?

Love and kisses, Sophie & Regina

p.s. we really can't wear these hats to the beach

Lucy suspected that last nudge had to be Regina's idea. She had inherited Ellen's snide edge. With one thing and another going on this week, Lucy hardly noticed the Earth about to shift on its axis. A minor detail, all things considered.

But she had made headway with the sock monkey hats, progress during the long night of Maggie's incarceration and more last night at the knitting meeting.

In fact, she'd noticed the hats were just about finished. All she had to do now was add the monkey faces and sew on long strands on each side that tied under the chin. She decided to make the chin straps look like braids, secured with red bows. The girls would love that.

If she stole a few minutes from beautifying, she could finish and send them off to Concord this afternoon at the post office, when she got to town.

She sent back a brief note:

Girls, Watch your mailbox!

Love, Aunt Lucy

P.S. Don't let your mom get to this package first, or these monkeys might not make it through Homeland Security.

Lucy washed the green paste off her face, which had now hardened to the consistency of wall spackle. A few more minutes and she could have easily screwed a picture hook into her forehead.

Pampering and polishing herself was hard. Knitting was easy.

She pulled out the hats and merrily set out braiding the tie strings, then attached them to the ear flaps. The monkey's face—sewed on stitches for eyes, red nostrils, and a smile—was going to be a bit harder, especially since she didn't seem to have the right color and weight of red wool in her knitting bag . . . or in any of the plastic containers under her bed and in various closets that held her stash.

She could pick some up later at the Black Sheep. But that meant she couldn't finish the hats until tomorrow. Then she practically tripped over the answer to her problems.

The box of dog sweaters. It still sat in the middle of her office. There had to be some red wool in there that she could snitch for monkey noses.

Lucy pulled open the flaps and dove in. She needed to sort out the contents anyway. Take a few out for Tink before she passed it on to the animal hospital.

It was the only box from the Knitting Nest that had not been taken away in the raid on Maggie's shop, she realized, as she picked through it. Lucy wondered if she should tell the police she'd taken it from the shop before their raid and wondered if Maggie had mentioned it the night she was questioned. She couldn't really see how it would matter. They had the hat block with Amanda's blood on it, which seemed to be the real prize.

The box contained a canine boutique. The designs were amazing, created with craft, humor, and style. Turtlenecks, simple wraps, capes, styled and sized for different breeds. She chose a dark blue poncho for Tink, trimmed in bright green with a stand-up collar and snap closure neck. She also chose a yellow wraparound coat that looked like it had been felted and was probably water repellant.

Tink was already nosing around, curious at what Lucy was doing, or maybe she smelled some former dog pals from the Nest on the carton. She stood very calmly as Lucy tried on her new outerwear but did try to chew on the fringe that trimmed the poncho.

Lucy knew Amanda had sold pet coats like this in her store but wondered if she planned on marketing them on a wider scale. She really could have made a fortune with this stuff. Maybe she had plans in the works but hadn't gotten things rolling before she'd been killed.

Lucy searched the sweaters for the red wool she needed without much success. At the very bottom of the box, she found a larger cape, a patchwork pattern made out of knitted squares. It was definitely not one of the best items. She decided she wouldn't feel too many qualms about pulling it apart to get some of the red yarn.

Lucy stretched out the piece on her lap and started to pick at a seam with a crochet hook. She felt something solid in one of the squares at a corner of the piece. Had Amanda put something inside the swatches to weigh the cape down, so it would stay in place?

Lucy was curious and looked closer at that square. It was made of purple wool, double sided, unlike the others, which were a single layer. She stretched apart the stitches and saw what looked like a piece of clear plastic, a case of some kind with something inside. She didn't realize what it was at first, then got it. A CD in a case had been sewed inside of the knitted square.

That didn't seem like a typical method someone would use to weigh down the corner of knitwear.

It did seem like a method someone would use to hide something.

Something important, that someone—like Amanda—didn't want anyone to find?

Chapter Eleven

Lucy ran over to her knitting bag, clutching the dog poncho. She dove into the assorted mess and came up with a small pair of scissors. She neatly snipped a seam on the purple square and slipped out the CD case.

She flipped open the cover. The disk had no label or writing on it. She wondered what it could be. What was so confidential Amanda needed to hide it in a dog sweater? Her diary, with all her private thoughts and yearnings about her secret love affair?

A list of grudges and revenge fantasies?

Confidential information she didn't want Peter to find during their divorce? Perhaps about her finances?

Lucy sat a moment with the disk in her hand. Reading it felt like a violation of Amanda's privacy, even though she was dead. Maybe *because* she was dead. But Lucy couldn't help herself and her curiosity finally overwhelmed her ethics. She returned to her office, stuck the CD in the computer tower, then clicked the icon.

Various folders appeared, named by numbered chapters. It looked like a manuscript. She'd seen enough of those to recognize the format. She remembered Peter saying Amanda was always tapping away on her computer and rarely let it out of her sight. She must have been trying to write a book. Maybe she even had a publisher interested.

Maybe that's why she was nicer to Maggie when she stopped at the Black Sheep the night before her murder. Their rivalry didn't seem as important to her anymore. She was on to a new arena. She was acting like the cat who ate the canary because she expected to finally trump Maggie with this victory.

Amanda's behavior the night before her death, when she'd surprised everyone at the Black Sheep, was starting to make some sense.

Lucy clicked on a file and a page of text appeared on the screen.

> *Chapter One*
>
> *Felting is easy and fun. Heat and agitation. That's basically all there is to it . . .*

She quickly scanned the page and then the next.

The words were stunningly familiar. She'd read this all before. Skimmed it, at least.

It was the manuscript of Cara's book, *Felting Fever*. But why was a copy of that file tucked away in one of Amanda's dog sweaters?

Lucy pulled up the file property information and checked the date the file was created. A little over a year ago, just the right time frame for book production. She considered the implications. Why would Amanda have a copy of Cara's book, in manuscript form, on her computer?

She could have been hired by the publishing house as an advisor, to review the material. Lucy had worked on lots of nonfiction titles. Editors, even the most savvy and chockful of miscellaneous knowledge, couldn't be expected to be an authority on every project they acquired. They sometimes hired expert readers to check information beyond what a regular copy editor could do.

Amanda could have been hired to review Cara's book. That was certainly possible.

But if that was the case, why did Amanda keep her connection to Cara and that sideline job—which had some status for her—such a big secret? From what Lucy knew of Amanda, she'd expect her to brag about it. Why did she act so eager to attend Cara's demonstration, as if she'd never met the woman before? Why didn't she mention her connection to the book and Cara to Maggie? That would have been more Amanda's style, trying to show up Maggie since she was even closer to Cara's success.

Finding the CD seemed to raise more questions than it answered. Lucy stared at the page on her screen for a while, then closed the file.

Tink nosed her elbow, nearly flipping Lucy's hand off the keyboard, her sign that she needed a backyard break.

Lucy checked the time.

Cripes . . . it was already past 3:00.

She still had to shower and dress before her hair appointment. Matt's office was open late tonight and it seemed easiest for them to meet in town at 7:00. Lucy dashed into the bathroom and jumped in the shower. She hadn't used even half of her beauty products, she noticed. She wasn't sure if that was a good sign, or a bad one.

Rubbing her skin raw with a new loofah and apricot-aloe dermabrasion grains, Lucy tried to focus on making "every part of her kissably soft and smooth." But she was more intent on sorting out her puzzling discovery.

Maybe this manuscript file explained why Amanda was making frequent trips to the city and how Amanda had enough money to cut back her hours at the Knitting Nest and afford a complete beauty makeover.

But expert readers didn't receive that large a fee, Lucy knew. Not even the really good ones. Unless Amanda was doing more for the publisher than just checking information. Supplying designs, perhaps? Maybe writing some sections with instructions? Cara had openly admitted that didn't come easily for her. Lucy hurriedly finished her shower, skipping a few more helpful products.

Dripping wet and wrapped in a big towel, she ran back to the computer and brought up the book file again. In a separate folder, she found the projects Cara showed off in her presentation. The cute little handbags decorated with felted flowers. The big tote bag and a scarf. Even the sweater coat Cara had been wearing.

She also noticed a folder that was just called "New." The start of a new book? She clicked and found patterns, novelty projects, including some of the dog sweaters in the box.

Goose bumps popped up on her bare skin.

Jumping to the Internet, Lucy Googled Amanda's name again. The same postings came up that she'd found in her first search.

She hit the first link and took a closer look at the information about Amanda's second-place prize in a design contest at a knitting conference, over two years ago.

The conference had taken place in Boston and was sponsored by *Stitchery* magazine, not Cara's magazine, *Knitting Now!* No obvious connection there. Lucy checked the information on Amanda's entry, "Felted tote bags with flowers."

Part of her wanted to jump up and shout, "Bingo!" Another part was sitting there saying, "Wha—?"

She still didn't understand what this all meant, or if it had anything to do with Amanda's murder. She did know that Amanda had definitely been way ahead of the curve on the felting trend. No wonder she didn't win first place. The judges didn't know what to make of her project.

She sat back from the computer, the towel slipping perilously low. Cara was the one who could explain what this all meant. But for some reason, the idea of approaching her with the discovery didn't sit well with Lucy.

Should she just bring the CD to the police and tell them where she found it? Maybe bring the entire box of dog sweaters?

That didn't strike her as the best option, either. The box had come from the Black Sheep and the last thing Lucy wanted to do was turn Detective Walsh's attention back to Maggie.

No, going to the police with this right now was not a good idea.

Lucy had no idea what she should do and didn't have any more time right now to try to figure it all out.

A quick glance at the clock in the corner of the computer screen made her jump out of her chair and run to the bedroom. She'd planned on wearing a pair of good black pants instead of jeans, but they needed ironing.

Damn. She didn't have time for that unless she skipped the haircut. Which was not an option now, since she hadn't bothered to wash her hair in the shower.

She pulled on jeans and a black tank top, and over that, a comfortable standby, a black, gray, and white sweater she'd made herself and was inordinately proud of . . . even though the sleeves had come out uneven lengths and she had to push them up a bit to hide the flaw.

Maybe it wasn't her most alluring piece of clothing, Lucy realized, as she slipped on some silver bangle bracelets. But it definitely made a statement—threw a gauntlet even?—at a prospective suitor.

What could you do? All the cleansing grains and waxing strips in the world wouldn't change that about her.

Lucy made it to the hair salon just in time. Friday afternoon was possibly the worst time of the week to schedule a haircut, like being the last patient to go under the knife at the end of the surgeon's long, hard week. Lucy had enough anxiety about anyone putting a sharp instrument to her hair as it was. And adding to that, now there was this latest bombshell discovery about Amanda.

But she had to go through with the cut. Figuring out who killed Amanda Goran was important . . . but so was her social life, right?

Besides, Lucy realized, she could mull over the meaning of the mysterious CD while she sat in the salon chair.

An assistant brought her back and introduced her to the stylist, Gary, who had been highly recommended by Suzanne. He greeted her with a smile of large white teeth that looked like Chiclets.

"So, let's see what's going on here, Lucy." Gary popped Lucy's hair clip with a flourish and thick, dark blonde hair poured out in all directions. "Nice. Some of my clients would die for this hair," he managed between yanks. "So, what are we doing today? Have something in mind, hon?"

"You mean, like a style?"

He stared at her in the mirror. Lucy could see he thought she might be joking. Then he realized she was not. "You have a picture or something?"

"Just a trim, please. Can you take off the split ends?"

He nodded, looking relieved. "Will do. How about a little angle over here, pick it up a little. Frame your face?"

"That would be fine. As long as it's not too short to clip back."

"No problem. You have a nice wave. I could put a few highlights in the front, bump up your color?"

Highlights? Wasn't that going over to the Dark Side?

"I do it real natural-looking, believe me." Gary's sincere expression reflected in the mirror. "It's a nice pick-me-up for the spring and it won't take more than an hour, promise."

She sighed and looked at her watch. This extra touch would be cutting it close. "Okay, what the heck." Living large now. Taking no prisoners. "Let's go for it . . . not too much, though."

"Don't worry. I'm the best." He leaned closer. "I could have my own shop, I just don't want the headaches. Know what I mean?"

Lucy nodded. "I do."

Two hours and nearly two hundred bucks later, Lucy staggered out of the salon, light-headed from the full hair styling experience and from inhaling various aerosols, anxious about the time it took.

It was nearly 6:30 and she had slightly over an hour to get home, feed and walk Tink, and put on some makeup before meeting Matt. But as she drove past the Black Sheep, Lucy couldn't help but notice that her friends had congregated inside. She saw Dana's car, Suzanne's, and Phoebe's. Had something happened to Maggie?

She pulled over and parked behind Suzanne's car. She could spare a few minutes. When she got inside, it was positively a party atmosphere.

Maggie greeted her with a wide relaxed smile. "Lucy, we called your cell. You didn't pick up."

"I was having my hair done. Guess I didn't hear the phone."

Maggie drew closer and gazed up at her in a wondering way. "It looks terrific."

"I got highlights . . . just a few," she clarified quickly. "It doesn't look too, you know—"

"Not at all," Dana cut in quickly. "I didn't even notice. I mean, I noticed it looks really nice, but it's just right. Where did you go?"

"Gary. At Cut Above, right?" Suzanne answered for Lucy. She looked very satisfied that her recommendation was garnering rave reviews. "The guy is an artist."

"He did a good job," Lucy agreed.

Phoebe was the only one who didn't shower her with compliments. She looked Lucy's hair over, her eyes getting squinty, perhaps thinking a streak of magenta would have been a better improvement.

"Guess what. Breaking news," Phoebe told her. "Peter Goran has finally been charged with Amanda's murder. They found his wife's computer in his truck. The one he kept saying was stolen by those random burglars? And he was definitely identified near Seabold's just before the alarm went off," Phoebe added. "Sweet, right?"

Lucy stared around at her friends. This was breaking news.

"Wow . . . how did you find out?"

"Christine Forbes heard about it. She called me just a few minutes ago," Maggie replied.

"Jack heard, too. Seems the police got a warrant to search Goran's house today. That's how they found the computer."

"Another anonymous tip?" Lucy asked.

"I think so." Dana shrugged. "It turns out there was someone in the garage at the auto repair shop after it closed and they recognized Peter, cutting through the back of the property. He finally did admit to breaking the window at Seabold's. He says he just wanted to get the police to call Amanda's case a robbery and give up, so he could get on with his life. Sounds a little unbalanced, right? And he still claims he had nothing to do with her death."

"I'm sure he does. His arrest is going to put a kink in his

plans. I wonder what he'll come up with now," Suzanne said in a singsong voice.

"Right. And now he's muddied the water and undercut his own argument, hasn't he?" Lucy agreed.

"The police might have something more than the computer. Something that hasn't gotten out yet. Maybe they tied him to the hat block," Dana suggested.

"I'm surprised it's took them this long." Suzanne let out a long breath. "And the way that Detective Walsh harassed poor Maggie. I think you could sue for that."

"I'd rather just get past it now, thank you. Anyone interested in taking this conversation over to the wine bar? I have a break before the class tonight. I'm buying," Maggie suggested.

"Sorry, I've got to get home." Lucy glanced at her watch. She really did have to run.

"Date night. Lucy has to finish primping," Phoebe said.

She glanced at Phoebe but didn't argue with her.

Lucy hated to ruin the festive mood, but she needed to tell them about the CD. "Before you all head out, I want to tell you something. I came across the strangest thing today when I was looking through that box of dog sweaters from the Knitting Nest."

Maggie stared at her, then slapped her forehead. "The sweaters . . . I almost forgot. Walsh asked if I had moved any boxes from the store and I completely forgot to tell him about that one."

Dana shrugged. "Doesn't seem to make a difference now. I wouldn't worry about it—"

"There was something in there that was . . . odd," Lucy cut in. "I was wondering if I should tell the police about it. But now that Peter Goran has been charged, it probably doesn't make any difference."

They stopped what they were doing and looked over at her.

Suzanne had been putting on her big wool coat and paused midway. "Tell the police? What do you mean?"

Lucy quickly explained how she'd been looking for red wool and finally found some in a patchwork design at the bottom of the box. Then she'd discovered the hidden CD, sandwiched inside the purple knitted squares.

"I put the disk in my computer and the manuscript of Cara's book came up." She looked at the others.

"The manuscript of her book? Or a copy of it?" Dana asked.

Lucy shook her head. "Not a copy. It looked like the original manuscript. For one thing, there were still a few typos and when I checked the dates on the files, they were created months before the book was published."

"What do you think that means?" Suzanne asked. "Was Amanda somehow connected to Cara's writing?"

"I thought she must be. Maybe as an expert reader? Someone who fact-checks special topics. But it seemed like she'd been making a lot of extra money lately. That type of freelancer doesn't get paid much," Lucy explained.

"Especially working on a craft book. And she seemed to have come into some extra money lately, getting her big makeover."

"So she must have been doing something more than fact-checking. Like maybe writing parts of it?" Dana suggested.

"Possibly. Or supplying designs. I found a posting on the Internet, about a contest she'd won a few years ago. The project was a handbag with felted flowers."

"Gooseflesh attack," Phoebe said.

"It's creepy, isn't it?" Suzanne agreed.

Maggie hadn't said anything so far, Lucy noticed. "It's all pretty confusing." She let out a sigh, her good mood now dispelled. She seemed disturbed by the idea, Lucy thought. "That would mean Cara's work isn't original," she said finally.

No one answered. They glanced at one another. Lucy had brought this skunk to the garden party and felt she should say something now, but didn't know what.

Maggie felt a strong bond with Cara and took pride in her success. Hearing Cara wasn't what she appeared to be was a disappointment. That was understandable. Learning that her prize student had been propped up by her arch enemy, well, that was practically . . . Shakespearian.

"A lot of people who write craft books or cooking books have support, Maggie," Lucy said finally. "Martha Stewart and Rachel Ray must have armies of people researching and writing things for them. It probably doesn't mean much."

It felt like it did, though, didn't it? Lucy couldn't deny that to herself.

"I find it odd that Amanda kept that relationship such a big secret," Dana observed. "It really goes against her character. She'd be the type to flaunt that connection. It gave her status."

"I did wonder about that," Lucy said. "But maybe she wasn't allowed to tell. Sometimes publishers asks ghost writers to sign disclosure agreements. I guess this accounts for her trips into the city. It wasn't some secret lover, after all. She was a ghost writer, going in for meetings."

"A ghost writer?" Maggie practically gasped. "Do you really think she did that much? That's a little different from just helping with the research, wouldn't you say?"

Lucy realized too late she had let that theory slip out. But now that she thought about it, it would be a logical explanation for their relationship. And the financial question. Cara had all the looks and charm and Amanda had all the knowledge, skill . . . and the real talent.

"Maggie . . . I honestly don't know," Lucy said finally. "All of these scenarios could be totally wrong. Maybe she was just . . . Cara's typist or something," she offered.

Phoebe made a scoffing face, but didn't say anything. Lucy felt the same. That notion was not bloody likely, but she was trying to make a point. She didn't want to upset Maggie by incriminating Cara further. She could certainly be wrong and totally jumping to conclusions.

"What are you going to do with the CD, Lucy?" Dana asked.

"I don't have time to do anything with it tonight. I guess the police should hear about it sooner or later. But it probably doesn't make any difference in the investigation."

"No, it probably doesn't," Maggie agreed.

"But they should be aware of it and determine that for themselves," Dana told Lucy. "If Peter goes to trial and some wild card like this comes out later, it could throw off his conviction. His defense could argue that the police didn't follow up on a possible lead."

"It's an embarrassment for Cara," Maggie pointed out, "but I don't see how it has anything to with Amanda's murder."

"I didn't mean it that way, Maggie," Dana said quickly. "It's just . . . a loose end, that's all. And I think we should keep this new wrinkle to ourselves for now," she added. "It's probably nothing. But there are privacy issues."

Maggie let out a long sigh. "Yes, there are issues."

"Are we still going out for a drink?" Suzanne asked the others. "I have to make it quick. I need to be home by seven."

Lucy nearly gasped. She'd forgotten all about the time . . . and Matt.

"I've got to run." She turned to Maggie. "I'll call you tomorrow, okay?"

Maggie nodded, then smiled. "Have a good time. I want a full report."

"We all want one," Phoebe added.

"I'm sure this guy is very nice, Lucy," Suzanne called after her. "But no whipped topping on the first date, right?"

They all started laughing.

"Suzanne, you're bad," Phoebe scolded her.

Lucy was glad her back was turned and no one could see her expression.

Lucy raced home, fed, and walked Tink. Then she ran into the bathroom and dabbed on some makeup. Just the usual, which was not much. No smokey eyes tonight, a makeup effect she'd studied carefully in a fashion magazine at the hair salon.

It was just as well. She felt shocked enough every time she looked in the mirror and caught sight of her new highlights. She hoped Matt would not decide he'd mistaken her for someone else.

They all want Malibu Barbie, Dana had promised her. Dana heard men's deepest, darkest fantasies so she should know, right?

Lucy checked her watch. Five to seven, just enough time to make it back into town. They were meeting at the Japanese restaurant near the harbor. It was showtime.

Matt stood outside the restaurant waiting for her. He greeted her with a smile as she walked closer.

"Hey . . . hi," he greeted her and she saw his eyes widen. "Did you do something to your hair?"

Lucy nodded and avoided his gaze. "Oh . . . just a trim," she fibbed.

"Looks great." He leaned over and gave her a quick hello hug, then held the door open for her and they went inside.

They were quickly led to a table and their waitress came by with hot hand towels and took their drink order. Matt asked for Japanese beer and Lucy asked for one, too.

Then they ordered a platter of sushi for two. It looked almost too artfully arranged to eat. Lucy focused on the interesting hand roll combinations while Matt worked on the sashimi. They covered a lot of conversational ground very quickly, too, bouncing from films to books to childhood ambitions. They took their time working through sushi and decided to skip the movie. It was more fun talking anyway, Lucy thought.

He asked how she had ended up a graphic artist and Lucy admitted that she'd tried for a while to make it as a fine artist. "I was working as a designer to pay the bills and trying to paint in my spare time. I guess I just got tired of getting beat up by gallery owners and pretty soon, my day job took over."

"That's too bad. Do you still paint?"

"Once in a while, when I have time," she said. "It's actually easier since I moved out here. I have lots of space in the cottage to keep my easel and paints out, which is half of the battle. And I do a lot of knitting," she added, with a sly grin.

"Did you make that sweater?" he asked. His smile was gentle, not at all condescending.

"Yes, I did."

"I like it. It's looks almost Peruvian . . . but sort of Nordic at the same time."

"That's exactly what I was going for." She gave him a serious look, then couldn't help smiling.

"I knit a little. I'm just learning," Matt said.

"You do?" Lucy couldn't hide her surprise.

"Dara got a kit for her birthday and it was my weekend with her. And that's what she wanted to do. So there we were." He laughed. "We made a scarf for a stuffed animal. It came out pretty good. I got sort of hooked," he confessed. "It's been relaxing during the breakup."

Lucy nodded, noticing he had not said "divorce." "Have you finished any other projects so far?"

"I made a sweater for Dara," he said proudly. "She's so small, it went fast."

"I love knitting for kids. The projects are fun. I just made sock monkey hats for my nieces. They were really easy. I can give you the pattern sometime."

From the way he spoke about his daughter, Lucy could tell Matt was a good father, close and involved.

He had the right politics, too. Her mother was going to love this guy.

They both ended the meal with ginger ice cream, both feeling full but unable to pass up the rare treat. After dinner, they decided to take a walk around the harbor, instead of going to a movie even though it had gotten quite cold.

When they came to the benches at the end of the old dock, they sat down close together and looked out at the lights of the next town, on the shoreline across the inky blue stretch of water. Lucy's two hundred dollar hairdo was no match for the damp wind off the water. Matt brushed a few strands of hair off her cheek with his hand. "I had a great time hanging out with you, Lucy."

Lucy turned toward him. His face was very close. "Me, too," she said. "Thanks for dinner," she added.

"Anytime." Then he leaned closer and kissed her.

It was good. Really good. Lucy closed her eyes and kissed him back. They soon had their arms around each other and she was suddenly glad they were out in the open and not alone at her house.

Finally, they decided to go. They walked back down the dock to the harbor park holding hands.

Matt suddenly slapped his forehead. "Some doctor. I never asked you about Tink. How's she doing?"

Lucy laughed. "She's doing great. You'd never know she just had a major operation."

"Sounds good."

Lucy glanced at him. "There's something I wanted to ask you,

Matt. When I brought Tink home and opened the envelope with the medications, did you really mean to give me that . . . that thing that came out of her stomach?"

Matt turned to her, wide eyed. "That was supposed to go out for lab work. No wonder I didn't get the report back yet."

Lucy laughed. "Whew . . . glad we cleared that up. I was worried that you had a really weird sense of humor."

"Well, it is weird . . . but not that weird," he promised her.

Lucy laughed, feeling relieved.

When they had reached her car, she got in and rolled down the window. "Well, good night. Thanks again."

He leaned over and quickly kissed her cheek. "Good night, Lucy. I'll call you tomorrow."

Tomorrow? Not just "I'll call you"? That was pretty definitive.

"Okay, I'll be around," she replied.

As Lucy drove off she saw him standing on the sidewalk, watching for a moment, then he turned and headed for his own car.

Wow, a really good date. How often did that happen? Next to never?

Lucy was practically giddy as she cruised down Main Street. She noticed the lights on at the Black Sheep. It was just a few minutes past 11:00 and she guessed Maggie was still at the shop, straightening up after her class. With Peter in custody, the scare among the shopkeepers in town had dispelled and Maggie was back to her old habits again.

Lucy considered stopping by, to report on the date, but then felt she just wanted to keep it all inside a little longer, savoring the feeling. Yes, this could be something good. Sometimes you just know. She would tell her friends in good time. But she just needed time to herself to let the experience settle and gel.

Starting a new relationship was a lot like making a Jell-O mold. One layer at a time. She'd have to tell Phoebe that.

As Lucy headed out of the village center to the cottage, she nearly laughed out loud, remembering the look on Matt's face when she'd asked why he'd sent her that disgusting specimen that had come out of Tink's stomach.

Lucy tried not to think of what it had looked like, squashed at the bottom of the little glass bottle, but the image came unbidden into her brain.

Suddenly, it hit her. The thing from Tink's stomach had looked just like Dana's ugly knitted flower. That's why a bell in her head had gone off the other night at the meeting, when they were all teasing Dana about how ugly her felted flower had turned out. Even Dana had said it looked like the dog's breakfast.

The thing from Tink's stomach was the same shade of reddish orange as the wool in Dana's flower and the pattern for the felted flowers on Cara's knitted jacket. The jacket that was missing a button . . . Lucy remembered now how she'd noticed that, looking over the photos that night.

It seemed impossible but the dots all connected in Lucy's brain at once and big lights were flashing, "Eureka!" She didn't need a lab report to confirm her conclusion:

The nasty glob that had come out of Tink's digestive tract had once been a pretty flower button on Cara's hand-knitted jacket.

Chapter Twelve

Lucy felt a bad taste in the back of her throat and it wasn't sushi reflux. She gripped the wheel and pulled over. Her hands were shaking and a cold sweat had broken out all over her body under her thick hand-knitted sweater.

All the time she'd been out with Matt, she hadn't given Amanda Goran's murder a thought. Apparently the pleasant distraction was just what her subconscious needed to put the pieces together.

But now she felt it in her gut with icy certainty.

Peter Goran had not killed his wife. Sure, he was a cheating husband and a gambler, eager to pay off his debts with his wife's life insurance benefits. Sales from his crafts were hardly enough to pay for his habit. He was a clumsy oaf who had tried to stage a break-in to persuade the police that Amanda was killed in a robbery and to help him get out of town.

Peter Goran was not a very nice guy but he wasn't a murderer.

The real murderer was Cara Newhouse.

Sweet, lovely Cara. Maggie's star student. The darling of the knitting world. The bestselling author and soon-to-be TV-show host. Cara had killed Amanda Goran, her secret ghost writer and pattern creator—and God only knew what else poor Amanda's contribution had been to Cara's success.

Lucy started the car, turned it around, and headed back into town. She had to tell Maggie her theory. It couldn't wait until the morning—it was too important. Maggie may have already broken her promise and spoken to Cara about the CD.

Lucy raced down the narrow winding side streets of town, taking a shortcut to Main Street. Her mind was piecing everything together as she drove. Cara must have stopped at the Knitting Nest on her way to the Black Sheep for her presentation. She obviously had fought with Amanda, probably over their business arrangement.

As the two women struggled, Tink tried to protect Amanda. Tink had jumped on Cara, taken a bite of Cara's coat, and swallowed the flower. Maybe Cara had been the one who'd injured her.

With Tink subdued, the rest of the dogs lost interest. Then Cara did Amanda in with the hat block Amanda had in her shop.

With Amanda knocked out, Cara ransacked the place and emptied Amanda's wallet, trying to make it look like a robbery.

What she really wanted was the computer. It must have had all the files of her book on it, e-mails, whatever. The book that Amanda—not Cara—actually wrote.

She must have looked through the office for any evidence of her relationship with Amanda and taken what she could find. That's why the police had never questioned Cara, not that Lucy had heard anyway.

Of course, she couldn't have guessed that Amanda had socked away some evidence in the dog sweater just in case she ever needed proof. In case Cara decided to cut her out of the picture.

The Sunday morning when Lucy had seen someone skulking around the Knitting Nest, had that been Cara, too? Looking for any evidence she may have left behind? For this very CD, or something like it?

Lucy came to a red light and had to stop. She pulled out her cell phone and tried Maggie's numbers, first the shop and then her cell. Maggie didn't pick up either call.

She tried Phoebe but there was no answer at her number, either. Phoebe must be with Josh tonight, she realized, which left Maggie alone in the shop.

Lucy rounded the final turn onto Main Street, her Jeep practically taking the curve on two wheels. She drove up to the Black Sheep and parked across the street. Maggie's Subaru was still parked in front and the lights shone brightly through the big bay window in front. Lucy didn't see any other cars on the street and breathed easier.

She felt foolish now, rushing over here like the place was on fire. Maggie was fine. She had kept her promise and had not called Cara. This revelation could definitely wait until tomorrow. But here she was, so . . .

Lucy headed up the walk to the porch. Before she reached the steps, she peered through the bay window. A woman stood in the middle of the front room, her back to the street. It wasn't Maggie. A chatty student, left over from the class? Wasn't it a little late for that?

Lucy drew closer and recognized the late-night visitor. It was Cara. Just as Lucy had suspected. Cara was alone with Maggie. Not good. And she had not parked her car in plain view. Even worse.

Lucy quickly slunk out of sight before either of the women could see her. Her heart pounded wildly and she could barely breathe. She didn't think it was a good idea to surprise them.

Cara was clearly dangerous. What if she had a weapon this time? A real one, not just knitting equipment.

Lucy crept down the driveway, heading for the back of the shop. She tried to keep her steps as silent as possible on the gravel but it was nearly impossible. Finally, she reached the rear of the shop and the back door that opened into the storeroom.

Lucy tried the handle. It was unlocked, thank goodness. She slowly and quietly turned the knob, then slipped inside, closing the door with the same care. The storeroom was dark. It took her eyes a moment to adjust. She crept toward the doorway that led to the shop and tried hard to still her breathing.

Luckily, Maggie and Cara were still standing toward the front of the shop and Lucy heard them talking about Amanda. Lucy flattened herself near the doorway, trying to make out their words. She gulped down a breath and focused.

"She was just a proofreader for me, Maggie. A fact-checker, that's all," Lucy heard Cara say. "You can ask the police if you like. They even spoke to my publisher. She had a contract and made good money, believe me. But she got very jealous when I started to have some success. You know how she could be. She was always jealous of you, too. I don't even want to repeat some of the things she said about you."

Good move. The old distraction tactic. Lucy hoped Maggie wouldn't fall for that.

"Amanda was insecure," Maggie agreed. "But why didn't you just tell me what was going on? I wouldn't have told anyone Amanda worked on your books if you needed to keep it confidential."

"Oh . . . I don't know . . . I wanted to tell you, I really did. But I knew how Amanda would exaggerate and take all the credit. I didn't want people to get the wrong idea. Especially with the TV show deal up in the air. It didn't seem the right time to admit I had any help. Even though she really didn't do much, I swear. The editor just wanted to cover herself, you know how it is, Maggie."

Lucy heard Maggie sigh. She knew Maggie really wanted to believe Cara, despite what her instincts and intuition might be telling her right now. "I knew how difficult Amanda could be, believe me," Maggie said.

"If only I'd come to you and asked for help with the books. We could have been an awesome team." Cara sounded her usual warm, sweet little self. "We can still write a book together, Maggie," Cara suggested. "There's so much I can still learn from you."

Lucy felt a yellowtail with scallion roll coming up again. Cara was shameless.

"You're very busy now. I don't see how you'd have the time." Maggie sounded as if she didn't know what to say. Did she have a clue about Cara's real involvement or her state of mind? Lucy couldn't tell. She sure as heck hoped so.

"So, what are you going to do with that CD? Can I have it back? I'd hate for someone else to find it and misunderstand."

Cara's tone was casual but underneath Lucy heard pure desperation.

"Oh, I don't have it," Maggie told her.

Lucy braced herself. It was going to get nasty now. She felt around her coat pocket for her cell phone, realizing she should have called 911 eons ago, before she'd even gotten out of her car. But her pockets were empty. She'd stupidly left her phone in the car, after she'd tried to reach Phoebe.

She did find the plastic CD case.

"You don't have it?" Cara sounded shocked. "I thought on the phone you said you found it, in a box from Amanda's shop?"

Lucy sucked in a breath.

Now she knew and sweet little Cara was about to go postal.

"Oh, you misunderstood me. Lucy found it. She just told me

about it tonight. Told a few of us." Maggie's tone was calm and matter-of-fact.

Cara seemed stumped. Lucy wondered if she was considering how she might knock off the entire knitting club . . . one by one . . .

Time to make my move, Lucy thought. Maybe she could grab Cara and Maggie could grab the phone and call the police?

Lucy stepped out of the back room, then waved the CD case to distract Cara.

"Here it is, Cara. All yours. No problem. Just tell us why you killed Amanda. Did you have some secret arrangement, besides the one she had with your publisher? Was she blackmailing you?"

Maggie's mouth hung open, staring at Lucy. She couldn't have looked more surprised if Amanda Goran's ghost had materialized in the middle of her shop.

Cara was frozen with shock. Then her fair complexion and pretty face turned red with rage.

"You're insane. I didn't kill Amanda. The police just arrested her husband, in case you didn't hear."

"I heard they found Amanda's computer in the back of his truck," Lucy replied. "I don't know how you got it there, but that was a nice touch."

"You have quite an imagination, Lucy. Maybe you should write a book, too."

"You mean like Amanda?" Lucy challenged her. "She was really writing your books and creating the designs, too, right? Doing everything," Lucy reminded her as she slowly tried to get closer. "This is proof enough," she said, holding up the CD, "but I'm sure if we call your editor we'll find out even more."

Cara didn't answer for a moment, then she did a silly-looking eye roll. "Big deal. I had some backup on the books. Everybody does that. Amanda just went psycho on me. She started making all these insane demands. Her name on the book covers and co-hosting the TV show. Can you imagine it? We had an agreement. She wasn't supposed to just . . . pop out of the closet. With her pathetic makeover and her new teeth . . . but I didn't kill her," Cara quickly insisted. "It was her husband, Peter. He needed the insurance money. He has a gambling problem."

"Yes, he does need the money," Lucy admitted. "But that was just a turn of good luck for you. I'm thinking now you framed him somehow, planting that computer in his truck. Like you tried to frame Maggie," Lucy told her. "Hiding the hat block in the shop. Perfect. You brought it here the day you came with the flowers and pretended to be looking for buttons to match your new sweater. You must have dumped it in one of the cartons while Maggie and I were in the storeroom together."

The idea had just come to Lucy as she recalled that morning in the shop. But as soon as she saw Cara's expression, she knew she'd gotten it right and the pieces all finally fit together.

"You bitch, that's not true! None of it. I could never do anything like that. Especially to Maggie." Cara's doe-eyed expression grew stone-cold.

Maggie gasped. Lucy noticed now that she had slipped behind the counter. If Cara got violent at least that would be some barrier between them, Lucy thought.

Cara put her hand into her pocket and pulled out a gun.

Lucy froze in place. She couldn't even dare to take a breath.

"Well, it's been nice chatting with you, Lucy. But it is late. Hand over the CD and I won't shoot Maggie."

Lucy's hands were shaking and she tried to play for some more time. She kept glancing at Maggie, hoping she'd duck down under the counter. But Maggie did the opposite and came out again from behind her thin protection.

"Cara, please. Try to just calm down. Put the gun down. Don't make an even bigger mistake," Maggie spoke slowly as she walked toward Cara.

"Stay right where you are, Maggie. I don't want to hurt you." Cara's voice was tight and menacing. She meant business.

Maggie froze in her tracks.

Lucy held her hands in a gesture of surrender, then gently leaned over to hand Cara the CD.

As Cara reached out for it, Lucy grabbed the folded-up umbrella swift that was sitting on the counter near the cash register and swung it, whacking the gun out of Cara's hand.

"Ow! Goddamn, you broke my hand . . ." Cara grabbed her hand, wincing in pain.

The CD went skidding across the bare wood floor and so did the gun.

Cara stared at Maggie and Lucy, then dashed for the front door.

She pulled it open and a swarm of policemen filled the shop entrance. Lucy saw a few more on the porch, peering through the window, then she turned at the sound of footsteps running into the shop through the storeroom.

Cara knew she was cornered. She didn't even try to resist, just buried her face in her hands and cried.

Lucy looked over at Maggie, who now stood close by. "Silent alarm. There's a button under the counter. I had it installed after Amanda's murder. Never thought I'd use it this way." Then Maggie's expression dissolved into tears.

Lucy stood beside her and put her arm around Maggie's shoulder. She swallowed hard. Lucy knew the truth about Cara had to be a shock and a painful revelation for Maggie. Lucy didn't know what to say. She thought it was best, just then, not to say anything.

• • •

Despite a late night at the police station, where she'd spent several hours with Maggie giving statements, Lucy woke up early on Saturday morning. She showered and dressed quickly, then walked Tink down to the village. She wandered along the paths in the harbor park for a while, then picked up the *Plum Harbor Times* at the stationery store. Part of her wanted to read the local news coverage and part of her didn't.

"Local Resident Confesses to Goran Murder" the grim headline read. While Lucy and Maggie told and retold the police the story of their standoff with Cara, Cara was in another interview room with Detective Walsh, telling her long sad tale.

Lucy scanned the article quickly. There wasn't too much in there that she didn't know and a lot was left out that she did. She walked down to the Black Sheep, wondering if she'd find Maggie there. Lucy had no doubt last night that Maggie would open today at her usual time, despite the fact that they had not gotten home until after two. Anyone else would have hung the "Gone Knitting" sign and taken the day off.

But Lucy knew Maggie. She needed to keep busy. That was her way of coping with a crisis. It wasn't such a bad method, either, Lucy decided.

When Lucy got to the shop, she tied Tink on the porch and went inside. Maggie and Dana were sitting in the front room, Maggie on the love seat and Dana in an armchair. They greeted her and Lucy took a seat.

"How are you doing today, Lucy?" Dana asked with concern. "You were a real hero last night."

Lucy had to think for a moment, then realized Dana was talking about the way she'd knocked the gun out of Cara's hand with the yarn swift.

"My martial arts moves are a little rusty, so I had to make do."

"It was fast thinking . . . and very brave," Maggie said. She glanced at Lucy for a moment. At the time, neither of them had realized the danger they'd been in, everything had been happening so quickly, but this morning it was starting to sink in.

"Where did Cara get that gun anyway? I'm not sure the police ever told me," Lucy asked Maggie.

"It was in her parents' house," Maggie explained. "Her family is quite well off. They have a big old house near the bluff. Her father kept a gun around for protection. I'm not sure she even knows how to shoot it, but still . . ."

"I'm glad we didn't wait to find out," Lucy finished for her.

The front door flew open. Suzanne ran in, holding a copy of the newspaper. "I thought I'd find you here. Thank God you're both okay . . ." She quickly hugged Maggie, then turned to Lucy, smothering her against her ample chest for a second. "I couldn't believe it. Cara Newhouse?" She dropped into an armchair and shrugged off her coat. "In a million years, could you ever imagine that?"

"Cara confessed to everything," Maggie said bleakly. "There's no question."

"How did it happen? I mean, how did she and Amanda even get together in the first place?" Suzanne asked.

"She told me she was in town, visiting her family while she was writing her first book, *Live, Laugh, Knit*," Maggie explained. "She was having trouble with the book and needed help. She said she wanted to come to me, but felt embarrassed. So she went to Amanda's shop instead. She pretended to be a novice knitter and asked Amanda all her questions."

Lucy had not heard all of Maggie's conversation with Cara, so she was interested in this part of the story. "So how did she end up hiring Amanda as a ghost writer?"

"Cara didn't really say." Maggie sighed. Lucy could tell it was hard for Maggie to talk about this. "I guess at some point she saw that Amanda was talented and had so much knowledge, she could be more useful to her than just as a problem-solving source. She did tell me that Amanda got good money out of their deal and had signed some kind of agreement with the publisher."

"But that agreement was only as a fact-checker," Lucy added. "Detective Reyes told me last night that Cara and Amanda had another agreement, a private one, which was basically a deal where Amanda wrote the books and created all the designs. The police found evidence of that on the computer, once they knew what they were looking for."

"And Cara got all the glory," Suzanne finished for her.

"Exactly," Dana nodded. "But when Cara's star began to rise, all due to Amanda's talent and knowledge, Amanda must have gotten peeved. Was that it?"

"Yes, she was jealous, pure and simple. Amanda's Achilles' heel," Maggie replied. "It was eating Amanda up inside to see Cara getting all the praise and attention from her hard work."

"Anybody would have felt the same. I mean, it wasn't really fair," Suzanne shrugged. "Did she try to blackmail Cara? Is that why she killed her?"

"No, it wasn't blackmail. At least that's what Cara told the police," Dana said. She looked at Maggie. "Is that what she told you?"

"Cara claimed it all came to a head with the TV-show offer. Amanda insisted that Cara share the spotlight and prepared herself to come out of the shadows. That's why she had that expensive makeover and bought new clothes. . . ." Maggie's voice trailed off. She took a breath and looked up at her friends again. "Amanda made Cara agree that they would announce their partnership at the Black Sheep, at her book signing event. Can you imagine that?"

"That's why Amanda came here the night before," Lucy said, "to check if the stage was set for her big debut."

"Exactly," Dana agreed. "She was going to be the first one here."

"She also made Cara promise they would do the TV show audition together," Maggie added. "But Cara wasn't taking any chances and probably called off the TV crew for the day. That's why they didn't show."

"So she agreed to share the spotlight with Amanda, then decided she couldn't stand the idea? Is that what happened?" Suzanne asked.

"More or less," Maggie replied with a sigh. "I'm not sure if she went to the Knitting Nest that morning intending to kill Amanda. She told me they'd agreed to meet there, so they could come to the Black Sheep together. Cara claimed she only wanted to talk Amanda out of going public but Amanda was impossible to deal with."

"Cara told the police pretty much the same thing," Dana added. "She tried to persuade Amanda to stay under wraps a bit longer. She even offered her more money. But Amanda got very angry. They struggled. The dogs got upset and Tink leaped at her. But she managed to push them off, too."

"That's when she probably kicked Tink," Lucy said.

"Probably," Dana agreed. "That made Amanda even more upset. She turned to check on her dog and Cara grabbed the first thing she saw—the hat block—and knocked her over the head. She told the police she didn't mean to kill her. But once Amanda was clearly dead, it seemed easy to make it look like a robbery. And she was thrilled to get her hands on the computer that held all the evidence of their relationship. So she grabbed it, then searched the office files to find anything else that might incriminate her."

"What about when Maggie came to the shop that morning? Was Cara still there?" Suzanne asked.

Lucy had forgotten about that. Cara was probably in a panic when she heard Maggie knocking. "Yes," Maggie said, looking very interested. "Did Jack hear that part of the confession?"

"Cara saw you, but you didn't see her, of course. She told the police she was worried at first that you'd seen her car. But once it was apparent you hadn't seen anyone at the Nest, she . . . she tried to turn the incident to her advantage," Dana summed up quickly.

Maggie stared at her. She didn't speak for a moment. "She tried to frame me for the murder, you mean," she said flatly.

Lucy's heart went out to Maggie. She could see how the betrayal stung.

"Cara had been lying when she told us she wasn't aware of any rivalry between me and Amanda. I guess I was a perfect suspect," Maggie said sadly. "It was easy for her to set me up, planting that hat block in the shop."

"Then the police got interested in Peter Goran and he looked even more likely to be the killer," Dana added. "So Cara figured out a way to plant the computer in his van. She called and asked to buy the spinning wheel from Amanda's shop. When he delivered it to her house and carried it upstairs to set it up for her, she must have snuck outside and hidden the computer in his van."

"Wow, I really thought he did it," Suzanne admitted.

"We were all willing to pin Peter," Dana agreed. "The police picked him out over Maggie, too. They were under pressure to arrest somebody."

"Cara would have gotten away with it. If Lucy had never found the CD with the manuscript," Maggie pointed out. Maggie sighed again. "What a waste. I still don't understand. She had talent. Why did she do such a thing?"

"Maybe Cara didn't have enough confidence in her own

ideas," Dana offered. "Or enough knowledge. Maybe she didn't want to work that hard. Or was pushed too far, too fast, and had to deliver. It seems she was terrified of being exposed as a fraud. Avoiding shame and humiliation are powerful motivators."

"Enough to make a person commit murder?" Maggie asked bleakly.

No one replied. Maggie shook her head. "Well, I was fooled. Taken in by her totally. I guess that makes me pretty gullible, right?"

"Oh, Maggie, don't say that." Suzanne leaned over and patted Maggie's shoulder. "I know you loved that girl. But she was . . . a bit of a psycho. She tricked you. She tricked all of us. But that wasn't your fault. It doesn't mean you aren't a great teacher."

"Suzanne's right. Think of how many people have come to this shop and been turned on to knitting and encouraged to express themselves. That's a great gift to the world, Maggie," Dana told her.

"If it wasn't for you, we wouldn't have all met here," Lucy reminded her. "We wouldn't have knitting night."

Maggie nodded. She wiped her eyes and nose with a tissue and stuck it back in her pocket. "What would I do without knitting night?" She glanced at Dana. "I'd need some real therapy, I guess," she quipped.

"Knitting is cheaper." Dana delivered the information with a grin.

"Especially if you get the yarn for free," Maggie countered. "Which reminds me, the police say they're going to return all that stock from the Knitting Nest next week. Which I practically did get for free. Sitting in the police station the other night, staring at those horrible green walls, I had an idea about what to do with it."

"What's that?" Lucy asked.

"I'm going to save most of it for our community services projects. Like those friendships shawls we knitted for the nursing home at Christmas?"

"What a great idea, Maggie," Lucy said.

"That is a nice idea," Dana agreed. "It is about time we started a new project like that. We ought to dedicate the contribution to Amanda Goran," she suggested.

"We should do that, definitely," Maggie nodded, looking solemn for a moment. "Poor Amanda. We didn't know her nearly as well as we thought. Maybe if she'd been publicly acknowledged for those books and designs, she would have been a different person."

"You might be right. No way of knowing now, unfortunately," Dana said quietly.

"Well, your good name is cleared, Maggie," Suzanne piped up. "You're not the black sheep in Plum Harbor anymore," she gently teased.

Maggie smiled self-consciously. "Oh, I don't know about that. I think there's more than a touch of the black sheep in all of you." She glanced at each of her friends in turn. "Snooping into crime scenes, gathering juicy gossip, analyzing criminal minds . . . Most of all, doing whatever it took to get me off the hook."

They laughed at Maggie's dramatic descriptions, but it was mostly true, Lucy realized. Knowingly or unknowingly, they'd all worked together to find Amanda's murderer and prove Maggie's innocence.

"Maybe that's what we should call our knitting group officially from now on, the Black Sheep," Dana suggested.

"I like it," Suzanne said, seconding the motion.

"May I see a show of hands?" Maggie asked. "All in favor?"

"Wait . . . Phoebe's not here," Lucy pointed out.

As if on cue, the shop door flew open. Phoebe marched in, her clothes wrinkled and disheveled, her peacoat crookedly buttoned. Her hair, with its streak of magenta against the pitch black, was partly gathered in an elastic, the rest hanging out down her back and shoulders. She looked seriously out of whack. Even for Phoebe.

"Why didn't somebody call me? You guys . . . you could have been killed or something. And *that* Cara. I always knew there was something off with that babe. Too plastic to be true, know what I mean?"

Lucy did know what Phoebe meant yet had never quite put her finger on it.

Maggie walked over and calmly slipped her arm around Phoebe's shoulder. "We're all right, Phoebe. Don't worry. We definitely would have let you know if something serious had happened. Sit down and take a breath . . ."

"We're just taking a vote on a new name for our group," Dana explained, patting Phoebe's hand.

"And I never got to tell you guys about my date last night. With the vet," Lucy added in a tantalizing tone.

"Oh man, I have to hear this." Phoebe sat down, looking a bit calmer.

"Okay, Lucy. Spill it," Suzanne urged her. "We old married ladies love a hot date story. With a doctor, no less . . . but I'm supposed to show a house at eleven."

"Just a minute. We can't just sit here without working on something." Maggie sat back, positively shocked. "Before Lucy spills the beans, I'm going to show you a gorgeous lace stitch I found in a spring pattern book. It's just exquisite . . ."

Maggie seemed energized again, casting aside her sadness over Cara and Amanda. She riffled through the pile of pattern books and papers on the tea table, then pulled out a sheet.

"Here it is. We can start right now. I already pulled out the right yarn and needles . . ."

Lucy took a pair of extrafine needles and some silky purple yarn that Maggie handed around in a basket. She sat back and smiled.

As Bette might say, it had been a bumpy night all right, but this flock of beloved black sheep had come through intact . . . their friendship even stronger.

Who could ever imagine they'd solve a murder case together? Who could predict what new adventures—in knitting and in life—awaited?

Notes from the Black Sheep Knitting Shop Bulletin Board

Glad you guys had fun dyeing wool with Jell-O. I found the instructions online, at a super knitting site, www.Stringativity.blogspot.com in a blog entry by Tracy Grawey Purtscher posted on 12/09/07. It's called "Jell-O is to Dye For." (You can read about other Jell-O-dyeing methods there, too.) Here are the instructions, for any slackers who didn't bother to take notes.

—Phoebe

Dyeing Yarn With Jell-O: The Microwave Method

SUPPLIES & INGREDIENTS

Large microwaveable bowl—nonporous

Long-handled spoon or fork to manipulate yarn—nonporous

1 package regular Jell-O Berry Blue

White vinegar—1 cup

Salt—1 teaspoon

Water—5 cups

Skein of white wool—70 to 80 grams

DIRECTIONS

In a large bowl, mix together in the order listed:

5 cups water

1 teaspoon salt

1 package regular Jell-O Berry Blue

1 cup white vinegar

Stir with utensil to mix. Add skein of wool and swish around to allow dye to soak into fibers.

Place bowl in microwave and heat on high for 2 minutes. Remove and let it cool for 1.5 minutes. Repeat process 3 times altogether.

Let wool cool before removing and hanging to dry.

Dear Customers,

Did you miss the "Felting Just for Fun" class we had? It was a big hit. I'll definitely hold another session soon.

If you want to get started on your own, check out some of these websites:

"Knitty" is a favorite. You can find felting instructions and free patterns for great projects here, including a wonderful French market tote. Go to www.knitty.com/ISSUEwinter03/FEATfelthis.html

Or you can click on the felting link from the navigation bar on www.mybagatelle.com

www.Michaels.com has felting instructions, too, and a free pattern. Just use the words "Fabulous Felted Knit Flowers" in the search box on the homepage.

And let me know if you have any questions. I'm always here to help.

Keep Knitting!

—Maggie

Sock Monkey Fans Unite!

Here's the pattern info about the sock monkey hats I made this winter. Go to www.knittingpatterncentral.com and search "Sock Monkey Hat."

These grinning little guys grow on you, don't they? There are some great sock monkey projects out there—toys, socks, Vintage Sock Monkey. Here are a few more links I found: www.sockmonkeyfun.com and www.sockmonkey.net

Enjoy monkeying around!

—Lucy

Okay, Everybody—here is that secret guacamole recipe you keep asking me about. Special tip: If the avocados aren't fully ripened, just peel, cut into pieces, and put them in a blender or food processor with a tablespoon of olive oil and a dash of lemon juice. Blend for a second or two—just until the pieces break up and mix with the oil. Don't make an avocado slushy out of it, okay? You can also add a spoonful of mayo to the recipe to fake a richer, riper texture.

—Ole! Suzanne

Suzanne's Chunky Guacamole Recipe

3 ripe avocados (Haas brand preferred)

2 to 3 tablespoons olive oil

Half a lemon

½ sweet onion, diced into small chunks

1 small ripe tomato, seeds removed and diced into small chunks

1 to 2 tablespoons fresh cilantro, finely chopped

Dash of Worcestershire sauce

Coarse salt

Choose the two ripest of the three avocados. Peel off skin and cut in half to remove pit. Place halves in a large mixing bowl and smash with a fork until smooth.

Add olive oil and squeeze in juice from half a lemon.

Add onion and tomato chunks and 1½ tablespoons of the cilantro.

Add a dash of Worcestershire sauce and about ½ teaspoon coarse salt, depending on taste.

Blend all ingredients. Mixture does not need to be perfectly smooth.

Peel the remaining avocado and remove pit. Chop into pieces about ½ inch in size and add to the mixture.

With a spatula, scoop guacamole into a smaller bowl suitable for dipping and top with remaining chopped cilantro and a small wedge of lime. If not serving immediately, store in the refrigerator. Cover with plastic wrap and press wrap flat to the top of mixture (this will prevent the dip from getting brown on top).

Serve with your favorite tortilla chips.